UNKNOWN SOLDIER

World War I

DAVID PRESTON

ISBN:
Hardcover 979-8-9905622-0-2
Paperback 979-8-9905622-1-9
eBook 979-8-9905622-2-6

Azalea City Publishing, LLC
Mobile, AL 36693
www.azaleacitypublishing.com
Cover photograph: Paula Lenor Webb edited by Jonathan M. Holt
Cover design: Artillery Design Company Ltd
https://www.artillerydesign.co.uk/

DEDICATION

To my father, whose love of reading, history, and politics helped mold me into the nerd I am today. I will be eternally grateful to you.

To Michelle Johnson, thank you for being the best friend anyone could ever ask for

ACKNOWLEDGMENTS

Even though many times a single person's name is on a book as the author, a book can never be a singular effort by one person.

This book could not have been possible without the encouragement and help of my traveling companion to historical places-- Paula Lenor Webb. Thank you for being in my "cheering squad".

It would also not be possible without the herculean editing efforts of Mary S . Palmer. I know it was a struggle to get through it, and for that I thank you.

For the review and input into the story to make sure the story flowed and the military stuff was as realistic as possible, a big thanks is needed to Kelly Johnson, Alabama National Guard (Ret.) and Mike Bunn, Author, Historian, and Director of Blakeley State Park.

Foreward

Alabama's remarkable military heritage is one of its most-deeply cherished traditions. In every one of our nation's wars dating from the time of the state's establishment in the early nineteenth century to the present day, Alabamians have participated and played prominent roles. Even in conflicts that predate Alabama statehood (1819), the state lays claim to its residents participation through the involvement of the pioneering settlers who fought in such consequential conflicts as the Creek War, the War of 1812, and even the Revolutionary War. The state's military heritage is, by any measure, rich, distinguished, and longstanding.

Those who have studied Alabamians' military stories will quickly realize they are not abstract tales. They are sagas of real people, who endured real sacrifice for real ideals, and made a real difference in the course of the fights in which they were engaged. Many of Alabama's war stories are familiar to even the most casual enthusiast of state history today, ranging from the thousands of rugged infantrymen and sailors who fought on battlefields across the nation and on the high seas in some of the most consequential actions of the Civil War to the determined Tuskegee Airmen, who fought in the skies during World War II with a special purpose. It is easy to overlook, however, the valiant men who fought for the cause of freedom in World War I. America's military involvement in the conflict was short by comparison to that of some of our allies, but it showcased American fighting men—and Alabamians in particular—in a special way that deserves our remembrance.

The legendary 167 th Alabama Infantry, for example,—the "Rainbow Division"—participated in some of the fiercest contests of The Great War and won the respect and admiration of fighting men on both sides of the Atlantic. What

they did on faraway battlefields such as Chateau-Thierry
and La Croix Rouge Farm, places in France very few back in
Alabama are familiar, are often overshadowed by the global
conflict known as World War II or more recent military
actions involving people still living.

In *Unknown Soldier*, my friend David Preston has made the
story of Alabama's World War I veterans comprehensible and
helps us appreciate the sacrifices represented by the
unidentified casualties of war commemorated in the "Tomb of
the Unknown Soldier." Inspired by multiple real stories and
portraying people that represent a mosaic of Alabama troops
of the period, the novel paints a picture of fictional characters
whose backgrounds, motivations, and experiences would no
doubt ring true to actual soldiers who fought the war. Students
of Alabama and military history will appreciate the research
that went into writing this novel, and all those who savor a
good tale well told will enjoy the author's easy style and even
pace in relating the story. In the pages that follow, readers will
be transported to a place and time in which the world seemed
to be engulfed in the "war to end all wars," and gain a better
understanding of the experiences of the men who fought its
battles. My understanding of Alabama's role in World War I
has been made richer due to David's work, and I am sure yours
will too.

Mike Bunn
Author, *The Fourteenth Colony*
Director, Blakely State Park

Prologue

The Andersons had always been deeply patriotic, with a profound respect for their country and those who had sacrificed their lives to protect it. Mrs. Anderson's Grandfather, Papaw Tommy and Grandmother's brother, James, even served in World War I together. So, when Mr. Anderson, a retired military veteran, suggested taking a family trip to Washington, D.C. to visit the Tomb of the Unknown Soldier at Arlington National Cemetery, everyone eagerly agreed.

The Andersons, consisting of Mr. and Mrs. Anderson and their two children, Emma and Jacob, embarked on their journey to the nation's capital. Excitement filled the air as they packed their belongings, ready for the memorable adventure that lay ahead.

Their road trip was filled with laughter at Mr. Anderson's corny dad jokes, games created from the minds of Emma and Jacob and interesting stories that may or may not have been true. Along the way, they marveled at the changing landscapes that started out with the flat gulf plains that turned into the rolling hills of the Appalachian and Smokey mountains and stopped at historical landmarks, immersing themselves in the rich tapestry of America's history. The Andersons made it a point to appreciate every moment and soak in the natural beauty of the journey and the vivid memories being made in the minds of the children.

Finally, they arrived in Washington, D.C. The family settled into a cozy chain hotel in the Virginia suburb of Falls Church and woke up early the next morning, eager to begin their day at Arlington National Cemetery. As they stepped onto the hallowed grounds, a sense of hushed reverence enveloped them.

They followed the winding paths through the rolling rows of white gravestones, each representing a hero who had made the ultimate sacrifice for their country. The silence was broken only by the gentle rustling of the multi-colored autumn leaves and the distant sound of a bugle solemnly playing taps. It was a somber reminder of the price paid by others for their freedom.

At last, they reached the Tomb of the Unknown Soldier. Mr. Anderson, his military training instilling a deep respect, explained the significance of the tomb to his captivated children. They stood in awe as they witnessed the Changing of the Guard ceremony, a solemn display of honor and dedication.

The Andersons stood in respectful silence near the Tomb of the Unknown Soldier. The air was heavy with respect, as they observed the ceremony, a ritual that honored the fallen heroes who lay beneath the hallowed ground. It was a moment of reverence and reflection.

As the ceremony progressed, the Andersons noticed a group of teenagers nearby who seemed oblivious to the solemnity of the occasion. They chatted loudly, laughed, and even took selfies, showing a lack of respect that deeply troubled them.

Just as the Andersons exchanged concerned glances, a Tomb Guard, resplendent in his crisp uniform, moved swiftly and silently towards the disruptive visitors. The atmosphere seemed to shift immediately, as if the weight of the moment had been recognized.

With calculated precision, the Tomb Guard approached the group, his eyes fixed on their startled faces. He paused for a moment, allowing the overwhelming weight of his presence to be felt. Then, in a firm but respectful voice, he addressed the disruptive visitors.

"Please maintain proper silence and respect within the premises of the tomb. This is a place of honor, where heroes rest. Let us all pay our respects with dignity," the Tomb Guard spoke, his words echoing through the air.

The disruptive teenagers, taken aback by the sudden admonishment, fell silent in stunned shock. Some looked embarrassed, realizing the magnitude of their actions. The Andersons watched in awe as the Tomb Guard maintained his composure, his dedication to the sacred duty evident in every movement.

The group quickly adjusted their behavior, offering nods of acknowledgment and whispered apologies. They became mindful of the sanctity of the place, realizing the impact their actions had on others who had come to pay their respects.

Jacob gazed at the solemn gleamy white marble beauty of the Tomb, his young mind filled with curiosity and questions. He turned to his father who stood beside him, a look of pride filled with reverence etched on his face.

"Dad," Jacob began, his voice filled with genuine curiosity, "who is buried here? Why is it called the Tomb of the Unknown Soldier?"

Mr. Anderson, a proud military veteran, knelt down to Jacob's eye level and placed a gentle hand on his son's shoulder. He took a moment to gather his thoughts, wanting to explain this painfully significant piece of history in a way that Jacob would understand.

"Son," he began, his voice soft and measured, "the Tomb of the Unknown is a place dedicated to soldiers who made the ultimate sacrifice for our country but whose identities remain unknown."

Jacob's eyes widened with a mix of awe and genuine confusion. "Unknown? How can they not know who they are?"

Mr. Anderson nodded, patiently empathizing with Jacob's curiosity. "You see, son, during times of war, there are instances when soldiers give their lives on the battlefield, but their identities cannot be determined. Sometimes, it's because they were badly injured or disfigured, and other times, their remains are simply not found."

Jacob furrowed his young brow, trying to comprehend the magnitude of such a sacrifice. "So, they are buried here to honor their sacrifice?"

"Yes, exactly," his father confirmed. "These soldiers represent all the brave men and women who fought for our country and made the ultimate sacrifice, even when their names are known only to God. They symbolize the valor, courage, and selflessness of all those who gave their lives to protect our freedom."

Jacob's inquisitive mind grappled with the weight of such sacrifice. He stood in silence for a moment, absorbing the significance of the Tomb.

His father continued, "It's important to remember that each time we visit this place, we honor not only the unknown soldiers but also all those who have served and continue to serve our country. Their bravery and dedication should never be forgotten."

Jacob nodded, a newfound appreciation for the significance of the tomb beginning to take hold. He understood that the tomb was a reminder of the countless sacrifices made by those who fought for their country, even when their names were lost in the annals of history, known only to God.

As they stood there together, the Andersons paid their solemn respects, their hearts filled with unending gratitude for the unknown soldiers and all the servicemen and women who had served their country with honor. Jacob felt a sense of pride and responsibility, knowing that he carried the legacy of their sacrifices within him.

Then Jacob asked a simple question to his father, "What were these men's lives like?"

Chapter 1

The sun cast its golden glow over the small town of Thomasville, Alabama. Thomasville, nestled within the heart of Clarke County, is a world marked by simplicity and a powerful sense of community. Life unfolds at a slower pace than most bigger cities even in the South, untouched by the modern conveniences and complexities of bustling cities.

The town's center is dominated by a quaint square, where locals gather on warm afternoons to share news, stories, and the latest gossip. Tall oak trees line the streets, casting dappled shadows upon the weathered sidewalks. The town's square buzzed on a daily basis with activity as locals went about their normal routines. Even though the town's charm lies in its close-knit nature, where everyone knows their neighbors and a friendly nod or wave is exchanged with each passing soul, James Reynolds, a young man on the brink of adulthood, stood at the heart of it all, gazing at the familiar sights and feeling a sense of restlessness stirring within him.

Thomasville exudes a rustic beauty, with sprawling cotton fields stretching as far as the eye can see. These fields serve as the lifeblood of the community, with families working tirelessly to cultivate the white gold that sustains their livelihoods. The rhythm of the seasons dictates the ebb and flow of life, from the spring planting to the autumn harvest, each stage celebrated with a sense of pride and shared responsibility. James had grown up amidst the cotton fields, with the scent of pine trees hanging in the air. However, as he watched the townsfolk going about their business on this particular day, a deep longing welled up inside him. He yearned to venture beyond the boundaries of this idyllic southern town, to explore a world beyond the comforts and constraints of his small-hometown life.

Each day, as the sun painted the sky in hues of orange and pink, James found himself daydreaming of distant places and grand adventures. The rhythm of Thomasville no longer sufficed; he craved the unknown, the thrill of new experiences, and the opportunity to make his mark on the world.

One evening, with his heart set on departure, James gathered his courage and approached his parents, Samuel and Elizabeth Reynolds, in their modest home. The air inside was filled with the aroma of his mother's cooking, and the comforting sound of conversation drifted from the sitting room.

"Ma, Pa," James began, his voice betraying a mix of excitement and apprehension. "I've made up my mind. I want to leave here and go to Mobile."

His parents exchanged a knowing glance, recognizing the spark of wanderlust that had been in their son's eyes for months now. They once had the same spirit of adventure when they were James' age.

Samuel, a weathered man with a gentle smile, placed a hand on James' shoulder. "Son, we understand your yearning for something more," he said, his voice filled with the understanding of someone who once had those same dreams and longing for a brand new world. " I will make you a promise. If you save up the money to get a room in the boarding house in Mobile for the first month you're down there, I will pay for your train fare to the big city. Just remember to stay true to yourself, and never forget to write your ma and sissy."

Elizabeth, a woman of quiet strength and a teacher of young children at the local community school, stepped forward, her eyes shimmering with a mixture of pride and concern as tears of excitement and love filled her eyes. "James, you've always had a curious spirit. We want you to be happy, but promise us you'll take care of yourself and not get in too much trouble" James smiled a bit with the coy smile of a young man knowing trouble found him way more often than he found it at this last comment asking himself "what teenage boy didn't get into trouble?"

James nodded, his resolve strengthening with each passing moment as he absorbed their words of wisdom and encouragement. He turned to his younger sister, Maggie, who stood nearby, her eyes filled with both sadness and admiration.

"Maggie, you're going to be alright here," he assured her, wrapping her in a tight embrace. "I'll write you letters, and someday, I'll come back to tell you all about my adventures in the big city. I promise to send you gifts and candy from Mobile that you can't get here. Who knows, I might even come back with a girlfriend that can be like a big sister for you to play with."

With child-like silliness Maggie responded, "You better not" wiping away tears from her eyes. "I'm the only girlfriend you ever need" she continued with a sly smile on her face, returning her brother's amused look.

Ever since she was born, James and Maggie had always been extremely close. Because the kids her age didn't like playing with her, James spent a lot of his free time entertaining her, and letting her tag along with him and his friends as she grew up. He knew that she would be the hardest to say his farewells too when the time came. When he left for the big city of Mobile, he knew that his leaving would be the hardest on her.

With tears glistening in her eyes, Maggie whispered, "I'll be waiting, James. Make sure you come back safe."

***

After James had saved up the money for the first two months' rent at O'Malley's Boarding House in Mobile, a place James had heard about from an advertisement in the Mobile Press Register, who's editions made it to Thomasville a day after they were printed. A man of his word, his father, Samuel, escorted him down to the train station in town and purchased his ticket to Mobile. After they shook hands, and a few reminders from his father for James to keep in touch with his Ma and Maggie, James noticed a group of his friends moving in his direction.

As James bid farewell to his friends, he found Tommy O'Connor, his loyal companion since childhood, waiting by an oak tree near the town square. Tommy, a jovial and steadfast friend who always helped James get into trouble and had always stood by James through thick and thin.

"So, you're really going, eh?" Tommy asked, a mix of apprehension and sadness evident in his voice.

Even though Tommy had always been skittish and saw the adversity in everything, the bond between James Reynolds and Tommy O'Connor was forged in the crucible of childhood, an unbreakable friendship that would endure the test of time. In the quiet town of Thomasville, their lives intertwined, and their paths became inseparable.

From the earliest days of their youth, James and Tommy were two sides of the same coin. Where one went, the other was sure to follow. They were mischievous partners in crime, exploring the nooks and crannies of the town, chasing adventure with reckless abandon. Together, they climbed the tallest trees, their laughter echoing through the branches, and raced their bicycles down the winding streets, the wind streaming through their hair.

As they grew older, their bond deepened, becoming a steadfast foundation in a world full of uncertainties. James, with his dreams of venturing beyond Thomasville's borders, found skepticism in Tommy's apprehensive support. Tommy, with his unyielding loyalty, provided a shoulder to lean on and a voice of caution amidst the tumult of adolescence.

Their conversations were legendary, held late into the night beneath the stars. They discussed the mysteries of the universe, contemplating the meaning of life and the complexities of love. They shared dreams and fears, their imaginations intertwining as they painted vivid pictures of the future, they hoped to carve out for themselves.

Through it all, James and Tommy faced life's trials together.

James nodded, his gaze lingering on the familiar faces around him. "I can't ignore this feeling, Tommy. I need to see what's beyond these cotton fields. Maybe it's where I'm meant to be. There's still time to change your mind and come with me."

Tommy clapped James on the back, a hint of a smile on his face. "You know I can't leave Patty here by herself, plus I'm not as brave as you." Patty Johnson was Tommy's longtime girlfriend whom he planned on asking to marry him when he turned eighteen in four months. "You better bring back some tales of your adventures, my friend. I'll be here, ready to listen and raise a glass in your honor or commiserate in your failed return. Oh, and one last thing, you sure as heck better come back for my wedding."

Before James could board the train, he saw his Ma and Maggie running down the street after him. Ma reached him first and they embraced as tears filled her eyes. Ma said, "I love you son and take care of yourself."

James knelt down so that he could look Maggie in the eyes as they said their goodbyes.

"Maggie, I want you to know how much you mean to me," James whispered, his voice filled with emotion. "You've always been my guiding light, my little sister whom I love more than words can express."

Maggie's eyes shimmered with unshed tears, her voice barely above a whisper. "James, I'll miss you so much. Promise me you'll come back and tell me all about your adventures."

James reached out, gently wiped away a tear from Maggie's cheek. "I promise, Maggie. No matter where life takes me, I'll always come back to you. You'll forever be my compass, my reason to return."

Their embrace held a mix of sadness and hope, their hearts

entwined even as the world threatened to pull them apart. In that moment, James realized that no matter the distance between them, their bond would endure.

It seemed like the town had gathered at the train station to bid James and the other passengers farewell. Amidst the crowd, Maggie clung to their parents, her small frame barely visible. James spotted her, and his heart swelled with a mixture of pride and longing.

As he boarded the train, James leaned out the window, his eyes locked with Maggie's. "I'll write you letters, sissy, I promise."

Maggie nodded, her eyes shining with a mix of love and faith. "I'll be waiting, James. Safe travels and remember, no matter where you are, I love you."

With final farewells exchanged, James made his way to his seat. The bustling atmosphere was filled with anticipation as passengers hugged their loved ones and collected their belongings. The departing train pierced the air, marking the beginning of James Reynolds' journey to Mobile, a city teeming with possibilities and the promise of a brighter future. As he sat down, his heart filled with a mixture of excitement and trepidation, he couldn't help but reflect on the years of hard work and sacrifices that had led him to this moment.

James felt a profound sense of gratitude for the love and support that had surrounded him throughout his life. His parents, Samuel and Elizabeth, had instilled in him the values of resilience, determination, and the pursuit of dreams. Now, it was his turn to make them proud.

As the train started to move, James took a deep breath and closed his eyes, scanning his thoughts about the adventures ahead. Feeling a surge of excitement as the train slowly started to pull away.

The passing scenery outside the window blurred into a kaleidoscope of colors, a reflection of the myriad emotions that swirled within James' mind. Thoughts of his family and friends in Thomasville brought a mixture of joy and sadness. He cherished the memories they had created together, from childhood escapades to shared dreams. But he also knew that this journey was essential for his personal growth and the pursuit of his own ambitions.

Mobile, with its bustling streets and urban buildings, promised a world far different from the tranquil simplicity of Thomasville. It beckoned him with the allure of new experiences, opportunities, and the chance to hone his craft as a carpenter. It was a city that whispered of untold adventures and the potential to carve out his own path in life.

As the train rumbled along the tracks, James couldn't help but imagine the future that lay ahead. He pictured himself in a workshop, surrounded by tools and the sweet scent of freshly cut wood. He envisioned his hands, calloused from years of dedication, transforming raw materials into works of art. And he imagined the pride and satisfaction that would come with creating something beautiful with his own hands.

The hours melted away as the train sped towards its destination. James occupied his time with thoughts of the challenges he might face in the city, but also the resilience he had inherited from his family. He reminded himself of the countless hours spent honing his skills, the unwavering support of his loved ones, and the burning passion that fueled his determination.

Finally, the train pulled into the GM&O terminal in Mobile, its brakes screeching and hissing as it came to a halt. James stepped onto the platform; his gaze fixed on the bustling streets that stretched before him. The city's energy enveloped him, and he felt a surge of both excitement and apprehension.

With each step he took, James embraced the uncertainty of the unknown, knowing that it was an essential part of his journey. He was ready to immerse himself in the vibrant tapestry that Mobile had to offer, to learn from fellow craftsmen, and to make a name for himself in the world of carpentry.

As the sun dipped below the horizon, casting a warm glow over the city, James found himself standing before a sign that read *Apprenticeship Opportunities Available*. He took a deep breath, a sense of purpose welling up inside him. With final farewells exchanged and the promise of a new chapter ahead, James Reynolds, fueled by love, support, and the fire of his dreams, stepped forward into the embrace of his future in Mobile.

Chapter 2

In 1916, Mobile, Alabama, welcomed James with open arms as he stepped off the train onto its vibrant streets. The city, a bustling hub of commerce and culture, thrived with a unique charm similar to the one found in New Orleans, which set it apart from other southern towns. As James took in his surroundings, he found himself transported to a world of the rich history exuded throughout the city by the distinct architecture of the buildings that distinguished the city's growth like rings around the core of one of the many oak trees that lined it's many streets, the Southern hospitality exhibited by its people that made anyone that experiences it feel instantly like family, and a blend of cultures scattered throughout the neighborhoods that created the vibrant tapestry that makes the characteristics of Mobile.

The aroma of freshly baked bread from Smith's Bakery on Dauphin Street mingled with the salty breeze from Mobile Bay, carrying whispers of the city's maritime roots. The stately oak trees that lined the streets, their branches reaching out like welcoming arms, providing respite from the Southern sun. Brick-paved roads echoed with the clatter of horse-drawn carriages and the occasional honking of early model automobiles, like Henry Ford's Model T. A testament to the city's progress and ever-changing landscape.

The city's architecture stood as a testament to its storied past. Victorian and Greek Revival mansions, adorned with ornate details and wraparound porches, graced the streets, reminiscent of a time when elegance reigned supreme. Colorful Creole cottages stood alongside, highlighting the influence of French and Spanish settlers who had left an indelible mark on the city's cultural fabric.

Mobile's lifeblood resided in its vibrant people. Beinville Square and Market Hall bustled with a lively atmosphere, where vendors sold fresh produce, spices, and handmade crafts. The aroma of gumbo and fried chicken wafted through the air, tantalizing passersby with the promise of mouthwatering flavors. On Dauphin Street, the city's main thoroughfare, department stores and boutiques beckoned with the latest fashions, catering to the city's well-heeled residents.

As James wandered through the streets, he encountered a mosaic of people from diverse backgrounds. Creole families conversed in a mélange of French and English, their vibrant dresses and flamboyant hats adding splashes of color to the landscape. African Americans, with their resilience and creativity, created an indelible mark on the city, their soulful music floating from juke joints and churches alike.

The heartbeat of Mobile, however, resided in its waterfront. The Port of Mobile buzzed with activity, a testament to the city's role as a thriving commercial center. Ships from around the world docked at its wharves, unloading goods that would find their way into the city's stores and homes. The sound of ship horns echoed through the air, symbolizing the interconnectedness of Mobile with the rest of the world.

In Mobile, the spirit of community thrived. Churches played a vital role, not just in spiritual nourishment but also as social centers where residents gathered for Sunday services and midweek social events. Fraternal organizations and social clubs dotted the city, offering a sense of camaraderie and support to those seeking connection in a bustling metropolis.

As James settled into his new life in Mobile, he found himself swept up in the city's rhythm, captivated by its vibrant energy. With each passing day, he discovered new facets of the city's character, forging friendships and connections that would shape his journey. However, would this new world provide the adventure and wonder that James sought, or would it teach him the harsh realities of adult life on his own?

***

The sun hung low in the sky as James made his way down the bustling streets of Mobile. Having arrived at his destination, O'Malley's Boarding House on Conti Street, he was eager to find a place to rest his weary bones after the long journey.

The boarding house, a three-story red brick building with a quaint white porch and a wooden sign hanging from one of the white porch posts, stood proudly amidst the vibrant neighborhood. Its windows glimmered in the setting sun, beckoning tired travelers like James to find solace within its walls.

As he climbed the wooden steps to the porch, a sense of anticipation swelled within him. He reached for the tarnished brass doorknob and gently turned it, the creak of the door announcing his arrival. Stepping into the foyer, he was greeted by the scent of a home that housed up to twenty-five men at one time and the murmur of conversation drifting from the common room.

Iris O'Malley, a plump and motherly woman with silver hair and kind eyes, stood behind a wooden counter, organizing papers and greeting guests with a warm smile. When her eyes met James', her smile widened, recognizing the look of a weary traveler in need of respite.

"Welcome, lad," she said in a melodic Irish accent. "Are you looking for a long-term or short-term stay? Come, let's find you a cozy bed for the night."

James felt an immediate sense of comfort in Mrs. O'Malley's presence. He followed her through the corridor, his footsteps muffled by the threadbare carpet that had seen countless weary travelers over the years. The walls were adorned with faded paintings and photographs, capturing the history and stories of those who had once called this place home.

They ascended a creaking staircase, each step leading James closer to the sanctuary he sought. As they reached the second-floor landing, Mrs. O'Malley gestured toward a row of arranged doors.

"We have a few beds available, dear," she explained. "Choose one that you feel you will be comfortable with."

James peered into each room, their simple furnishings hinting at the stories of previous occupants. He finally settled on a room with a view of the street below, where he could catch glimpses of the city's vibrant pulse flowing by with the passing of each person who walked by.

Mrs. O'Malley handed him a small, iron key, its worn edges a testament to the many hands that had held it before. "This will be your sanctuary during your time with us, James. Make yourself at home."

Grateful for her hospitality, James thanked her and entered the room. The space, though modest, radiated a sense of warmth and welcome. Two sturdy bunk beds stood against the wall; the frames polished to a smooth shine. One of the four beds was occupied with a sleeping older gentleman, so James selected the top bunk next to the window, inviting James to rest and watch the world pass by as he nodded off to sleep.

As he settled onto the bed, a sense of relief washed over him. He knew he had found more than just a place to lay his head; he had found his temporary home while here in Mobile. A place where he could find a community of kindred spirits within the walls of O'Malley's Boarding House or just a place to sleep and wash up if the occasion called for it.

After relaxing for about fifteen minutes, James knew it was time to start making a game plan for finding work and establishing himself.

***

The morning bathed the streets of Mobile in a golden glow as James stepped out of his new home. With determination in his eyes and a sense of purpose in his stride, he set out on his quest to find work as a carpenter apprentice.

Armed with his modest demeanor and a confident knowledge of woodworking taught to him by his father, James began his journey through the bustling city. He walked from workshop to workshop, his optimism fueling his determination despite the weight of rejection weighing on his shoulders.

His first stop was Davis & Sons Carpentry, a renowned establishment known for its fine craftsmanship. James entered the workshop, his gaze sweeping across the busy scene of carpenters diligently at work. He approached the foreman, a burly man with a weathered face.

"Good morning, sir," James greeted, his voice steady and confident. "I'm James Reynolds, a carpenter by trade. I'm looking to become an apprentice."

The foreman glanced at James, his eyes lingering on the young man's worn but well-maintained outfit. He sighed, shaking his head. "Sorry, lad. We've got a full team at the moment. No openings for apprentices."

Undeterred, James thanked the foreman for his time and continued his search. He visited several more workshops and each time met with similar responses. Some were kind enough to offer advice or suggest other places to try, but the reality remained: there were no apprenticeship opportunities available for James.

As the day wore on, the sun began its descent towards the horizon, casting a warm glow over the city. James, undeterred by the string of rejections, decided to try his luck one last time. He arrived at the waterfront, where the cotton docks bustled with activity.

He noticed a group of men loading bales of cotton from a ship, their muscles straining with the effort. The work was grueling and demanded strength, but James was not one to shy away from hard labor. Determined to put food in his belly and a roof over his head, he approached the dock supervisor.

"Excuse me, sir," James called out, his voice carrying above the clamor of the docks. "I'm James Reynolds, new in town. I'm willing to work hard and lend a hand if you have any positions available."

The dock supervisor, a stout man with a rugged appearance, sized James up with a discerning eye. He nodded; his voice gruff but welcoming. "We could use an extra set of hands. The work's tough, but if you're up for it, we'll give you a shot."

A sense of relief washed over James as he joined the group of dock workers. With sleeves rolled up and a newfound determination, he eagerly embraced the physical demands of the job. Together, they loaded and unloaded bales of cotton, their sweat mingling with the scent of the raw fibers.

The hours passed, and as the day dipped below the horizon, James found himself in the rhythm of the dockyard. He marveled at the camaraderie among the workers, their banter as they shared stories to ease the fatigue in their muscles.

As the day came to an end, the dock supervisor approached James, a glimmer of respect in his eyes. "You held your own today, Reynolds. You've got a decent work ethic. Stick with us, and we'll take care of you."

James nodded, a smile of gratitude spreading across his face. Though his dream of becoming a carpenter apprentice had been put on hold, he had found a temporary path forward. The docks would provide him with a steady income and a sense of purpose while he continued to search for the opportunity to pursue his true passion.

As the final rays of sunlight painted the sky with hues of orange and pink, the weary dockworkers began to trickle away from the cotton docks, their day's work complete. James Reynolds, his clothes smudged with dirt and sweat clinging to his brow, joined the exodus, ready to return to the boarding house.

As he walked, a group of his fellow dockworkers, their boisterous laughter filling the air, caught up to him. They exchanged playful banter, teasing and jostling one another in good spirits. But as James approached, their laughter turned into whispers and sidelong glances.

"Hey there, newbie," one of the workers called out with a smirk. "Thought you could handle a day's work, huh?"

The others chuckled; their laughter laced with a hint of mockery. James felt a knot forming in his stomach, his confidence momentarily faltering under their gaze. He clenched his fists, unsure of how to respond.

However, amidst the teasing and laughter, a voice of kindness emerged. Louie, a seasoned dockworker with graying hair and a weathered face, stepped forward, placing a hand on James' shoulder.

"Leave him be, lads," Louie interjected, his tone firm yet gentle. "We were all newbies once. Ain't no need to give him a hard time."

The others paused, their expressions shifting from amusement to curiosity. James looked at Louie, gratitude welling up within him. Louie, sensing the unspoken question in James' eyes, leaned in and offered some words of wisdom.

"Listen, kid," Louie began, his voice filled with empathy. "This job ain't easy, and the fellas here can be a rough bunch. But they respect hard work and loyalty. Show 'em what you're made of, and they'll come around."

James nodded, absorbing every word as if they were precious nuggets of advice. He recognized the significance of Louie's kindness, a lifeline of acceptance in an otherwise uncertain environment.

"Thanks, Louie," James said, his voice filled with gratitude. "I appreciate your guidance. I'll do my best."

Louie patted James on the back, a smile tugging at the corners of his mouth. "That's the spirit, kid. Now, go on and rest up. Tomorrow's another day, and the docks won't wait for no one."

With those parting words, Louie rejoined the group, his presence diffusing the tension that had hung in the air. James walked away; his spirits lifted by Louie's encouragement.

Over the coming days, James followed Louie's advice. He worked diligently, proving his worth with every bale of cotton he lifted and every task he completed. Slowly but surely, the teasing and mocking subsided, replaced by nods of acknowledgment and occasional words of friendship.

James began to find his place among the dockworkers, sharing stories and laughter during breaks. He discovered common ground with each passing day, building friendships forged by the shared hardships of the dockyard.

And Louie, true to his word, became a mentor and friend to James. He taught him the tricks of the trade, from the best ways to lift heavy loads to the shortcuts that saved time during the long shifts. Their bond grew stronger with each passing day, a testament to the power of kindness and guidance in an unfamiliar world.

As James walked back to O'Malley's, the teasing of his first day a distant memory, he couldn't help but feel a sense of gratitude. The docks had been a baptism of fire, but through it all, he had found acceptance and camaraderie.

***

The third Friday of James' time as a dockworker had arrived, and the air buzzed with anticipation. It was payday, a momentous occasion that marked both the end of a grueling workweek and the start of a weekend filled with possibilities. As the sun dipped below the horizon, James found himself surrounded by a group of his fellow dockworkers, their faces etched with smiles and mischief.

"Hey, James!" shouted Frank, a burly man with a hearty laugh. "You've been doing a fine job around here. We thought it was about time you joined us for a celebration!"

The others nodded in agreement, their camaraderie evident in their gestures and friendly banter. They shared tales of past Friday night revelries, emphasizing the jovial atmosphere of The Hurricane Tavern, a local bar nestled amidst the heart of Mobile's entertainment district.

Intrigued by the prospect of joining his newfound friends for an evening of merriment, James hesitated for a moment. He hadn't ventured out beyond the confines of O'Malley's Boarding House since his arrival in Mobile, but the warmth and acceptance he had found among the dockworkers emboldened him.

"Count me in," James replied with a smile, his voice filled with enthusiasm. "I could use a night of laughter and good company."

The group cheered in response, their spirits soaring as they made their way through the streets of downtown Mobile. The Hurricane Tavern loomed ahead, its flickering sign casting a warm glow on the sidewalk.

Inside, the tavern buzzed with life. The air was thick with laughter, the clinking of glasses, and the lilting melodies of a lively piano. The scent of tobacco and the aroma of freshly poured drinks mingled in the air, creating an atmosphere of unadulterated revelry.

James and his newfound friends settled around a worn, wooden table, their voices rising above the cheerful cacophony. Pints of frothy beer were passed around, clinking in celebration as they toasted to a hard week's work and the bonds of friendship forged on the docks.

As the night wore on, the dockworkers engaged in raucous card games, their competitiveness accompanied by laughter and good-natured taunting. James found himself immersed in the spirited games, learning the intricacies of each hand and celebrating small victories with his companions.

The hours slipped away unnoticed, marked only by the rounds of laughter and the clatter of coins exchanged in good-natured wagers. The Hurricane Tavern became a sanctuary, a place where worries were forgotten, and the bonds of camaraderie grew stronger.

Amidst the revelry, Louie, ever the guiding presence, leaned toward James and spoke in a muffled voice. "See, kid," he said with a chuckle, "this is what it means to be part of the dockworker's family. We work hard, and we celebrate even harder. Remember, it's not just about the sweat and toil, but the friendships we forge along the way."

James nodded, his heart brimming with gratitude for the community he had found in Mobile. These were more than just drinking buddies; they were his brothers in arms, comrades who had shared the struggles and triumphs of the docks.

As the night came to a close, the dockworkers bid farewell to The Hurricane Tavern and to each other, their spirits high and their laughter lingering in the night air. James walked alongside his friends; the weight of the week's labor temporarily lifted from his shoulders.

He knew that the bonds he had formed on this night would transcend the walls of the tavern. The Hurricane Tavern had become a place of kinship, a testament to the resilience and solidarity of those who called the docks their home.

Lost in his thoughts, and probably a little bit drunk, James did not notice Mrs. O'Malley sitting in the common room of the boarding house as he walked in, sitting with a disapproving look on her face.

***

The night air hung heavy with a mixture of warmth and restlessness as James walked the final stretch back to his room. The celebratory evening at The Hurricane Tavern had stretched longer than anticipated, and now he found himself navigating the quiet recesses of the hallway.

As James entered the dimly lit foyer of the boarding house, he was met with the disapproving glare of Iris O'Malley. Her stern expression spoke volumes, conveying her concern and disappointment with a single glance, even though he was oblivious to it.

James shuffled his feet, feeling the weight of the night's

merriment settling on his shoulders. Her genuine care for the residents of the boarding house with her maternal instincts on full display. But little did James know the turmoil that her disapproval stirred within her.

Iris's eyes softened, her gaze filled with a mix of exasperation and something deeper, a hint of sorrow. She was determined not to let him go down the same path as her son. James' fleeting resemblance to Iris's son was undeniable. Their shared dark hair and determined eyes bore a striking similarity.

Patrick used to be just like James. Iris thought to herself. He was full of life, always looking for adventure. However, one night, in a drunken brawl at the bar, he took a life, and his freedom was lost forever.

James felt a shiver run down his spine.

Iris sighed, her gaze softening as she looked at James. "He reminds me so much of Patrick, and it frightens me. I don't want to lose another young man to the grip of tragedy," She said to herself.

***

The first rays of sunlight peeked through the windows of O'Malley's Boarding House, gently caressing the slumbering faces of James and his bunkmates. Little did they know that their blissful rest was about to come crashing down most unexpectedly.

At precisely 6:30 a.m., a cacophony of noise erupted outside the bedroom door. It was the unmistakable sound of pots and pans clanging together, accompanied by the boisterous singing of a tune that sounded suspiciously like "The Early Bird Catches the Worm."

The door flew open, and there stood Iris, her eyes sparkling with a mixture of mischief and determination. She brandished a wooden spoon, serving as her makeshift conductor's baton, as she led a parade of her helper, Ms. Higgins, and a procession of brooms and dusters.

"Rise and shine, sleepyheads!" Iris bellowed, her voice reverberating through the room. "It's wash day, and there's work to be done! No time for beauty sleep!"

James and his disoriented bunkmates stumbled out of bed, his hair askew, and his eyes bleary from the remnants of the previous night's indulgences. They exchanged groggy glances, struggling to comprehend the absurdity of the situation.

Iris seemed oblivious to the consequences of her actions, her primary focus on executing her grand plan to perfection. She waltzed around the room, twirling her wooden spoon with gusto, directing her team of cleaners like a maestro conducting a symphony.

Adelaide Higgins, who had an uncanny resemblance to a tornado in an apron, expertly whisked away the bedsheets, making them disappear with a magician's flair. Meanwhile, the brooms and dusters given to the bunkmates danced through the air, sweeping away cobwebs and dust bunnies.

James, still rubbing his temples to tame the pounding headache that accompanied his hangover, couldn't help but marvel at the spectacle unfolding before him. The sheer absurdity of it all threatened to bring a smile to his weary face, despite the discomfort.

As the room filled with the sound of exaggerated coughs and sneezes from the dust and dander in the air, Iris finally turned her attention to James. She cocked an eyebrow, her eyes gleaming mischievously as she saw his haggard appearance.

"Ah, young James," she said with a theatrical sigh. "Seems like last night's merriment didn't sit too well with you, did it? Well, consider this a friendly reminder that sometimes the price of revelry is a pounding headache and a rude awakening!"

The room erupted in laughter, a chorus of chuckles and groans mingling with the sound of brooms tapping against the floor. James couldn't help but join in, his own laughter mixed with a hint of self-awareness. Iris had certainly found a creative way to teach him a lesson about moderation.

As the morning unfolded, the bunkmates found themselves caught up in the frenzy of "wash day" their weariness slowly giving way to amusement. They took part in the cleaning rituals, scrubbing away stains and sharing tales of their adventures.

Iris, satisfied with the chaos she had sown, stood back to admire her handiwork. The room now sparkled with newfound cleanliness, a testament to the power of teamwork and the unorthodox methods of their indomitable matron.

Later in the day, after the boarding house had been cleaned, James sat on his bed and started writing a letter to his sister, Maggie, while periodically glancing out the window.

Chapter 3

Three months had passed since James arrived in Mobile, and he had settled into a rhythm that felt like second nature, like waking up on time without the help of a friend, roommate, or alarm clock. Life in the city had become his new normal, and he couldn't help but marvel at the changes in his life, like growing a beard for the first time, which had unfolded since his arrival.

At the cotton docks, James had become an integral part of the team. His strong work ethic and willingness to go the extra mile, like always volunteering to do extra tasks when someone was needed, had earned him the respect and admiration of his coworkers. They recognized his dedication and rewarded him with a sense of friendship that made the long, grueling hours that came with the hot and humid summers in Mobile seem more manageable.

Each day, James would rise with the sun, the hues of dawn that peeked over the towering treetops that lined the waking streets of Mobile. James enjoyed walking down those streets from the boarding house to the docks, which served as a reminder of the opportunities that lay ahead. Scarfing down a breakfast of scrambled eggs, bacon, biscuits and gravy and grits at

O'Malley's Boarding House, he would fuel himself for the day's physical demands. Mrs. O'Malley, despite her initial stern demeanor, had grown fond of James and would occasionally slip him an extra slice of pie and a warm, heartfelt smile as he prepared to head out the door. "Have a great day down at the docks and don't work too hard, James" Iris said as she waved him a hearty goodbye on his way out.

At the docks, the air was thick with the scent of cotton and the sound of the bustling activity of workers hard at their crafts and merchants conducting business. James would join his fellow dockworkers, his trusted friend Louie always by his side, as they tackled the laborious tasks that awaited them. Together, they unloaded bales of cotton from the ships, their muscles straining but their spirits unwavering most of the time.

Through the sweat and toil, James found solace in the unity of purpose that permeated the dockyard. The shared laughter and the occasional friendly banter eased the burden of the backbreaking work. He had become part of a tight-knit brotherhood, a mosaic of diverse personalities, each with their own stories and aspirations.

During their lunch breaks, James and his newfound friends would gather under the shade of an old oak tree, exchanging stories and sharing meals brought from homes. They spoke of their families, their dreams, and the trials they had overcome. James would share stories about his parents, Maggie. "One time, Maggie was running after my friends and I through the woods and she didn't see us turn right before the pond on ole man Cooks' place and she ran right into the pond and fell face first." James recalled with a hearty laugh at the memory. Their conversations were laced with laughter and camaraderie, forming bonds that transcended the confines of the dockyard.

Outside of work, Mobile offered a vibrant tapestry of sights and sounds, especially during the Mardi Gras season even though James never really celebrated the season he did enjoy festive fun, music and food. James would often spend his evenings exploring the city, discovering hidden corners, like Hurricane Tavern which James continued to visit with his coworkers, he just never stayed too long or overindulged which seemed to assuage Mrs. O'Malley and immersing himself in its rich culture. He marveled at the bustling markets that seemed to spring up in every square and park in the city, the lively music emanating from street corners, and the tantalizing aromas that wafted from local eateries.

On weekends, James would take a respite in the natural beauty that surrounded Mobile by spending as much of his free time exploring the woods and bayous as possible, an activity that gave him a sense of normalcy. At home, which was something he and Tommy loved to do. He would venture out to the nearby bayou, casting a fishing line and allowing the tranquility of nature to wash over him. These moments of solitude provided him with a sense of balance, a reminder of the simpler joys that lay beyond the demands of work.

With each passing day, James felt himself grow stronger, both physically and emotionally. The challenges he faced had honed his character, teaching him resilience and perseverance. He had learned the value of challenging work and the profound sense of accomplishment that came with it. He even started to become friendly with some of the young ladies around town, most of their fathers turning their noses up at a meager dockworker.

As the months rolled on, James continued to thrive in his newfound life. He had become an indispensable member of the dockyard crew, trusted and respected by his peers. The confidence that radiated from him was a testament to the transformation he had undergone since leaving Thomasville.

James missed his family dearly, although he found solace in the knowledge that he was building a life for himself. Mobile had welcomed him, sometimes with open arms and sometimes with a swift kick in the rear, offering opportunities for growth and connection that he had never imagined.

However, James was starting to grow weary and bored by the repetitive and tedious work that the cotton docks offered.

***

As the days turned into weeks and the weeks into months, James Reynolds found himself caught in a relentless cycle of work at the cotton docks. The initial excitement and sense of purpose that had accompanied his arrival in Mobile started to wane.

The physical demands of the dock work were taking their toll on James' body. His muscles ached from the long hours of heavy lifting, and his hands were calloused from handling rough ropes and bales of cotton. The once novel experience had transformed into a monotonous routine, leaving him longing for something more.

Despite his dedication to the docks and his newfound friends and coworkers, James couldn't shake the dream of becoming a carpenter. He continued to search for apprenticeship opportunities, but those doors remained closed. The demand for carpenters in Mobile was scarce, and those few openings were fiercely contested by seasoned craftsmen.

During his rare moments of respite, James would take out his toolbox and work on small projects, keeping the flame of his passion alive. Each stroke of the hammer and every careful measurement served as a reminder of the dream he held onto so dearly.

As weeks went by, James confided his feelings of restlessness to his friend Louie. The older dockworker listened attentively; his wise eyes filled with empathy. "I understand your yearning, lad, many young men like yourself have come through these docks with similar dreams and felt the same burnout" Louie said, "but remember, Rome wasn't built in a day. Sometimes, we have to weather the storms before the sun breaks through."

Despite Louie's comforting words, James couldn't shake the growing sense of disillusionment. He missed his family and the familiarity of Thomasville. The bustling streets of Mobile had lost some of their luster and just become crowded spaces full of people consumed in their own lives and families oblivious to the feelings and pains of the others around them, and the constant noise and commotion grated on his nerves at times, especially on the days that seemed to get warmer earlier as the summer dragged on.

One evening, after a particularly arduous day at the docks, James found himself strolling along the riverside alone, the setting sun casting a glow over the water. His mind was lost in contemplation, wrestling with the conflicting emotions of camaraderie, homesickness, and adventure that swirled within him.

As he watched the ships sail into the horizon, a newspaper flew up and lodged itself on James' lower leg. A feeling of discontent washed over him. "Is this all there is?" he thought, "Is this what I left home for? A life of labor without a glimmer of my true passion?"

The uncertainty gnawed at James' heart, and he felt a deep longing for change. He knew that life was an ever-changing tapestry, but the threads of his current reality were beginning to unravel.

That night, as James lay in his bunk at O'Malley's Boarding House, he felt the weight of the world upon his shoulders. His dream of becoming a carpenter felt like an impossible feat, and the sense of defeat threatened to consume him.

But in the darkest hours before dawn, a glimmer of hope would flicker even though James would not realize it yet.

James had been an avid reader of the newspaper since the age of ten. He loved keeping up with events from around the world and it made him feel more important and educated than his formal education might lead you to believe. It was a habit that he picked up from his father and one that his mother, the teacher, encouraged. James would spend breakfast every morning he was home sitting at the table eating whatever his mother had fixed and reading the sections of the paper his father would pass to him after he was done with it. That's why James picked up the newspaper that flew into his leg when he was walking alone on the cotton docks. There was a lot of stuff going on in the world, especially with the Great War raging in Europe, not to keep up with the newspaper.

As the first light of morning broke through, James rolled out of bed and after wiping the sleep away from his eyes, he reached for the newspaper that he had brought back to the boarding house with him the previous night that he had folded and put on his nightstand. He opened the paper up and started to read.

***

PANCHO VILLA INVADES!

March 10, 1916

Columbus, New Mexico - In the early hours of March 9, the tranquil town of Columbus was shaken by a thunderous onslaught as famed Mexican revolutionary leader, Pancho Villa, and his five hundred raiders stormed the border, leaving death and destruction in their wake.

Under the cover of darkness, the raiders crossed the U.S.-Mexico border, launching a surprise attack on the unsuspecting residents of Columbus. The quiet town turned into a battleground within moments, as Villa's forces launched an assault on the U.S. Army garrison and civilian targets alike.

The attack was swift and ruthless, catching both military and civilians off-guard. The raiders set fire to buildings, looted stores, and engaged in fierce gun battles with the outnumbered U.S. forces stationed in the area.

The garrison's defenders, valiantly led by Lieutenant Colonel Slocum, put up a brave resistance against Villa's raiders, but the sheer force of the attack overwhelmed them. Chaos ensued as residents fled for their lives, seeking shelter wherever they could find it.

In the midst of the mayhem, 18 Americans and numerous civilians injured. The raiders struck with a ferocity that left no room for mercy, causing immense grief and anguish among the survivors.

As the news of the invasion spread, panic and fear rippled through other border towns and communities. Residents braced for potential attacks, unsure if Villa and his forces would continue their campaign of violence beyond Columbus.

The swift response of the U.S. government will be felt as President Woodrow Wilson has ordered General John J. Pershing to lead an expeditionary force into Mexico in pursuit of Villa. The incident threatened to escalate already tense U.S.-Mexico relations, leading to concerns of further instability and conflict along the border.

President Woodrow Wilson addressed the nation, condemning the invasion and promising a resolute response to bring Villa to justice. He emphasized the need to protect American lives and property, ensuring that such aggression would not go unpunished.

In the aftermath of the Columbus invasion, the nation mourns the loss of innocent lives and the devastation left in the wake of Pancho Villa's raiders. It stands as a stark reminder of the challenges posed by international borders and the fragility of peace.

As the U.S. military launches its pursuit of Villa, uncertainty looms over the region. The residents of Columbus and neighboring towns grapple with the aftermath of the attack, with scars that may take years to heal. It is likely that National Guard units from around the country will be called up to participate in the upcoming expedition.

Today, the streets of Columbus are filled with grief and the echoes of gunfire have been replaced by the somber tolling of church bells. As the nation seeks justice for the fallen, the memory of March 9, 1916, will forever be etched in history as a day of chaos and tragedy that shook the American Southwest to its core.

Chapter 4

The morning sun had barely risen when James stepped into the communal area of O'Malley's Boarding House. He habitually glanced at the table, expecting to find the usual spread of breakfast treats of eggs, grits, bacon and biscuits that Mrs. O'Malley lovingly prepared for her lodgers. However, today was different. The newspaper folded under his arm revealed the headline about Pancho Villa's invasion of New Mexico that James had just read in his room.

James' intense stare and clinched jaw betrayed the surge of anger and frustration welling up inside him. The invasion was an unsettling reminder of the conflict and turmoil that loomed. He had hoped to find a sense of stability and peace in Mobile, away from the tensions of the outside world while experiencing the adventure and wonder that the world had to offer, but now it felt like even that sanctuary was slipping away.

"Damn it," James muttered under his breath, taking the newspaper in his hands from under his arm. He felt an overwhelming urge to do something, to take action, but his restlessness and the frustration etched on his face showed he didn't know where to direct his energy.

Mrs. O'Malley, busy in the kitchen, noticed James' agitation and approached him with a concerned expression. "James, my dear, what's got you so worked up?" she asked gently.

"It's this news about the Pancho Villa invasion," James replied, showing Iris the newspaper in his hand, his voice tinged with frustration. "It feels like a gut punch and slap in the face at the same time, and it pisses me off."

Mrs. O'Malley sighed, placing a comforting hand on his shoulder. "WATCH YOUR LANGUAGE YOUNG MAN!" Iris sternly rebuked him. "I understand your concerns, James. The world can be a tumultuous place, and it's natural to feel overwhelmed. But getting angry won't change anything. Sometimes, all we can do is take care of ourselves and our responsibilities."

James nodded; the weight of the world still heavy on his shoulders. "You're right, Mrs. O'Malley. I just wish there was something I could do to make a difference." Thinking to himself that while he did have responsibilities at the cotton docks, he had no ties that bound him permanently to Mobile.

"Sometimes, the most significant impact we can have is through our actions," Mrs. O'Malley said, as her voice filled with wisdom. "Focus on your work at the docks and be a good friend to those around you. That alone can make a difference in the lives of others."

As Mrs. O'Malley turned back to the kitchen, James took a deep breath, trying to let go of his frustration. He knew she was right, but the turmoil in his heart remained.

Lost in his thoughts, he walked out of the boarding house without realizing that he had completely missed breakfast. This oversight was highly unusual for him, and the offended look on Mrs. O'Malley's face was noticeable.

***

The cotton docks buzzed with activity as James and Louie worked side by side, unloading bales of cotton from a nearby ship. The midday sun beat down on them, intensifying the already strenuous labor. Beads of sweat glistened on their foreheads as they heaved the heavy cargo.

As they took a momentary break, Louie noticed the distant look in James' eyes. "Something's eating at you, lad," Louie remarked, as he wiped his brow with the back of his hand.

James sighed, a mix of frustration and weariness evident in his voice. "It's this Pancho Villa invasion business," he said, his jaw clenching with anger. "I just can't understand why a fool from Mexico would want to even antagonize us."

Louie nodded, understanding James' sentiments all too well. "I hear you," Louie said, his voice carrying a tone of empathy. "It's a harsh reality we're living in, and it's easy to feel overwhelmed by it all."

"I left Thomasville hoping for a fresh start, a chance to see all the wonders and excitement the world has to offer," James said, his voice tinged with disappointment. "But it seems like there's no wonder, just nonsense like this no matter where I go."

Louie placed a reassuring hand on James' shoulder. "I know it's tough, but sometimes, we have to confront the darkness to appreciate the light," he said. "We can't change the world overnight, but we can make a difference in our own little ways."

James pounded his fist into his other hand as he let out a frustrated sigh. "I'm just tired, Louie," he admitted. "Tired of the hardships, tired of the uncertainty, and tired of feeling like there's no escape from it all."

Louie nodded again; his eyes filled with understanding. "Life can be a heavy burden, that's for sure," he said. "But remember, you're not alone in this. We're all in this together, and we lean on each other for support when times get tough."

As James took in Louie's words, a sense of friendship washed over him. It was true; he wasn't alone in his struggles. The friendships he had forged at the docks had been a source of strength and comfort, reminding him that he was part of a community that faced life's challenges together. However, his fellow dockworkers were not the only friends he had in life. James knew that his childhood friend from Thomasville, Tommy, would be just as upset about the Villa raid as he was.

"I appreciate your words, Louie," James said, his voice softening. "It's just hard sometimes, you know?"

Louie nodded, his eyes reflecting the shared weariness James could tell they both felt. "Believe me, I know," he replied. "But remember, it's okay to feel burdened and weary. It's part of being human. The important thing is to keep moving forward, even when it feels tough."

As the day wore on, James found solace in the company of his fellow dockworkers. They exchanged stories and jokes, sharing the weight of their burdens in the form of shared laughter and camaraderie. However, James could not shake the feeling that there was something he should and could do personally to right the wrong done in New Mexico.

As the day began to set on the workday, James felt a glimmer of hope in the midst of his weariness. The weight of the world hadn't lifted entirely, but he knew he had the strength to carry on, supported by the friends he had made and the resilience that lay within him.

The cotton docks would continue to be a place of hard work and toil, but James was already dreaming of ways to fight back against the turmoil the world was throwing his way.

***

Later that evening, as James returned to the boarding house

after a long day at the docks, Mrs. O'Malley approached him with a stern look.

"James, I must say, I'm quite disappointed that you missed breakfast this morning," she said, her voice firm but tinged with hurt.

"I'm sorry, Mrs. O'Malley," James replied, feeling guilty for his oversight. "I was just so caught up in the news and everything that I completely lost track of what I was doing."

"I understand that you're digesting a lot of news and emotions, but it's easier to digest that on a full stomach," Mrs. O'Malley expressed with the wisdom of an older Southern mother. "Breakfast is important, and it's my way of taking care of you all."

James nodded as he hung his head feeling remorseful for missing breakfast. "You're right, Mrs. O'Malley. I should have been more mindful."

Mrs. O'Malley's expression softened, and a small smile appeared on her face as she patted James on the back. "I know you have a lot on your mind, but don't forget that I do care about you like my own child. If you ever need someone to talk to, I'm here."

With those words of comfort, James felt a sense of gratitude for Mrs. O'Malley's care and understanding. He knew that he was lucky to have such a supportive place to call home, even in the face of the world's troubles.

***

With the awkward breakfast conversation a few months in the rearview mirror and James having settled back into his normal daily routine, James returned to the boarding house one evening and Iris led James to the dining table for supper. Mrs. O'Malley knew James liked reading the newspaper with breakfast but since he had missed it that morning due to an early morning ship arrival at the docks, she saved that day's copy for his supper. As James sat down to a meal of flat iron steak, mashed potatoes, collards, and cornbread, he started to flip through the headlines in the paper. Most of the news was about the latest goings on in The Great War in Europe, which seemed like a world away from Alabama, but then James saw something that stopped him as he read it.

***

Alabama National Guard Mobilized for Mexican Border Service! Attention, Volunteers! Answer the Call of Duty

Montgomery, Alabama - In response to the recent raids by Pancho Villa along the Mexican border and in the wake of his violent incursion into New Mexico, the Federal War Department has officially mobilized the Alabama National Guard to join the Punishment Expeditionary Force.

The call to duty extends to all able-bodied and patriotic citizens of Alabama who are willing to serve their country in this crucial mission to bring Pancho Villa to justice and defend the nation's border. Your service is needed to support the efforts of the U.S. Army in restoring peace and security along the border with Mexico.

Mobilization Date: June 16, 1916

Location: Vandiver Park, Montgomery

If you are ready to take up arms and stand united against aggression, make your way to Vandiver Park in Montgomery starting on June 19, 1916, to enlist in the Alabama National Guard. Show your commitment to the nation and join your fellow citizens as we embark on this historic expedition to uphold the honor of our country.

This is an opportunity to serve with valor and demonstrate your dedication to the United States of America. The Punishment Expeditionary Force will be tasked with hunting down the infamous Pancho Villa and ensuring that justice prevails for his raids and attacks on American soil.

The Federal War Department emphasizes the urgency of this mission, calling upon the bravery and resolve of the men of Alabama to defend the border and preserve the nation's safety.

Inquiries and enlistment applications can be made at Vandiver Park on the specified dates, where officials from the Alabama National Guard will be present to guide and assist you.

Let the spirit of patriotism guide your decision, and together, we shall stand strong against those who threaten our nation's peace and security. Your service will be remembered as a testament to the strength and unity of the people of Alabama.

***

After reading that announcement, James knew what he needed to do. Ever since he was a young boy, he would listen to stories from his grandfather about the different battles his grandfather fought in the Civil War with the 30th Missouri "Irish Brigade". From the riverbanks of Port Hudson and Vicksburg to the bay shores of Spanish Fort and Blakely, James' grandfather had seen a lot of action and destruction in the war and wasn't shy about sharing it with his grandkids and their friends. James' grandfather's service in the Mobile Campaign is how James' family ended up in Clarke County, Alabama.

James and Tommy spent many Sunday afternoons sitting on the front porch at the feet of James' grandfather's rocking chair. Listening to him regal them with stories about the many different battles he participated in during the war as a member of the Union Army. It was listening to these stories and "recreating" some of these battles in the front yard as children that James developed his deep sense of patriotism. After reading the announcement about the call-up of the National Guard, James knew he had to enlist, and that Tommy would want to as well, even though doing so would make him anxious. However, he had to figure out how to get to Montgomery first.

That evening, as the sun dipped below the Mobile skyline, James found a quiet moment to talk to Louie about the decision that had been weighing on his mind. They sat on an empty crate near the edge of the cotton docks, their tired bodies seeking respite from the day's toil.

"Louie," James began hesitantly, "I've been thinking about joining the National Guard. With all that's happening in the world, I want to do it."

Louie looked at James thoughtfully, nodding in understanding. "That's a noble decision, lad," he said. "Serving your country is a significant responsibility, and it takes courage to step up."

"I just want to make a difference," James said earnestly. "And maybe, just maybe, I'll find some direction and purpose in my life."

Louie smiled, his eyes glimmering with pride. "I have no doubt you'll make a fine soldier, James," he said. "To get to Montgomery, you'll need to take the train. It's a long ride, but it's worth it."

"The train, huh?" James pondered, his mind calculating the logistics.

"Yes, the train," Louie confirmed. "And you'll need a little something to ensure a free ride."

"A free ride?" James raised an eyebrow.

Louie leaned in closer, his voice lowering conspiratorially. "Find the fella who feeds the coal furnace on the train," he said. "He's the one you want to talk to. A friendly word and a bit of help might just earn you a ticket without cost."

James grinned at the clever suggestion. "You're full of surprises, Louie," he said with admiration.

"Years of experience, my boy," Louie chuckled. "Now, about asking Tommy to join you in Montgomery. Be straight with him, and don't sugarcoat anything. Tommy seems like a practical fella, and he'll appreciate honesty."

"You're right," James nodded. "I'll tell him about the decision I've made and why I feel it's important. Maybe he'll see the value in joining too."

"That's the spirit," Louie encouraged. "And remember, Tommy's always been one to stand by you. If you present it as an opportunity for both of you to make a difference, he just might be swayed."

As the conversation carried on, James felt a sense of gratitude for Louie's guidance and wisdom. Louie had become not just a friend, but a mentor, offering invaluable advice that James couldn't find anywhere else.

With renewed determination, James prepared himself for the journey to Montgomery. Also, he needed to prepare for the conversation with Tommy. The day that followed was a whirlwind of preparation, both mentally and practically, as he readied himself for these new adventures that awaited him in life.

The next day, James approached the conductor of one of Southern Railways' train that had stopped at the cotton docks to unload. James struck up a conversation with him and explained to him that he wanted to hitch a ride to Thomasville and then on to Montgomery.

The conductor said "Ain't no free rides on this train, boy, so either pay up or get on out of here with that nonsense."

With a slight grin on his face James continued to press, "I understand, and I would never ask you to give me a free ride. I'm willing to work for my passage."

"Well, I guess my stoker would appreciate the respite. If you're willing to shovel coal into the furnace, I guess I can get you a ride to Thomasville," responded the conductor. "Be back here in two hours ready to go, or you'll be left behind, boy."

After having run back to the boarding house, telling his goodbyes to Mrs. O'Malley, and gathered his things, James returned to the cotton docks an hour and a half later, informing the foreman that he was leaving town and probably would not be back.

"Well dang it, You're one of the best young workers to come through these parts in a very long time. You'll be sorely missed, and if you ever come this way again and need a job, you'll have one on my crew." The Forman said shaking James' hand as he began the process of leaving. James walked up to Louie as he was walking towards the train, Louie standing there with a knowing expression on his face of pride for James and his next adventure, and sorrow that he would not see his young friend again for a while, if ever. "Look here. Lad, you better keep in touch and don't be a stranger," Louie said as they shook hands. "I won't, and I promise to come back as soon as everything's over." A smile formed on his face.

The conductor blew the whistle for the train engine, and James made his way toward the track. As he climbed on board the train engine, he turned around and waved goodbye to Louie, and the rest of his crew who had unexpectedly stopped what they were doing and gathered behind Louie to send him off.

James got situated in the boiler room of the train engine, put his stuff in the corner, and grabbed the shovel. The fireman for the train engine showed him how to load coal into the steam engine and explained how much coal needed to be in the steam engine to keep it going. James quickly realized that this was not going to be an easy trip back home, but one that was well worth it.

***

As soon as James had collected his things and stepped off the train from the boiler room at his first destination, he immediately saw Tommy milling around downtown Thomasville, almost like he was waiting for James to get there. James immediately called out to Tommy who swung around and suddenly had a grin from ear to ear. When he saw James getting off the train. Tommy immediately started running towards the train depot and they embraced like brothers when they met.

"How the heck have you been, James?" Tommy asked as soon as the embrace was over.

"I've been pretty good, and I've got tons of stories to tell." James quipped.

"I'll be back through here tomorrow around the same time to pick you up," the train conductor interjected. James nodded at the conductor in recognition and immediately turned his attention back to Tommy. The two gathered James' belongings and started down the street towards his parents' house.

As soon as they turned on to the street where his parents' house was located, Maggie immediately recognized James and Tommy as she started running down the street towards them. Screaming James' name, causing his mother to stop hanging the wash on the line, and look up with a smile on her face. As soon as Maggie reached James and Tommy, she immediately jumped into James' arms and gave him a big hug around his neck. "James, what are you doing back here?" Maggie asked inquisitively.

"Would you believe I came back just to see you?" James responded teasingly with a smile on his face.

"Not in a million years," she responded playfully slapping his chest with the back of her hand.

"I'm on my way to Montgomery, and I wanted to stop by and see everybody while I had the chance," he finally said truthfully.

By this time James' mother had caught up with the crowd on the street, she asked, "This is an unexpected surprise, what are you doing back here James?" Bewilderment and concern started to crawl across her face.

"I'm on my way to Montgomery, and I wanted to stop and see everybody while I had the chance," he responded. "Why are you headed to Montgomery?" she quizzed. "We can talk about that this evening when Pa gets home," He returned. That concerned look on his mother's face only grew deeper knowing the real reason he was headed there.

"Well, at least let me get some dinner on the stove for you." She said as she turned back towards the house.

At the house, James' mother and Maggie went into the kitchen to fix dinner, Tommy, and James settled into rocking chairs on the front porch. James regaled Tommy with stories about Mobile, the cotton docks, the boarding house, Mrs. O'Malley, and the Hurricane Tavern. In turn, Tommy relayed stories to James about things going on around town and the story of how he asked Patty to marry him. With both boys caught up on things going on in their lives, the time had come to speak with Tommy about Montgomery and the National Guard. James took Louie's advice to heart. He was straightforward and honest, laying out his reasons for wanting to join the Guard and explaining the sense of purpose he sought in doing so.

Tommy listened intently, his serious demeanor giving way to contemplation. "I dunno know James, that sounds pretty dangerous." Tommy responded. "Life is dangerous and unrelenting," James retorted. "This way, we can spend life doing something important that is greater than ourselves." "Yeah, but I have Patty to think about now and what if something happens to me out West?" Tommy questioned. "Do you think that Patty will be impressed by someone that runs away from a fight?" James returned. After a moment of silence, he looked at James with determination in his eyes. "Alright, James," he said. "If you think this is something we can do together, count me in."

James grinned, a surge of camaraderie swelling up inside of him. "Together," he repeated. "We can make a difference, Tommy. I'm sure of it."

That evening after supper was over, James approached his parents who were sitting on the front porch swing enjoying the muggy warm summer air in southwest Alabama and told them that he wanted to talk to them. "Yes, son?" Samuel inquired. "The reason I am heading to Montgomery is because the National Guard is enlisting men there for a stint of service out West to hunt down and punish Poncho Villa and his gang of murderous thugs." James started. "I want to join." "Are you sure about this, James?" his mother asked. "That sounds like it is awfully dangerous, and it would kill your Ma if something happened to you," his father added. "I'm sure," James said matter of flatly. "Tommy has agreed to go with me, so I won't be alone, and if Mobile taught me anything, it's that life is dangerous anywhere you go, it's what we do with life that matters most." "Well son, you're an adult now, so I can't stop you, but I don't want you to go off and get hurt," his father said. "I promise I will be careful, Pa."

With the decision made, James and Tommy began their journey to Montgomery the next afternoon, ready to face whatever challenges lay ahead. As they boarded the train, James couldn't help but feel a sense of excitement mingled with trepidation. But he knew that with Louie's advice and Tommy by his side, he was on the path to something meaningful and transformative.

Tommy and James stepped off the train when they reached the Vandiver station and walked the short distance to Vandiver Park. When they arrived, they realized that they were not the only Alabamians to heed the call.

Chapter 5

As the train rolled to a stop at Vandiver Station in Montgomery, James and Tommy stepped off the platform with anticipation. They had spent their time on the train, catching each other up on events since James had left for Mobile, and shoveling coal into the train furnace. The journey had been long, but they were finally here, ready to embark on their new path as members of the National Guard.

"Feels like we've come a long way, doesn't it?" Tommy remarked, stretching his arms and taking in the new surroundings of a mass of people moving from the train platform to the makeshift military camp at Vandiver Park.

James nodded, a mix of excitement and nerves bubbling inside him. "It sure does, maybe that's because we spent the whole time burning up keeping that train going" he quipped. "This is where it all begins."

They walked through the station and onto the hustling and bustling streets of Montgomery enveloping them. The noise of carriages and the chatter of passersby that buzzed around them as they walked created a symphony of life that was a far cry from the quiet simplicity of Thomasville.

Following the directions they had received, James and Tommy soon found themselves on the street leading to Vandiver Park. The sun cast a warm glow on the trees that lined their way, and a sense of determination washed over them.

"This is it," James said, his voice filled with conviction. "We're about to start a new chapter in our lives. So, if you want to back out now is the time."

Tommy nodded, his eyes reflecting a mix of excitement and trepidation. "I never thought I'd end up here, but let's do this," he admitted.

As they approached the entrance of Vandiver Park, the sight of the National Guard Camp came into view. Tents were pitched, flags flew high, and soldiers in uniform moved with purpose. It seemed like thousands of young men in a wide assortment of regular clothes just like them lined up at tables.

Taking a deep breath, James and Tommy got at the end of one of the lines, their footsteps echoing in the air. A sergeant approached them, his stern expression softened by a hint of warmth.

"Are you here to enlist?" the sergeant asked, sizing them up. "Welcome to Vandiver Park. I'm Sergeant Jones."

James and Tommy introduced themselves, their nerves subsiding slightly under Sergeant Jones' reassuring demeanor.

"Well, you're just in time," the sergeant said, a twinkle in his eye. "We've got a training session starting in half an hour. Let's get you settled into your quarters, and then you'll be joining the ranks." Sgt Jones led them out of line and directly to one of the tables where a soldier was taking down the names of people wanting to enlist.

After having given the soldier all of the pertinent information he needed, and going through the physical and medical processes, they settled into their designated tents. James and Tommy couldn't help but exchange glances of excitement and a hint of apprehension. This was the moment they had been preparing for, the chance to serve their country.

The training session was rigorous and demanding. The officers put them through a rigorous regimen of calisthenics and other exercises. They also taught the new recruits how to navigate the obstacle course, disassemble their weapons, clean them, and reassemble them. The camaraderie they started to experience among their fellow recruits made the challenges more bearable. They bonded with the others, sharing stories of their backgrounds and hometowns they left behind.

As the sun dipped below the horizon, marking the end of their first day at the camp, James and Tommy sat by the campfire exhausted.

"It's a whole new world, isn't it?" Tommy said, his eyes glistening with excitement and unease.

"It is," James replied, a sense of pride swelling in his chest. "And I'm grateful we're in this together, Tommy."

Tommy clapped James on the shoulder with a grin. "You and me, partners in this crime," he said. "I have a feeling we'll make a great team."

As the night settled around them, James felt a sense of purpose and belonging that they had never experienced before. They knew that the road ahead would be challenging, but with each other's support and the friendship of their fellow soldiers, they felt like they were ready to face whatever came their way.

And so, under the watchful stars and the enclosure of Vandiver Park, James and Tommy embraced their new roles as members of the Guard. Their journey had just begun, and they were eager to stand strong in service to their country, however, it was a long uncertain road ahead for them.

***

Life at Vandiver Park was an immersive and transformative experience for James and Tommy. From the crack of dawn to the setting sun, they immersed themselves in the rigorous training that molded them into National Guard soldiers.

Their days began with the blaring of trumpets, signaling the start of physical training. James and Tommy joined their fellow recruits in a series of grueling exercises. Push-ups, sit-ups, and long runs tested their physical endurance, but they pushed through, knowing that their strength and resilience were being honed.

As they caught their breath after the morning workout, Sergeant Jones approached them with a stern expression. "Now that you're warmed up, it's time for breakfast and then gun training," he announced.

James and Tommy, along with hundreds of their fellow recruits, devoured metallic trays of lukewarm eggs, bacon, a biscuit, and grits. They washed it down with a big glass of warm water. Because the camp did not give them much time to eat, only 30 minutes, they pretty much weren't able to carry on extensive conversations with each other or their fellow recruits.

At the firing range, James and Tommy familiarized themselves with their weapons. They learned how to handle rifles with precision and accuracy, their instructors emphasized the importance of safety and discipline. Because James and Tommy were new soldiers, they had difficulty picking up the nuances of the bayonet.

"Remember, a weapon is only as good as the soldier who wields it," Sergeant Jones said, watching them closely. "Respect your firearm, and it will serve you well."

Over the weeks, James and Tommy grew more confident in their shooting abilities. They became adept at hitting targets from various distances, each successful shot reinforcing their sense of responsibility as soldiers. They even became moderately proficient attaching their bayonet quickly.

Survival training was another crucial aspect of their regimen. Under the guidance of seasoned instructors, they learned essential wilderness skills, from building shelters to finding food and water in the wild.

The forest surrounding Vandiver Park became their classroom. They navigated through dense underbrush, learned to start fires with flint and steel, and identified edible plants. They even swam across the Alabama River several times so that they could get used to swimming with their gear on.

During one particularly intense survival training exercise, Tommy got lost in the woods. Panic started to creep in as he struggled to find his way back to camp. Just as worry threatened to overwhelm him, James appeared from behind the trees.

"Hey, Tommy! Over here!" James called out, waving him over.

Relief washed over Tommy's face as he rushed toward his friend. "James, I was lost. Thanks for finding me," he said, his voice filled with gratitude.

"We're a team, just like back home. Remember that time you got lost in the woods near Choctaw Corner?" James replied, clapping Tommy on the back. "We look out for each other."

The bond between James, Tommy and the other recruits that stuck it out through the training grew stronger with each passing day, and they found comfort in knowing they had trusted allies by their side.

As their training continued, they delved into tactical exercises and learned about military strategy. They practiced maneuvering in formation, coordinating movements, and responding to simulated enemy attacks.

In the evenings, as the sun dipped down to its resting place, James and Tommy gathered with their fellow recruits around the campfire. They shared stories, exchanged laughter, and forged friendships that transcended their individual backgrounds.

"This feels like a second family," Tommy remarked one night, looking around at his comrades.

James nodded, a smile playing on his lips. "It does," he agreed. "We come from different places and walks of life, but here we are, united in a common purpose."

As the weeks turned into months, James and Tommy underwent a transformation they had never anticipated. They became more disciplined, resilient, and focused. They were no longer the boys who had left Thomasville in search of direction and purpose; they were now soldiers ready to face whatever the world threw their way.

***

As their training at Vandiver Park progressed, James and Tommy eagerly anticipated the day they would be assigned to their respective units. The camp buzzed with excitement as the recruits completed their final evaluations and assessments, and the time for their assignments drew near.

One morning the recruits gathered in the main courtyard, as they did every morning. Sgt Jones stood before them, a clipboard in hand, ready to announce their assignments.

"Alright, listen up, everyone," he called out, his voice authoritative yet encouraging. "Today is a big day. You've all worked hard, and now it's time to put that training to use."

He began reading off names and unit assignments, each announcement met with anticipation and a mix of emotions. James and Tommy exchanged anxious glances, eager to find out where their paths would lead.

"James Reynolds, you'll be part of B Company, 1st Battalion, 167th Regiment," the sergeant said, a nod of approval in James' direction.

James felt a surge of pride at his assignment. He had worked tirelessly during training, and now he was being entrusted with a role in B Company.

As the list continued, Tommy's name was called out next. "Tommy O'Conner, you'll be part of A Company, 2nd

Battalion, 167th Regiment."

Tommy's face broke into a wide grin. "A Company, here I come," he said, his voice tinged with anxiety from being separated from his friend.

As the assignments were finalized, James and Tommy realized that they would be part of different companies, but they were determined to make the most of their separate journeys.

Over the following days, they settled into their respective units. James met his fellow soldiers in B Company, finding a mix of seasoned veterans and fellow newcomers like himself. The men of the unit welcomed him with open arms, hearty laughs, and practical jokes. He felt a sense of belonging among them.

Tommy, too, quickly integrated into A Company. His friendly and approachable nature endeared him to his fellow soldiers, and he soon forged bonds that felt like family.

In their respective companies, James and Tommy underwent further training, honing their skills and growing as soldiers.

They became familiar with their specific roles within their platoons, learning to work as a cohesive unit.

As the weeks dragged on, they participated in joint exercises with other companies, becoming part of a larger battalion and division. The sense of brotherhood they had experienced during basic training only intensified as they connected with soldiers from diverse backgrounds and areas of the state.

During a joint training exercise, James had the opportunity to reunite with Tommy. Their companies were collaborating on a tactical mission, and the excitement of working together again was palpable.

"Tommy! Over here!" James called out, spotting his friend across the field.

Tommy grinned and hurried over, clapping James on the back. "It's good to see you again," he said. "I've missed being in the same company."

"Me too," James replied, his eyes shining with enthusiasm. "But you know what? Our training has given us the skills to work together no matter where we are."

Tommy nodded in agreement. "You're right," he said. "We've both changed so much since we left home. I can't believe how far we've come."

As they worked side by side in the exercise, James and Tommy felt a deep sense of pride and accomplishment. Their journey from small-town boys to dedicated soldiers had been transformative, and they knew they were part of something much greater than themselves.

At the end of the day, as they bid each other farewell and returned to their respective units, James and Tommy felt a renewed sense of unity with a tinge of homesickness, for James, missing his family, especially Maggie and Tommy missing Patty.

***

Dear Maggie,

I hope this letter finds you well back home. Life here in Montgomery has been quite an adventure, and I can't wait to share all the exciting details with you.

First and foremost, let me tell you about the National Guard. It's been everything I hoped for and more. The training at Vandiver Park has been intense, but it has prepared me well for my role in B Company, 1st Battalion, 167th Regiment. The camaraderie among my fellow soldiers is incredible, and I've made some loyal friends here.

There's a guy named Jack in my squad who hails from up north. He's got a quick wit and a profound sense of humor that keeps us all laughing even in the toughest of times. Then there's Sam, a fierce and skilled soldier who happens to be the best shot in our company. He's become like a brother to all of us in the squad, always looking out for everyone.

But, of course, I haven't forgotten my friend Tommy. We're in different companies, and I have to admit, I miss him a lot. We used to spend every day together, and now our paths don't cross as often. However, when we do get the chance to see each other during joint exercises, it's like no time has passed at all. Tommy is doing well in A Company, 2nd Battalion, 167th Regiment, and I'm proud of him.

Life in the National Guard is challenging, but it's also rewarding. Our training has given me a sense of purpose and direction that I didn't have before. I feel like I'm part of something bigger, and it's a responsibility I take seriously. We've been on several exercises and maneuvers, and each one has taught me the importance of teamwork and trust.

Montgomery is a bustling city with its own charm. The streets are always filled with people, and I've had the chance to explore some of the local spots with my newfound friends. You should see the State Capitol Building! It is huge! It's bigger than anything you can find in Thomasville. Maybe Ma and Pa can bring you up here one day to see it. We even got to participate in a military parade down the streets of downtown Montgomery on the 4th of July weekend in front of thousands of onlookers.

The friendships I've formed here are unlike any other. We share a bond that only comes from experiencing the challenges of training and serving together.

I think about you, Ma, and Pa often, especially during the moments of quiet reflection. I miss the comfort of home, the familiar faces, and the peacefulness of Thomasville. However, I know that my journey here is important, and it will shape the person I become.

Please give my love to everyone and know that you're always in my thoughts. I'll write again soon and share more about my experiences here. Until then, take care and know that I'm doing well.

With all my love,

James

***

The glaring sun hung high in the sky as B Company assembled in perfect formation on the parade ground. James stood tall, his uniform crisp, and his boots polished to a shine. The anticipation in the air was palpable, for today was the day of the inspection by none other than Lieutenant Colonel William Screws, the esteemed commander of their division, the 4th Alabama Infantry, and of Camp Vandiver Park.

As James looked around at his squad mates, he could see the mixture of nerves and excitement mirrored in their expressions. Lieutenant Colonel Screws had a reputation for being a formidable but fair leader, and his presence commanded respect.

"Remember, boys, stand tall and look sharp," Sergeant Jones whispered to the squad, his voice a mix of encouragement and sternness. "This is our chance to show the colonel what we're made of."

James nodded, steeling himself for the inspection. He adjusted his uniform once more and took a deep breath, trying to quell the butterflies fluttering in his stomach.

Just then, the sound of marching boots filled the air, and all eyes turned toward the approaching figure of Colonel Screws. He was an imposing man with a commanding presence, his uniform adorned with medals and insignia that spoke of his seasoned experience.

As Lt Colonel Screws made his way down the ranks, he scrutinized each soldier with a keen eye. His gaze was unwavering, and James could feel the weight of his stare as he approached. It was the moment of truth, a test of all the training and discipline they had undergone.

At last, Colonel Screws stopped in front of James, his piercing blue eyes locking onto his. "Private Reynolds, isn't it?" he asked in a deep, authoritative voice.

"Yes, sir," James replied, his voice steady despite the nerves.

Lieutenant Colonel Screws circled him, examining every inch of his uniform and gear. "You seem to be standing tall, soldier," he commented, a hint of approval in his voice.

"Thank you, sir," James said, trying to hide the pride in his voice.

Colonel Screws paused for a moment before speaking again. "Hell son, your company has an impressive record, Private. I've heard good things about your dedication and discipline. If you keep this up, son, we're going to have to make you a damn corporal!"

James felt a surge of pride and relief at the compliment. "Thank you, sir. We take our training seriously, and we strive to be the best."

Lt Colonel Screws nodded, seemingly satisfied with his inspection. "That's the spirit," he said. "Keep up the good work and remember that discipline is the cornerstone of any successful soldier." Screws said to the entire company.

"Yes, sir," James replied in unison with the rest of his company, feeling a newfound sense of determination.

As Lieutenant Colonel Screws continued his inspection, James felt a sense of pride in being part of the 4th Alabama Infantry. The presence of their esteemed commander instilled in him a sense of purpose and duty, reminding him of the responsibility they all carried as members of the Guard.

Later that evening, as James and his fellow cohorts gathered around the campfire, they exchanged stories about the inspection and their encounters with Lieutenant Colonel Screws. Despite the initial nerves, they all felt a sense of respect and admiration for their commanding officer.

"He's tough," one of the soldiers remarked.

"Exactly," James agreed. "He expects the best from us, and it's up to us to rise to the challenge."

And so, with the image of Colonel Screws etched in their minds, James and his fellow soldiers continued onto bed for the evening.

***

The day after the inspection by Colonel Screws, the atmosphere at Vandiver Park was filled with a sense of accomplishment and friendship. James and his fellow soldiers from B Company had proven themselves worthy of their commander's approval, and the pride in their unit was palpable.

As the sun rose over the camp, the company received orders to visit the medical tent for a routine check-up. Excitement buzzed among the soldiers as they made their way to the designated area, eager to find out why they had been summoned here.

Inside the medical tent, rows of cots were set up, manned by medics ready to conduct the check-ups. James approached one of the cots with a mixture of curiosity and nervousness. He had never been through a military medical examination before, and he wasn't sure what to expect.

"Name and rank?" the medic barked; his tone professional but terse.

"Private James Reynolds," James replied, standing at attention.

The medic nodded and motioned for James to sit on the cot. "Alright, let's get it over with," he said, looking impassively at his clipboard.

The examination was thorough but quick. James had his blood pressure taken, his reflexes tested, and his medical history reviewed. Documenting his medical history was easier than he thought it was going to be, as it was just answering a bunch of questions as the medic made notes. He also had his height and weight recorded, ensuring that he was physically fit for duty. After it was determined that he was, James received his inoculations and vaccinations including those for smallpox and typhoid fever.

Once the examination was complete, the medic gestured toward a table nearby. "Next, we'll find out your blood type," he said.

James had never known his blood type before, and he watched with curiosity as the medic prepared the necessary equipment. A small prick on his finger yielded a few drops of blood, and the medic placed the sample on a testing strip.

"Congratulations, Private Reynolds," the medic announced with a small hint of sarcasm. "You're blood type O."

"Blood type O? What does that mean?" James asked, still unfamiliar with the significance.

The medic explained, "blood type O is considered the universal donor, meaning that your blood could be given to anyone in need, regardless of their blood type." It was a valuable trait, and James felt a sense of relief knowing that it wasn't anything serious that would keep him from serving in the Guard.

After learning their blood types, the soldiers were given another important item: metal identity tags, which would later be called dog tags. Each soldier's dog tags contained their name, rank, serial number, and blood type. These tags would serve as a means of identification in case of injury or death on the battlefield.

James watched as the medic stamped the information onto his

dog tags. Holding the cool metal in his hand, he felt a solemn weight settle on his shoulders. These tags represented not only his identity as a soldier but also a reminder of the risks that came with his commitment to the National Guard.

Leaving the medical tent, James rejoined his fellow soldiers, each one now adorned with their own dog tags. As they continued their training at Vandiver Park, James wore his tags with pride, knowing that they were a testament to his dedication to serving his country. Every time he felt the weight of those metal tags against his chest, he was reminded of the responsibility he carried as a member of the Guard, and the trials they would face going forward.

***

As the evening set in the next day on the mess tent at Camp Vandiver, James and Tommy found themselves sitting by themselves, reminiscing about their recent experiences. They had just completed their medical evaluations, and the day's activities had left them with a mix of exhaustion, apprehension and excitement.

"So, Tommy, what did you do last night after we got back from downtown Montgomery?" James asked, a playful grin on his face.

Tommy chuckled nervously, looking around to make sure no one else was listening. "Well, you see, James, I had a little adventure," he replied sheepishly.

James raised an eyebrow in curiosity. "An adventure? Tell me more," he urged.

Tommy leaned in, lowering his voice to a conspiratorial whisper. "I went to this hotel downtown, called The Bama," he said with a mischievous twinkle in his eye. "And, well, I spent the night with a lady, if you catch my drift."

James couldn't help but burst into laughter, surprised by Tommy's bold confession. "You sly dog! You went to The Bama, huh? How was it?"

Tommy's cheeks turned bright red, but he grinned anyway. "It was something else, James. Something I'll never forget, but probably regret," he said with a wink.

"Just be careful, Tommy," James cautioned, his tone serious now. "You know that kind of thing can get you into trouble."

"I know, I know," Tommy replied, his demeanor becoming more somber. "It was just a moment of weakness, you know? We've been training so hard, and I wanted to let off some steam."

James nodded understandingly. "I get it, Tommy. We all have our ways of coping with the pressure. Just make sure you don't leave me out of it, alright?"

"You're right, I won't," Tommy admitted, a hint of remorse in his voice. "I promise I won't leave you the next time we go downtown again."

James patted Tommy's shoulder reassuringly. "We're in this together, buddy," he said. "We'll watch out for each other and make sure we stay on the right path or at least get into trouble together."

As they sat together in the mess tent eating the slop that passed for dinner, James and Tommy shared stories and laughed about the lighter moments of their training. Tommy's escapade at The Bama became an inside joke between them, a reminder of the bond they shared and the camaraderie that kept them going through the challenges they faced.

***

A week had passed since Tommy's candid confession, and life at Vandiver Park had resumed its usual routine of training and drills. The soldiers of B Company were focused on their duties, but there was a sense of unease in the air as rumors of upcoming medical inspections spread like wildfire.

One morning a stern-faced medic approached the soldiers of B Company. "Listen up, men," he called out, his voice firm and unwavering. "We'll be conducting a 'short arm' inspection today. That means everyone lines up and follows instructions to the letter."

James exchanged a worried glance with his fellow soldiers, aware of the implications of the inspection. It was an uncomfortable and intrusive procedure meant to identify any potential cases of venereal disease among the men. While it was an essential measure to maintain the health and readiness of the troops, it was still an embarrassing ordeal that no one relished.

The soldiers lined up in neat rows, apprehension etched on their faces with vertical wrinkles on their foreheads, mouths stretched closed, and eyebrows furrowed together. James could feel his heart pounding in his chest as the medic explained the process.

"We'll go one at a time," the medic instructed. "When it's your turn, step forward and follow the doctor's instructions."

As the inspection began, James did his best to maintain his composure, but he couldn't help feeling a mix of embarrassment and discomfort. One by one, the soldiers went through the procedure, and while everyone tried to remain stoic, the awkwardness in the air was palpable.

As Sam's turn approached, James couldn't help but offer him a supportive pat on the shoulder. "You'll be fine, buddy," he whispered reassuringly.

Sam managed a weak smile. "I hope so," he replied, trying to appear brave despite his nerves.

Finally, it was James' turn. He stepped forward, his expression a mix of apprehension and resignation. The doctor conducted the inspection with utmost professionalism, but there was no denying the discomfort in the air.

As the inspection concluded, James saw relief wash over Sam's face. He knew how tough the experience had been for his friend and was relieved that it was over.

Later that evening, as the soldiers gathered around the campfire, there was an air of solemnity. The "short arm" inspection had been a humbling reminder of the realities of military life and the sacrifices they made for bad decisions.

"Nobody likes going through that, that's for sure," one soldier remarked, breaking the silence.

"I guess it's just part of the job," another soldier replied, trying to shrug off the unease.

James spoke up, his voice calm and resolute. "It might be uncomfortable, but it's crucial for our health and readiness if we are going to keep making decisions like that," he said. "We need to stay strong and focused, no matter what challenges come our way."

The soldiers nodded in agreement, A week had passed since Tommy's candid confession, and life at Vandiver Park had resumed its usual routine of training and drills.

In the days that followed, life at Vandiver Park resumed its usual rhythm, and the memory of the "short arm" inspection slowly faded. James remained steadfast in his dedication to the unit, knowing that their commitment to the Guard demanded sacrifices and perseverance.

***

Dear Ma and Pa,

I hope this letter finds you well back home. I have some exciting news to share with you! Our unit, B Company, has been deployed to Nogales, Arizona. It's a long way from home, but I wanted to let you know that I am safe and eager to serve.

The journey from Montgomery to Arizona will be quite an adventure. We board a train that will take us across the vast landscapes of our country. The train ride will be long and tiring, but we are filled with anticipation as we head towards our assignment.

The friendship among the soldiers is stronger than ever. We have trained together, laughed together, and now we are ready to face the unknown together. There is a sense of unity and purpose among us, knowing that we have each other's backs no matter what.

As we get ready to settle into our new surroundings, the excitement is palpable. We have undergone additional training and briefings, preparing us for the specific challenges we would face in Arizona. Every day, we feel more and more ready to put our training into action.

I want to assure you both that I am well and in good spirits. The thought of being away from home and the comfort of Thomasville is tough, but I draw strength from knowing that I have your love and support.

Please pass on my love and regards to Maggie. I will write again soon and keep you updated on my experiences in Nogales. I am honored to be serving our country and proud to be part of the National Guard.

Take care and know that I am always thinking of you.

105

With all my love,

James

Chapter 6

The day of departure from Vandiver Park was marked by a mixture of excitement and solemn grimaces of the soldiers' faces, who knew it would be a while before they saw their loved ones as they prepared for the journey. The soldiers of the Alabama National Guard, including B Company, were gathered in formation, their bags packed and their faces a medley of determination, anticipation, and anxiety.

Lieutenant Colonel Screws stood before them, his voice projecting authority and pride. "Men, the time has come for us to embark on a new chapter," he declared. "We're heading to Arizona, to fulfill our duty to our country."

A cheer erupted among the soldiers, the culmination of weeks of training and preparation. The thought of finally being deployed in a theater of war filled the air with a tangible sense of purpose.

As the day came to a close across the camp, the soldiers boarded the train that would carry them across the vast expanse of the country. The train's sleek exterior exuded power. The excitement among the soldiers was infectious as they settled into their assigned compartments. "Are you ready to ride Tommy?" James quipped. "Let's get these wagons headed West!" Tommy responded nervously as they made their way down the train car and sat down.

James and Tommy found themselves side by side, their expressions a mixture of excitement and nerves. "Can you believe it, Tommy? We're actually on our way," James remarked, his voice tinged with awe.

Tommy nodded as a grin spread across his face. "It's like nothing I could ever imagine, James. All those days of training, and now we're heading into the real thing. Let's hope that it doesn't become a nightmare."

The train's whistle blew, signaling the start of their journey. With a lurch, the train began to move, and the soldiers waved goodbye to Vandiver Park and the throngs of citizens that had turned out in Montgomery to see them off.

As the train journeyed westward, the landscape out the windows changed dramatically. Fields of cotton and forests of Pine, Oak and other hardwoods gave way to vast open plains and rugged terrain. The soldiers watched the scenery in awe, the realization of the distances in which they were sinking in.

Sam turned around in his seat and asked, "Ever left the state of Alabama, boys?" "Nope, this is going to be fun exploring new places and meeting new people" James responded. "Parts will be fun, but war is never a cakewalk," Sam admonished, turning back around in his seat.

However, the journey was not without its challenges. One such challenge presented itself immediately. The reason they got off to such a late start was relayed to them by their commander. Colonel Screws approached the soldiers, a stern expression on his face. "Men, I have received word that the transport cars provided by the rail company are unsatisfactory," he announced. "They are filthy and full of debris. We cannot travel in such conditions." In addition to the unsanitary conditions, every hundred miles or so, the train would come to a halt to refill its water supply and restock on coal for the steam engine. These pauses allowed the soldiers time to stretch their legs and mingle outside the train while some of them smoked, but they also served as a reminder of the logistical intricacies of such a massive operation.

As the train continued its westward trek, the soldiers settled into a rhythm of camaraderie. Conversations filled the air as the young men got to better know each other. Laughter echoed through the compartments as they traded humorous stories about their lives and families back home, and the sense of unity among the soldiers grew stronger with each passing mile.

The journey to Nogales was not only without its challenges and delays but also its celebrations and wonder. The stops for water and coal became opportunities to bond amongst themselves, continuing to trade stories as well as cigarettes and get good exposure to diverse cultures, for some of them the very first time. Most of the guys had difficulty understanding the accent and French annunciations of the Cajuns they came across in Louisiana, and many of them chuckled at the Texas drawl of many of the oil workers and their families that came out in Houston. Some even admired the freedom and resilience of the cowboys tending to the cattle of the planes of West Texas.

After several days of travel, the train finally rolled into Nogales, Arizona. The soldiers disembarked, their eyes taking in the unfamiliar surroundings. The realization that they were not in Alabama anymore brought a mix of emotions — excitement, determination, and a deep sense of nervousness.

The train's rhythmic clatter slowed as the Alabama 4th Infantry approached Camp Little in Nogales, Arizona. The soldiers peered out the windows, their anticipation palpable. "Have you seen anything like this before?" Tommy asked bewildered. "No Tommy, this place is way bigger than even the camp back in Alabama!" James responded. The journey had been long, but they were finally at their destination.

As the train came to a halt, the soldiers filed out of the cars, their boots crunching on the desert gravel. The air was dry and warm, a stark contrast to the familiar humidity of home. The landscape stretched out before them, a mix of rugged terrain and sweeping vistas.

James and Tommy walked side by side, their eyes taking in the sight of Camp Little. Tents dotted the landscape, and soldiers bandied about, setting up their new home where the California National Guard had just vacated. It was a scene of organized chaos, a melding of determination and purpose.

"Here we are, Tommy," James said with a mix of excitement and awe. "Camp Little, Nogales, Arizona."

Tommy nodded, his gaze sweeping over the camp. "It's a far cry from home, that's for sure."

The soldiers of the 4th Infantry quickly fell into the routine of setting up camp life, setting up tents, getting the layout of the land memorized and generally familiarizing themselves with their surroundings. Because the California Guard had previously occupied Camp Little, their new home already had many necessities that an army camp would need including a netted tent for a mess hall, medical facilities, and even the layout necessary for tents. Tents were erected, equipment was organized, and bonding filled the air as soldiers from different units mingled and shared stories.

One evening, James and Tommy found themselves sitting by a makeshift fire, their faces illuminated by the flickering flames.

"We're a long way from home, James," Tommy remarked, his voice tinged with what sounded like homesickness to James.

James nodded in agreement. "But hasn't it been fun, Tommy? Did you ever think in a million years that you'd leave Thomasville?"

Tommy leaned back, staring up at the star-studded sky that was growing crisper and colder by the minute. "Nope. It's just... it's a lot to take in."

Their conversation was interrupted as Col. Screws approached, his presence commanding attention. "Men," he began, his voice steady. "I want you all to know that you're here for a reason. Our duty is clear, which is to secure our border and protect our fellow Americans, and we will face the challenges ahead with resolve and courage."

The soldiers listened intently, their respect for their commanding officer evident. They knew that their time at Camp Little was just the beginning, a prelude to the trials and tests that awaited them.

As the days turned into weeks, the soldiers settled into their new routine. Camp Little became their home, the foothills of Nogales their backdrop. The challenges of desert life were met with resourcefulness and determination. They learned to adapt to the arid climate that could get bone-chilling cold in the winter nights.

James and Tommy's units found themselves stationed next to one another, their friendship growing stronger with each passing day. The soldiers shared meals, stories, and the weight of their shared mission.

"We may be far from home," James said one evening as they

watched the sunset over the desert horizon, "but we're not alone. We have this whole new family of brothers."

The sun-driven heat bore down on the vast training grounds of Camp Little as the soldiers of the Alabama Guard prepared for another day of rigorous training. The camp had become a hub of activity, with soldiers from different units engaged in the various exercises and drills, like the morning calisthenics routines army life is infamous for.

James and Tommy, now well-acquainted with the routines of military life, stood in formation with their fellow soldiers, their expressions a mix of focus and discipline.

"Attention, men!" barked Sergeant Jones, his voice cutting through the air like a whip. "Today, we're moving on to more advanced training. We've got a lot to cover, so let's get to it."

The soldiers snapped to attention; their eyes fixed on their sergeant. They knew that the days of basic training were behind them, and now they were stepping up to a more specialized realm of instruction.

Their training began with weapons. The soldiers honed their marksmanship skills, firing rifles and pistols with precision and discipline. The crack of gunfire echoed through the training grounds as they practiced hitting their targets with unwavering accuracy.

As they progressed through the training, the soldiers were introduced to artillery. They learned the mechanics of howitzer and cannon fire, understanding the intricacies of aiming, loading, and firing these powerful weapons. The thunderous booms and reverberations served as a reminder of the sheer force they were learning to wield.

One day, as James and Tommy took a break from their training, they watched in awe as a group of soldiers prepared an observation balloon. The massive balloon, with its intricate rigging and sandbags, was a marvel of engineering. It would serve as a vantage point for scouting enemy positions and mapping out the battlefield.

"Can you believe that thing?" Tommy exclaimed; his wide eyes fixated on the befuddling site.

James nodded, equally impressed. "It's incredible, Tommy. The technology they're using out here is beyond anything we could've imagined."

Their training wasn't limited to weaponry either. The soldiers were put through more sophisticated bayonet training, learning advanced techniques for close combat. The sound of metal clashing against metal filled the air as they practiced lunges, parries, and strikes, mastering the art of the bayonet.

As the weeks passed, the soldiers absorbed a wealth of knowledge and skills. They trained tirelessly, determined to excel in every aspect of their instruction. The challenges were intense, but the soldiers were unwavering in their commitment to becoming the best soldiers they could be.

One evening, as James and Tommy sat by the campfire, exhaustion etched on their faces, they reflected on their journey.

"Who would've thought we'd be learning all of this?" Tommy mused, rubbing his sore muscles.

James chuckled, a mixture of pride and exhaustion in his voice. "It will come in useful the next time Peggy gets mad at you."

Their conversation was interrupted by the arrival of Col. Screws, his presence commanding the air.

"Men," he began, his voice carrying the weight of authority, "your dedication and progress have not gone unnoticed. You've shown remarkable growth, and I do not doubt that you will continue to excel."

The soldiers listened intently, a mix of pride and determination swelling within them. Col Screws' words were a validation of their hard work and a reminder of the importance of their mission.

As the sun hung high in the sky the next day, the soldiers of James's unit gathered for their daily briefing. Lieutenant Colonel Screws stood before them, his gaze steady and commanding.

"Men, we've received new orders," he announced. "We're to construct trench works near camp. These trenches will serve as practice grounds for trench warfare training."

A murmur of anticipation and trepidation rippled through the ranks. Trench warfare was a critical aspect of modern combat, and the soldiers understood the importance of honing their skills in this challenging environment. However, James recalled stories of trench warfare his Grandfather shared with him at places like Vicksburg, Spanish Fort and Blakely during his time in the Civil War, and James wasn't looking forward to it.

With their orders in hand, the soldiers set to work immediately. Shovels bit into the dry Arizona soil as they dug, their movements synchronized and efficient. It was a grueling task, but their determination never wavered. They were driven by a sense of duty and a shared goal – to create trenches that would prepare them for the realities of the battlefield.

James and Tommy worked with their companies, sweat trickling down their brows as they dug deep into the earth. The heat bore down relentlessly, but its efforts started losing steam as the winter months approached, their spirits remained high, however. The camaraderie among the soldiers was palpable, a bond forged in the crucible of shared effort.

As the work progressed, the trenches took shape. They wound through the desert landscape; their zigzag patterns designed to minimize exposure to enemy fire. The soldiers lined the trenches with sandbags, creating protective barriers against potential attacks.

In record time, the trenches were completed, a testament to the soldiers' dedication, teamwork, and abilities. As the work was finishing up, they stood back, surveying their handiwork with a sense of pride. "Can you believe we did all this digging, Sam?" James asked. "It was a hell of a task, but we got it done" Sam returned.

These trenches were more than just dirt and sandbags – they were a tangible manifestation of their commitment to their training and each other.

With the trenches in place, the Alabama National Guard shifted their focus to trench warfare training. The soldiers lined the trenches, donning their uniforms and equipment. Colonel Screws oversaw the training, his voice steady as he guided them through the intricacies of trench life.

"Remember, men, in warfare, especially in trench warfare, every movement counts," he emphasized. "Your survival depends on your ability to navigate these trenches with speed and precision."

The soldiers listened intently, absorbing every word. They practiced traversing the trenches, crawling through narrow spaces, and firing their weapons from protected positions. The training was intense, pushing them to their limits and honing their instincts for combat.

James and Tommy found themselves immersed in the training, their bodies moving with a newfound agility as they navigated the trenches. The sand and grit became a familiar sensation, a reminder of the challenges they would face on the battlefield.

As the training sessions continued, the soldiers grew more adept at trench warfare. They learned to communicate effectively within the confines of the trenches, coordinating their movements and responding to simulated attacks.

One evening the soldiers gathered around a campfire, exhaustion etched on their faces. Lt Colonel Screws addressed them, his tone filled with pride.

"You've all shown exceptional progress," he said. "These trenches are a testament to your dedication and hard work. Trench warfare is a harsh reality of modern combat, and I do not doubt that you are all prepared to face it head-on."

The soldiers exchanged glances, a sense of unity and purpose prevailing. The trenches that had once been a challenging construction project had transformed into a training ground, a place where their skills were sharpened, and their resolve fortified.

One evening near the end of trench warfare training, the soldiers of James' company had been granted a rare night off from their rigorous training. Excitement buzzed through the air as they prepared to head into downtown Nogales for a well-deserved evening of fun and entertainment.

James and his friends gathered near the camp's entrance; their uniforms exchanged for more casual attire. Laughter and banter filled the air as they shared stories and speculated about the adventures that awaited them in town.

"James, you're coming with us, right?" One soldier clapped a friendly hand on his shoulder.

James hesitated, his gaze shifting to the bustling streets of

Nogales beyond the camp. He had heard whispers of what went on in town – the bars, the brothels, the raucous revelry. It was a stark contrast to the disciplined life of the camp, and a part of him was both curious and apprehensive.

Sam, who had been standing nearby, chimed in with a grin. "Come on, James, it's our night off. We deserve a little adventure, don't you think?"

James couldn't help but chuckle at his friend's enthusiasm. "Alright, alright, you've talked me into it. I'll join you guys."

The soldiers cheered and exchanged triumphant glances; their bonds unbreakable. With that, they set off for downtown Nogales.

The town was alive with activity, its streets lined with colorful signs and bustling establishments. Laughter and music spilled out from the saloons, and the tantalizing aroma of food wafted through the air.

The soldiers moved as a group; their spirits high as they explored the town's offerings. They entered a lively saloon, the air thick with cigarette smoke and the clinking of glasses. James felt a rush of excitement as he took in the scene — the boisterous conversations, the lively music, the energetic dance floor. It reminded him of The Hurricane Tavern and his dockworker buddies back in Mobile, they would really enjoy this place.

Amidst the revelry, a group of soldiers gathered around a table, their focus intent on a game of craps. James watched, intrigued by the dice and the shouts of victory and defeat. Tommy leaned in, a mischievous glint in his eye. "Want to give it a shot, James?"

James hesitated for a moment before nodding. "Why not? Let's see if I have any luck."

With Sam's guidance, James learned the rules of the game and placed his bets. The dice were cast, and the group watched with bated breath as they tumbled and rolled.

Miraculously, luck seemed to be on James' side that night. With each roll, his pile of winnings

grew, and he couldn't help but get caught up in the thrill of the game. The cheers and jeers of his companions added to the excitement, creating an atmosphere of friendly competition.

As the night wore on, the soldiers enjoyed the various diversions that downtown Nogales had to offer. They visited a local brothel, where laughter and music filled the air, and they indulged in the lively atmosphere. Sam and the other soldiers of B Company started to peel off one-by-one with different ladies as one of the ladies approached James who was sitting on a couch, drinking a glass of whiskey, which James had overheard his buddies complaining about the $4 a pint price, in the parlor of the salon called 'Madam Octavia's' and struck up a conversation.

"Hey darlin', I'm Daisy, what's your name, Handsome?" "James" he responded nervously, not knowing how to act. James wasn't used to such a beautiful woman showing him attention. Daisy could feel James' nervousness and put a hand on his knee to try and put him at ease. "Don't be nervous darlin', I promise I won't bite, okay maybe just a little." She said with a sly smile on her face and a slight giggle. James smiled back and said, "I'm not nervous, it's just a little nippy in here." He tried to recover some sort of manly demeanor but failed to get rid of that boyish nervousness from his face. "Well, I have a place in the back that is a little more comfortable," Daisy said with a reassuring smile on her face.

Eventually, as the hour grew late, James bid Daisy a good night who hugged him and kissed him on the cheek as she led him back to the parlor. As the soldiers began to make their way back to camp, his company mates teased James about his adventure with Daisy and revealed to him that they had pooled their money and paid Daisy to ply her trade with him. The night had been filled with laughter, camaraderie, and a taste of the town's vibrant nightlife.

As James settled into his tent, a smile tugged at his lips. The night had been a departure from the disciplined routine of camp life, a chance to let loose and embrace the camaraderie of his fellow soldiers.

***

Dear Maggie,

I hope this letter finds you well and in good spirits back home. I wanted to share with you the wonderful Christmas celebration we had here at Camp in Nogales. Despite being far from home, the spirit of the season managed to find us, and it was a day filled with merriment, joy, and a taste of home.

Our camp was transformed into a festive haven. Soldiers had gathered whatever decorations they could find, and the sight of makeshift wreaths and paper ornaments hanging around our tents brought a touch of holiday cheer to the desert landscape.

The highlight of the day was, of course, the Christmas dinner. The mess hall was abuzz with activity as we lined up our plates and spirits eager for the feast that awaited us. The aroma of roasted turkey filled the air, and my mouth watered in anticipation.

As we sat down to eat, I couldn't help but be amazed at the spread before us. There, on our plates, were slices of succulent turkey, golden brown and glistening. Next to it was a generous serving of dressing, warm and fragrant, with hints of sage and thyme. And let's not forget the cranberry sauce — a burst of tart sweetness that perfectly complemented the savory flavors.

The feast continued with all the fixings — creamy mashed potatoes, rich gravy, buttered corn, and green beans. I piled my plate high, savoring each bite as if it were a taste of home itself. It was a reminder that, even in this distant desert, the traditions and flavors of the season could find their way to us.

The bonding around the table was heartwarming. Despite being far from our families, we created a sense of togetherness that made the day special.

There were stories shared, laughter echoing through the hall, and a feeling of gratitude that we were able to celebrate in each other's company.

After dinner, we gathered for a makeshift gift exchange. Soldiers had crafted small tokens of appreciation — hand-carved trinkets, knitted scarves, and heartfelt notes. The gifts were simple, yet they carried a profound sense of thoughtfulness and care.

As the day drew to a close, I found myself reflecting on the meaning of Christmas — the spirit of giving, the joy of shared moments, and the importance of connection, even amid challenging circumstances. While we may be far from home, the bonds we've formed here are strong, and they carry us through.

I hope your own Christmas was filled with warmth and love, surrounded by family and friends. Know that even in this distant desert, the spirit of the season managed to touch our hearts and bring us a taste of home.

Take care, dear sister, and know that you're always in my thoughts. Wish Ma and Pa a Merry Christmas for me and may God's blessings be upon you as we celebrate his son's birth.

With love,

James

***

The order came down with a mix of anticipation, apprehension, and determination – the Alabama 4th Infantry was to embark on a march from Nogales to Tucson and back. The soldiers knew it would be a grueling journey, but their spirits were high as they prepared for the march ahead that was slated to take 15 days but ended up taking only nine.

James and his fellow soldiers fell into formation, their backpacks secured, and their faces set with resolve. The morning light had just begun to peek over the horizon as they set off from Camp Little, their boots kicking up the desert dust as they marched in unison.

The first few days of the march were a test of endurance. The soldiers moved with purpose, the rhythm of their steps a steady cadence that carried them through the arid landscape. The desert sun shining down on them. Bright as ever, they pressed on, their shared determination fueling their progress.

As they covered an average of fifteen miles a day, the Alabama 4th Infantry exceeded even the army regulations for marching distances. The soldiers were relentless, pushing themselves to new limits and proving their resilience in the face of the challenging terrain. On the third day of the march, a commotion from A Company got the attention of the men of B Company when James noticed Tommy hunched over on the side of the march. His instincts immediately kicked in and he ran towards his childhood friend. "Are you okay, buddy?" he asked Tommy as he arrived to his friend about the same time the medics got there. "Yeah, I just feel sick and worn down," Tommy responded. "It's probably just dehydration," the medic chimed in as Sgt. Jones came stomping up. "Private Reynolds, get back into formation and let the medics do their job!" the sergeant barked.

Amidst the march, there were moments of friendship and levity. Chants echoed through the ranks, and laughter filled the air as soldiers shared stories and jokes to lighten the mood. Even in the midst of their arduous journey, the bond between them remained strong.

On the fourth day of the march, the soldiers reached the outskirts of Tucson, their fatigue temporarily forgotten as the city came into view. The feeling of accomplishment was palpable, a mix of pride and relief as they realized they had made it to their destination.

Upon their arrival in Tucson, the soldiers were met with a sense of celebration. They paraded through the city streets, their footsteps echoing against the adobe walls. The townspeople lined the streets, offering cheers and words of encouragement as they passed.

As the parade culminated, a review of the troops was held, with the brigadier and regimental commanders present to oversee the proceedings. James and his comrades stood tall and proud, their uniforms a testament to their dedication and discipline.

After the review, the soldiers were given a brief respite to rest and replenish their supplies. The streets of Tucson came alive with activity as the soldiers explored the city, relishing the opportunity to experience a change of scenery.

As the day began to come to an end on the ninth day, the Alabama 4th Infantry arrived back toward Nogales. The return journey was no less demanding, but the soldiers faced it with the same determination that had carried them this far.

The march back to Camp Little was a mix of exhaustion and

satisfaction. The soldiers had proven their mettle, exceeded expectations and demonstrated their readiness for whatever challenges lay ahead. As they returned to camp, they carried with them a sense of pride – not just in completing the march, but in the bond, they had forged through shared the effort.

***

The soldiers of the 4th Alabama gathered in formation at Camp Little in Nogales, Arizona. Lt Colonel Screws stood before them, his voice carrying the weight of authority.

"Men," he began, his gaze sweeping over the assembled soldiers, "our mission has taken a new direction. We are to be split into two groups and deployed for border patrol."

A ripple of anticipation and anxiety spread through the ranks. Border patrol was a critical duty, a chance for the soldiers to demonstrate their readiness and vigilance along the border between the United States and Mexico.

James and Tommy exchanged glances, resolve and uncertainty passing between them. They had faced many challenges together, and this would be no different.

"As part of this deployment, Colonel Screws continued, "one group will head east to Lochiel, and the other will head west to Arivaca."

The soldiers listened attentively, their minds processing the new orders. Lochiel and Arivaca – two points along the border that would now become their focus.

James found himself assigned to the group heading to Lochiel. The landscape stretched out before them as they set off, their boots kicking up the desert dust. The air was dry and warm, the desert heat unforgiving, but the soldiers pressed on.

As they patrolled the border, James and his unit maintained a watchful eye, scanning the horizon for any signs of activity. The vast expanse of the desert seemed to stretch on forever, a reminder of the challenges that came with their duty.

One evening, as they set up camp near Lochiel, James and his fellow soldiers gathered around a makeshift fire. The night was alive with the crackling of flames and the quiet murmurs of conversation.

"It's a different kind of challenge out here," Sam remarked, his gaze fixed on the distant border.

James nodded in agreement. "It's a reminder that we're here to protect our country and ensure its safety."

The days turned into weeks as James and his group continued their border patrol. Lochiel became their temporary home, a point of vigilance along the vast expanse of the border.

Meanwhile, Tommy and his group headed west to Arivaca. The landscape was equally unforgiving, the desert sun a constant presence as they patrolled the border on that side.

As weeks dragged on, the soldiers navigated the challenges of the terrain, endured the scorching sunlight, and stood watch with unwavering determination.

One day, as James and his group gathered for a brief respite, he found himself looking out at the horizon. The border stretched out before him, a reminder of the vastness of their duty.

Tommy's voice in his mind interrupted his thoughts. "It's tough out here, but we're making a difference."

The days had turned into weeks, and James and his fellow soldiers of the Alabama National Guard continued their vigilant border patrol duties. The desert sun shone down relentlessly, but their determination remained unwavering.

One afternoon, as they cleaned up camp near Lochiel, a murmur of excitement rippled through the group. A rider approached, kicking up dust as they sped towards the camp. James and his comrades watched with curiosity, their expressions expectant.

The rider pulled up, dismounting from the horse and approaching Col Screws. Hushed conversations ensued, and James strained to catch snippets of the exchange.

"News from home," one soldier whispered, his voice tinged with anticipation.

Eventually, Lieutenant Colonel Screws addressed the soldiers, his voice carrying a mixture of urgency and gravity. "Men, we have received word that our presence is required back in Alabama. Our service on the border has come to an end."

James exchanged glances with Sam, the weight of the news sinking in. Their time on border patrol had been a mix of challenges and bonding, and now a new chapter was about to unfold.

The news spread through the camp, and a mixture of emotions filled the air – excitement at the prospect of returning home, mingled with a sense of duty to the task at hand.

As the day of departure drew nearer, preparations were made for the journey back to Alabama. The camp that had become their temporary home was dismantled, and their gear was packed in anticipation of the long return journey home.

One evening, as James and his comrades sat around a campfire, the sound of a bugle echoed through the desert air. The soldiers fell into formation, their eyes fixed on Lieutenant Colonel Screws as he addressed them.

"Men, the time has come. We've received our orders to return to Alabama," he announced, his voice carrying a mixture of pride and authority. "Our duty here is complete, and now we must turn our sights towards home."

The soldiers exchanged glances. The journey back to Alabama would be long and arduous, but the prospect of reuniting with loved ones and returning to familiar terrain was a powerful motivator.

And so, with their orders in hand and a sense of purpose in their hearts, the soldiers of the Alabama National Guard began their journey back to their home state.

Chapter 7

The air was charged with a sense of anticipation as the soldiers of the Alabama 4th Infantry Regiment bustled around Camp Little in Nogales. Orders had come down from higher command, and the time had finally arrived for them to leave the border and begin their journey back home.

James and Tommy, like their fellow soldiers, were caught between excitement and a tinge of bittersweetness. The friendships they had built during their time on the border had become a part of them, but the prospect of returning home was a powerful pull.

Amid the flurry of activity, Lieutenant Colonel Screws addressed the soldiers. "Men, we've completed our duty here on the border. It's time to return to Alabama, to our families and our homes."

A cheer rose from the ranks, echoing the sentiment that had been building among the soldiers. The news of their impending departure had spread quickly, and the sense of unity was palpable.

The days that followed were a whirlwind of preparations. Tents were disassembled, gear was packed, and final farewells were exchanged with the townspeople and soldiers from other National Guard units from other states that had been stationed in Arizona as well, all who had become familiar faces during their stay.

One evening, as the sun began to dip below the horizon, James and Tommy found themselves sitting by their makeshift fire, the crackling flames casting a warm glow on their faces.

"It's hard to believe we're really leaving," Tommy remarked, his gaze fixed on the dancing flames.

James nodded, a hint of nostalgia in his voice. "Yeah, it feels like just yesterday that we got here."

Their conversation was interrupted by the sound of laughter and music in the distance. The soldiers had gathered for one last evening of camaraderie, a makeshift celebration to mark their departure.

James and Tommy joined the festivities, their laughter

mingling with that of their friends. Stories were shared, songs were sung, and the spirit of togetherness that had defined their time on the border seemed to reach its pinnacle.

As the night wore on, James found himself standing amidst a circle of fellow soldiers, their voices raised in song. The tune was familiar, "Alabam, My Heart of Dixie," a melody that spoke of home and the journey that lay ahead.

The next morning, the soldiers of the Alabama 4th Infantry Regiment stood in formation, their bags packed, and their faces turned toward the horizon. Colonel Screws addressed them one final time, his voice steady.

"We may be leaving this place, but the bonds we've formed here will remain with us," he said. "We go back to Alabama as a stronger unit, ready to face whatever challenges come our way, and make no mistake, those challenges are coming."

With those words, the soldiers began their march out of Camp Little, the dust swirling around them as they moved forward. The landscape that had once been unfamiliar was now etched in their memories, a chapter in their journey that had shaped them in ways that would prepare them for the coming storms.

The rhythmic clatter of train wheels against tracks echoed through the air as the Alabama 4th made their way from Nogales to Montgomery. The journey was long, the landscape shifting from the arid desert of the borderlands to the lush greenery of their home state.

James gazed out of the window, his thoughts a mix of anticipation and nostalgia. The bonds he had built with his fellow soldiers during their time on the border had become a cherished part of his journey, and now he was headed back to Montgomery.

As the train made a scheduled stop in Mobile, James' heart quickened. This was his adopted city before his service in the Alabama 4th, and he couldn't help but feel a sense of excitement at the thought of stepping back onto its streets.

The moment he stepped off the train, he was met with a familiar sight – the bustling docks, the sound of seagulls in the air, and the salty breeze that carried the scent of the sea. His dockworker buddies were toiling away at the day's tasks, their faces lighting up as they caught a glimpse of James strutting down the street with Tommy.

"James! You old rascal, look who's back!" Louie said as he clapped James on the back with a hearty laugh.

James grinned, the warmth of the reunion washing over him. "Louie, it's good to see you, my friend."

Amidst the clamor, James introduced Tommy to his dockworker buddies. Handshakes were exchanged and stories were shared about their experiences with James, the camaraderie seamless as if Tommy had been a part of their circle all along.

"And this," James said, turning to Tommy, "Is Mrs. O'Malley, the woman who practically took me in as her own here in Mobile." Pointing to an older lady milling around the streets carrying on with her daily errands.

Tommy extended his hand, a respectful smile on his lips. "Ma'am, it's a pleasure to meet you," as she noticed James' familiar face and came strolling over to give her former boarder a big hug.

Mrs. O'Malley regarded Tommy with a twinkle in her eye. "Oh, you're a friend of James, are you? Well then, you come here, young man." As Iris wrapped her arms around Tommy and gave him a big ol' southern granny bear hug.

As the soldiers mingled with the dockworkers and familiar faces from Mobile, the atmosphere was one of shared kinship and a sense of homecoming. It was a fleeting but precious moment of connection, a reminder that even amidst the rigors of duty, the bonds of friendship endured.

The stop in Mobile also held a grander purpose. The soldiers were welcomed with a reception that had been organized by the city, a gesture of appreciation for their service. The streets were lined with cheering crowds, and banners fluttered in the breeze, proudly welcoming the Alabama 4th back home.

At the heart of the reception, speeches were given by the Mayor of Mobile and Lieutenant Colonel Screws. Their words echoed with gratitude and pride, acknowledging the sacrifices of the soldiers and the honor they had brought to their city and their state.

James listened intently with a mix of pride and gratitude etched in his smile. He looked around at his fellow soldiers, the faces of his comrades illuminated by the spirit of the moment. The journey from Nogales had been a long one, however their journey wasn't over, and it was time to resume their trek to Montgomery.

As the train resumed its journey toward Montgomery, James settled into his seat with a sense of contentment. The reunion in Mobile, albeit short, had been a testament to the power of friendship.

The landscape continued to shift outside the window, carrying James and his comrades closer to their ultimate destination. Montgomery awaited them, and with it, a new chapter in their journey – one that held the perils of war for some of them.

The warm brightness of the day cast over the city of Montgomery as the Alabama 4th Infantry made its triumphant return. The streets were lined with cheering crowds, their cheers and applause echoing through the air. The soldiers, weary from their long journey, marched with precision and unity through the heart of downtown.

James' and Tommy's units marched together in the formation, their eyes taking in the familiar sights of their units' hometown, like the State Capitol and the numerous shops and restaurants that lined the streets of the downtown area. The streets that had once been so ordinary now felt transformed, each step a reminder of the journey they had undertaken and the community that had rallied behind them.

As they marched, the rhythm of their footsteps seemed to match the beating of their collective heart. Banners and flags fluttered in the breeze, displaying the red, white, and blue colors of the state and the nation. The crowd's cheers swelled, a chorus of gratitude and respect for the soldiers who had returned.

At the head of the procession, Lieutenant Colonel Screws rode on horseback, his posture reflecting a mixture of pride and humility. The soldiers followed him with unwavering determination, a testament to the training and strength that had defined their time in Arizona.

As they reached the heart of downtown Montgomery, the parade culminated at the State Capitol Building on Goat Hill where a platform had been erected. The soldiers came to a halt, standing tall and resolute as the cheers of the crowd enveloped them.

A hush fell over the crowd as the Governor of Alabama

stepped forward, his voice carrying a sense of gravitas. "Ladies and gentlemen, today we gather to welcome back the brave men of the Alabama 4th Infantry National Guard. These soldiers have served with honor and dedication, upholding the values that define our great state."

The Governor's words were met with thunderous applause, the thanks of the community palpable in the air. As the applause subsided, Colonel Screws stepped forward, his presence commanding attention.

"Today is a testament to the unwavering commitment of these soldiers," he began, his voice carrying the weight of their shared journey. "We faced challenges and overcame obstacles, but through it all, we stood together as a united force. Our duty may have taken us far from home, but it has also brought us back with a renewed sense of purpose and pride."

James exchanged a glance with the soldiers standing at attention next to him, their shared experiences and the journey they had undertaken forming a bond that would endure.

Lt Colonel Screws continued, his words resonating with each soldier and each member of the crowd. "We return to Montgomery not as individuals, but as a unit, a testament to the strength of our community and the spirit of our state. Our duty is not over – it is a responsibility that extends beyond our time in uniform."

As the ceremony drew to a close, the soldiers of the 4th Alabama stood united, a living embodiment of duty, honor, and service. The cheers of the crowd seemed to lift them up, carrying them forward on a wave of appreciation and support.

James and Tommy joined their comrades in a final salute, their hearts filled with gratitude for the community that had welcomed them back home.

About a week after arriving back at Camp Vandiver, the Alabama 4th received orders to deploy to different strategic infrastructure points around the state to protect vital lines of communication and transportation from German sabotage. While many of the soldiers believed that this was just guard duty to calm the fears of the average citizen around the country, they still took it seriously. James and Tommy's units were both dispatched to the Bay Minette sector, about a 45-minute train ride to Mobile, to protect vital railroad lines in the southwest part of the state. Their companies were assigned to protect the span over the Mobile-Tensaw Delta.

The Mobile-Tensaw River Delta stretched out before James and Tommy, a vast expanse of waterways and marshes that seemed to go on forever. Their units guarding the railroad span that connected Mobile to the rest of the state through the delta against any potential sabotage.

The tension in the air was palpable as the soldiers set up their posts along the railbank. The news of escalating tensions in Europe had reached American shores, and the specter of war loomed on the horizon. The mission was clear – to protect this vital link that could be targeted by those who sought to disrupt America's involvement in the conflict.

James adjusted his rifle, his gaze scanning the horizon. "Seems like we've gone from guarding the border to guarding our own backyard," he remarked to Tommy, who was walking beside him.

Tommy nodded; his expression serious etched in his face with focused eyes on the horizon. "It's a reminder that our work is never done. From border patrol to guarding this bridge, we're doing our jobs."

Their units were a mix of soldiers from diverse backgrounds, united by a common purpose. As the days turned into weeks, they settled into their roles, maintaining a vigilant watch over the railroad span.

One evening, as darkness started to set beyond the tree line of the delta, James and Tommy sat by the campfire, the crackling flames casting flickering shadows on their faces.

"This is different from anything we've done before as soldiers but reminds me of camping along the riverbanks of the Tombigbee near Coffeeville as boys," James said, his voice reflective. "Guarding a bridge against potential sabotage – it's like a whole new kind of duty."

Tommy nodded again; his gaze fixed on the distant horizon. "It's a reminder that a threat can come from anywhere, even close to home."

As the days passed, their vigilance remained unwavering. The soldiers patrolled the perimeter, their eyes scanning for any signs of suspicious activity. The quiet of the delta was punctuated by the creaking of the bridge and the sound of water lapping against the banks of numerous marshy islands that dotted the entire river delta.

One night, as James and Tommy stood guard, they heard a rustling sound nearby. Their training kicked in, and they exchanged glances before moving silently toward the source of the noise.

They found a figure hunched near the edge of the span, attempting to tamper with the rail tracks. Without hesitation, James and Tommy sprang into action, approaching the intruder with their weapons drawn.

"Freeze! Identify yourself!" James commanded, his voice firm.

The figure turned; his hands raised in surrender. "I mean no harm," a voice called out, revealing a local man who had wandered too close to the bridge.

Tommy lowered his weapon, his expression a mix of relief and frustration. "You scared the living daylights out of us, you know."

The intruder's eyes widened as he took in the uniforms of the soldiers. "I didn't realize this area was off limits."

James studied the man for a moment before speaking. "Well, now you know. We're here to make sure nothing happens to this bridge."

The man nodded; his demeanor respectful. "I had no ill intentions, I promise."

As they allowed the man to leave in his boat, James and Tommy exchanged glances. "It's a reminder that we're here for a reason," James said quietly. "Even in our own backyard, we've got to be on guard."

Tommy agreed, his gaze fixed on the bridge. "You're right, James. Our duty is to protect, no matter what, but that doesn't make it any easier."

The journey back to Montgomery a few months later from the Mobile-Tensaw Delta was a mix of weariness and anticipation. James and his unit had completed their sentry duty, standing guard over the railroad span day and night, and now they were making their way back to camp.

As the city came into view, James felt a sense of relief wash over him. The return to Montgomery held the promise of rest and a break from the vigilance of their recent mission.

The streets of Montgomery were lined with bustling crowds of people going about their daily lives of shopping, eating, and sharing the latest news and gossip as the soldiers roamed through the heart of the city. The informal parade of soldiers returning was a testament to the community's acceptance for the troops and their presence in their city.

James walked alongside his comrades; the noise of the crowd echoed in his ears. At the end of the street, the platform that had been set up for their return from Nogales stood. The soldiers came to a stop, standing tall and resolute as the crowd's background noise subsided.

"Men," Colonel Screws began, his voice carrying a tone of authority, "we are back in Montgomery after completing an important duty."

James exchanged glances with Tommy, both of them recalling the long hours of sentry duty.

Lt Col Screws continued, his voice growing sterner, "I am disappointed to report that our time on sentry duty has had an impact on our regiment's discipline."

James tinged with a little bit of surprise at the Colonel's words. He had always prided himself on his unit's discipline and dedication, but it seemed that their recent mission had taken its toll.

"I have received reports of laxity in adherence to regulations and a general slackening of standards," Colonel Screws continued. "This is not the standard of excellence that the Alabama 4th Infantry Regiment upholds."

While the units assigned to the Bay Minette sector had taken their duty seriously and unit commanders demand their soldiers maintain army discipline, rumors of other sectors giving into the boredom of sentry duty and allow their men to slack off and relaxed uniform requirements had made their way to all stations around the state.

James shifted uncomfortably. He knew that sentry duty had demanded their utmost attention, but he also understood the importance of maintaining discipline at all times.

"As we return to our barracks," Screws declared, his gaze staring into the souls the soldiers, "I expect a renewed commitment to our code of conduct and a return to the standards that define us as a regiment."

The soldiers saluted in agreement, their expressions a mix of understanding, embarrassment, and determination. James exchanged a glance with Tommy, a silent pact passing between them.

As the meeting concluded and the soldiers dispersed, James walked alongside Tommy, the weight of Col Screws' words lingering in the air.

"Did we let our guard down?" Tommy remarked, his voice inquisitive.

James shrugged; his gaze fixed on the path ahead. "Sentry duty was important, but we can't let it be an excuse for slacking."

Whispers swept through the camp like an unrelenting wind the following week, carrying with them a rumor that seemed too astonishing to be true. Lieutenant Colonel William Screws, the steadfast commander of the Alabama National Guard's 4th Infantry Regiment, was allegedly being relieved of his command. James and his fellow soldiers huddled in small groups, their voices hushed as they exchanged speculation and concern.

James found himself standing with Tommy, their brows furrowed in disbelief. "Can you believe this?" Tommy muttered; his gaze fixed on the whirlwind of activity around them.

"It's hard to fathom," James replied, his voice tinged with unease. Colonel Screws had become a figure of respect and guidance for the soldiers, his leadership unwavering in the face of challenges.

The rumor seemed to gather momentum in the following days, spreading from tent to tent like wildfire. Some soldiers shook their heads in disbelief, while others exchanged worried glances. The rumors claimed that the reason Screws was being relieved was because the Alabama 4th was about to be mustered into the regular army and a Colonel was too low of a rank for a commander. The air was thick with uncertainty, and even the routines of camp seemed disrupted by the weight of the news.

Later that week, James and Tommy found themselves sitting by their makeshift fire, the flickering flames casting shadows on their faces.

"Do you think there's any truth to it?" Tommy asked, his voice barely above a whisper.

James sighed; his gaze fixed on the dancing flames. "I don't know, Tommy. It's hard to tell what's fact and what's just idle talk."

Their conversation was interrupted by the approach of Sam, his expression a mixture of curiosity and urgency. "Hey, have you guys heard the latest?"

James and Tommy exchanged a glance before nodding. "We've been hearing things," James replied cautiously.

The soldiers leaned in close to Sam as his voice lowered. "Word has it that it's all due to some War Department order. They're saying that no regular army soldier under the rank of General can serve in a National Guard unit."

Tommy's eyebrows shot up in surprise. "Is that even true?"

The soldier shrugged, his expression grave. "I can't say for sure, but that's what folks are saying."

As Sam moved on, James and Tommy exchanged a confused glance. The intricacies of military regulations and bureaucratic orders were often complex and difficult to understand.

The following days were a mix of tension and speculation as the rumor continued to circulate through the camp. However, amidst the uncertainty, a glimmer of hope emerged. Prominent politicians, including the Governor of Alabama, the state's Senators, and influential Congressman, rallied to Screws' defense, determined to ensure that he remained at the helm of the Alabama National Guard.

One evening James and Tommy stood among a gathering of soldiers. Colonel Screws stepped forward, his expression a mix of gratitude and resolve.

"Men, I want to address the rumors that have been

circulating." His voice carried a sense of determination. "While it's true that orders have been issued, I want you all to know that I am committed to leading you, regardless of the obstacles that may come our way."

A collective sigh seemed to sweep through the soldiers, the tension of the past days gradually dissipating. Lieutenant Colonel Screws' words were met with resounding applause and cheers, a testament to the respect and loyalty he had inspired.

As the days went by, the camp slowly returned to a sense of normalcy. The rumored order that had once threatened to disrupt the regiment's unity never materialized.

The announcement rippled through the camp like a shockwave, leaving an air of surprise and apprehension in its wake. James and his fellow soldiers gathered around, their expressions a mixture of curiosity and concern as they listened to the news that had just been delivered.

Tommy stood among them, his gaze fixed on Colonel Screws, who stood at the center of the gathering. A campfire crackled nearby, its flickering light casting dancing shadows on the faces of the soldiers.

"As part of a reorganization effort," Screws explained, his voice carrying a measured tone, "we are making some adjustments to the company assignments within the regiment."

James exchanged a glance with Tommy, their unspoken communication a testament to the bonds of friendship they had forged since childhood. Tommy and James had been a part of different companies, ones that had become like family to them. The thought of them getting new assignments was met with a mix of apprehension, nervousness and excitement.

"Effective immediately," Colonel Screws continued, "Private O'Conner will be joining Company B, under the command of Lieutenant Birch."

The announcement hung in the air, and a hushed silence fell over the gathered soldiers. James stepped forward; his gaze fixed on Tommy. "Well, it looks like you're joining the ranks of my company, my friend."

Tommy managed a small smile, though the unease in his eyes was evident. "Guess I'm joining your family."

James clapped Tommy on the shoulder, a gesture of support and friendship. "We'll make it work, Tommy. Company B will be lucky to have you. You've always been like a brother to me anyway."

As the soldiers began to disperse, James and Tommy found a quiet corner where they could talk privately. The campfire's glow illuminated their faces as they spoke.

"It's a big change," Tommy admitted, his voice tinged with apprehension. "I've grown close to the guys in my old company."

James nodded, understanding Tommy's feelings. "I know it won't be easy, but we're all here to support each other. Company B is like a family too. Many of your old buddies will still be out there with us when we deploy."

Tommy sighed; his gaze fixed on the flames. "I guess change is a part of this military life, huh?"

James chuckled, a hint of wistfulness in his smile. "It sure is.

But one thing that won't change is the bond we've built, Tommy. No matter which company you're in, you're still my best friend."

Tommy looked up, a grateful expression on his face. "Thanks, James. I'll do my best to fit in with Company B."

As the days turned into weeks, Tommy settled into his new role within Company B. The transition was not without its challenges, but with each passing day, he found himself becoming a part of a new family – one that welcomed him in.

***

War Department Renames Alabama's Illustrious 4th National Guard Unit as U.S. Army's 167th Infantry Division

By Matthew Jones, Staff Writer

Location: Montgomery, Alabama

In a significant and historic move, the War Department has officially announced the transformation of Alabama's esteemed 4th National Guard Unit into the prestigious U.S. Army's 167th Infantry Division. This change, signaling a new phase of duty, pays homage to the unit's legacy while aligning its efforts with the nation's growing involvement in the global conflict.

This transition comes as the international landscape continues to shift, with the United States finding itself drawn into the turmoil of the Great War. The renaming of the unit, previously known for its dedicated service as the 4th National Guard, reflects a deepening commitment to the nation's defense and its role in the global theater.

The 167th Infantry Division's storied history, dating back to its origins in Alabama's heartland, serves as a testament to the dedication and courage of its soldiers. Having witnessed their unwavering vigilance on both domestic and international fronts, this rebranding underscores the unit's integral role in safeguarding American values and interests.

Lt. Col. William Screws the division's esteemed commander, expressed his sentiments on the momentous occasion. "The soldiers of the 167th Infantry Division have consistently exhibited the highest standards of professionalism, dedication, and selflessness. Renaming our unit reaffirms our commitment to our nation's call and the protection of our way of life."

Prominent state officials, military leaders, and citizens alike have applauded this transformation, recognizing the depth of sacrifice and service that the division represents. The Governor of Alabama conveyed his support, stating, "The 167th Infantry Division exemplifies the indomitable spirit of Alabama's sons. This renaming reflects their unwavering commitment to our great state and our nation."

The legacy of the newly christened U.S. Army's 167th Infantry Division continues to be shaped by the dedicated soldiers who stand ready to answer the call of duty. As the global conflict rages on, this storied division will undoubtedly play an essential role in defending American ideals and securing a brighter future for generations to come.

Chapter 8

The orders had come down like a thunderclap – the 167th Infantry Division was to ship out to Camp Mills, New York, marking the beginning of their journey into the heart of the conflict in Europe. The atmosphere in the camp was a mixture of anticipation, uncertainty, and a deep sense of duty.

James and Tommy stood amidst the flurry of activity, watching as their fellow soldiers made preparations for the journey ahead. Tents were being dismantled, supplies were being loaded onto trucks, and soldiers hurried back and forth, each step carrying the weight of the mission ahead.

"It's hard to believe it's finally happening," Tommy remarked skittishly, his gaze fixed on the chaos around them.

James nodded; his expression solemn. "Yeah, we knew this day would come, but it's still a shock when it actually does."

As the soldiers made their final preparations, James found himself at a makeshift table, a stack of paperwork before him. Among the forms was one for war insurance – a sobering reminder of the risks that lie ahead.

"Insurance, huh?" Tommy commented as he approached, his tone a mix of curiosity and dismissiveness.

James shrugged; his gaze fixed on the form. "Yeah, it's something I want to do for Maggie in case something happens to me. You never know what might happen out there."

Tommy's expression softened, understanding the weight of the decision. "Did you name Maggie as your beneficiary?"

James smiled, a mixture of pride and affection in his eyes. "Yeah, I did. If anything happens to me, at least she'll be able to go to college or afford to start a family when she gets older."

As the paperwork was completed and filed away, the soldiers were called to the medical tent for a different kind of preparation – inoculations against a range of diseases that could pose a threat on the battlefield.

James winced as the needle pricked his arm, the sting a small reminder of the challenges they were preparing to face. "Seems like a small price to pay compared to what's coming," he quipped.

Tommy agreed, a sense of unease in his eyes. "It's all part of the process. We're getting ready to go kick some German butt and we can't do that if we're lying in a hospital bed puking our guts out because we're sick."

As the days whisked by, the soldiers of the 167th Infantry Division continued to make their preparations. The camp buzzed with a mix of anxiety and excitement, the camaraderie among the soldiers growing stronger as they faced the unknown together.

One evening, as the darkness crept in on the camp, James found himself sitting by the campfire, a letter in his hands. It was a letter to Maggie, a heartfelt expression of his feelings and hopes for the journey ahead.

Tommy approached and took a seat beside him, his own letter to his family in his lap. "Writing home?" he asked as he jabbed James in the side.

With a small smile on his lips. James responded "Yeah, letting them know we're fixing to head up north to Yankee country."

Their conversation was interrupted by the approach of a fellow soldier, Sergeant Jones, who had been with them since before they went to Arizona. "Boys," he said, his tone serious, "we're about to embark on a journey that will test us in ways we can't imagine. But remember, we're in this together. Lean on each other when times get tough, because they will get much tougher than they ever have to this point."

James and Tommy exchanged glances as the weight of the sergeant's words sank in. As the campfire crackled and the stars began to emerge in the night sky, they found solace in the bonds they had forged going back all the way as young boys growing up in Thomasville.

The morning cast a golden hue over the camp as the 167th Infantry Division made their final preparations to leave Camp Vandiver, their home for months that had become a crucible of training, camaraderie, and anticipation. Soldiers moved with a sense of purpose, securing gear, double-checking supplies, and exchanging nods that spoke volumes without saying a word.

James and Tommy stood among the throngs of soldiers, their expressions a mixture of anticipation and somberness. The orders to depart had come swiftly, leaving little time for prolonged preparations and lollygagging.

"I can't believe the day's finally here," Tommy remarked.

A hint of mischief in his eyes, James responded, "Feels like just yesterday we were getting our inoculations."

The departure was shrouded in an air of secrecy, a stark contrast to the fanfare that usually accompanied such send-offs. The local newspaper, the Montgomery Advertiser, had been barred from announcing the departure, leaving only a few people in the streets who had somehow managed to catch wind of the event as the soldiers departed and were able to make their way to send them off.

As the soldiers gathered at the L&N Railroad Shed in Montgomery, the crowd remained subdued, their hushed conversations punctuated by glances toward their departing soldiers and loved ones. Some of the local soldiers' families stood among them, their eyes fixed on their sons, brothers, and husbands and their friends who were about to embark on a journey into war.

The trains stood ready, their engines billowing plumes of smoke that mingled with the emotions that hung heavy in the air. Guards had been posted at the doors of each train car, a stark reminder that once they boarded, there would be no turning back, some of them for good.

James and Tommy found themselves next to one another as they boarded one of the train cars, their footsteps resonating on the wooden platform. They exchanged a knowing glance as they entered the train.

"Guess we're riding up north together," Tommy quipped, his attempt at levity not lost on his friend.

James chuckled, though his smile held a hint of nostalgia. "Seems like we've shared just about everything on this planet, why would this be any different?"

As the train's whistle sounded, the vibrations underfoot signaled the journey's beginning. The soldiers found themselves waving to their families and onlookers through the windows, their farewells tinged with a sense of determination that transcended words.

The train's wheels set into motion, the gradual acceleration carrying with it the weight of the soldiers' commitment and sacrifice. The scene outside the windows shifted from the familiar surroundings of Montgomery to the landscapes that would soon blur by on the three-day journey to Garden City, New York.

James and Tommy settled into their seats, the rhythmic clatter of the train's wheels lulling them into a deep sleep that neither one of them had experienced in an exceptionally long time. Outside, the world passed by mile by mile, a reminder that their journey was just beginning. As they dozed off, the changing scenery seemed to strengthen, a testament to the friendships forged through a lifetime of shared experiences in Alabama and the friendships that would be forged by fire on the battlefield to come.

The arrival at Camp Mills marked a significant transition for the 167th Infantry Division. The journey had been long and arduous, the train's constant movement and the passing landscapes a testament to the miles they had covered. As the soldiers disembarked, the weariness in their bones was worked out of their systems by stretching their muscles and popping knuckles and bones.

However, the reception at Camp Mills was unlike what they had anticipated. Instead of a warm welcome, the soldiers were met with the strict protocols of quarantine. An air of frustration

"Quarantined? You've got to be kidding me," Tommy exclaimed, his voice a mixture of disbelief and frustration.

James sighed, understanding Tommy's sentiments. "Seems like the devil isn't quite done testing us yet."

The camp was a hive of activity, as soldiers underwent thorough medical examinations and were assigned to temporary quarters. The looming threat of disease was a concern, prompting health officials to take every precaution.

Days dragged on as the soldiers navigated the new routine of quarantine. Group activities were suspended, and the camaraderie that had sustained them through training now faced the challenge of isolation. James and Tommy found themselves confined to their quarters, their conversations and interactions limited to the confines of their immediate surroundings.

One evening, as a warm glow over the camp receded, Tommy

sat on his bunk, his expression subdued. "You know, I never thought I'd say this, but I miss the chaos of training."

James chuckled, a shared sentiment in his eyes. "Yeah, there's something to be said about the controlled chaos of Camp Vandiver."

Their conversation was interrupted by a knock on the door. A medic entered; his expression serious as he glanced at Tommy. "You're showing signs of the measles, Private. We're going to have to move you to the medical ward for observation."

Tommy's face fell, the frustration evident in his eyes. "Just when we thought things couldn't get any worse."

James placed a hand on Tommy's shoulder as he cast a glance at the medic. "He'll be alright, won't he?"

As the days passed, Tommy's condition was closely monitored and the medical ward became his temporary home, the rhythm of quarantine continued with a sense of monotony and vigilance. Despite the challenges, the soldiers found ways to pass the time, sharing stories, playing cards, and finding solace in the bonds that had carried them through the trials of Camp.

One morning, Tommy reappeared at the doorway, a hint of exhaustion but also relief in his eyes. "I've been given the all-clear. Looks like I'm no longer a threat to you, guys."

James grinned, a mixture of humor and relief in his expression. "Well, you're still a threat to us, you're just not going to kill us," he said with a chuckle. "We always knew you had a way of standing out, Tommy."

As the quarantine period drew to a close, excitement built in the air as the guys realized that they were going to be able to get back into the daily life of training and preparing for war.

After being released from the purgatory of quarantine and amidst the sprawling landscape of Camp Mills, the soldiers of the 167th Alabama Infantry Division found themselves plunged into a whirlwind of training unlike anything they had experienced before. The cacophony of military orders, clattering boots, and shouted commands filled the air, mingling with the early morning mist that hung over the camp. It was a place where the soldiers from the South would be transformed into battle-hardened soldiers, ready to face the harsh realities of the European theater in The Great War.

Sergeant Raines, a grizzled veteran with a chest full of ribbons, stood before a group of fresh-faced Alabamians, his voice booming across the training field. "Listen up, boys! We're here to turn you into lean mean fighting machines, and that means you're gonna have to work harder than you've ever worked in your lives."

James exchanged a glance with Tommy, the two childhood friends, having followed each other from Thomasville to Camp Mills. James was determined to face this new chapter together, and Tommy apprehensively followed.

As the training progressed, the Alabamians were subjected to a relentless regimen of physical fitness, marksmanship training, and grueling marches. The Alabama sun had been exchanged for the brisk air of New York, and the soldiers soon found themselves navigating the unfamiliar terrain of the northern training grounds.

One of the most critical aspects of their training was preparing for the potential horrors of chemical warfare. Instructors, clad in ominous gas masks, demonstrated the proper technique for putting on and sealing a mask in seconds. The soldiers practiced this ritual tirelessly until they could do it blindfolded.

Once, James had commented to an instructor that they could do it blindfolded and the instructor responded, "Good, because trying to put one of these on in the trenches with gas releasing from a projectile is going to feel like doing it blindfolded." The specter of gas attacks loomed large in their minds, and the importance of this training was drilled into them relentlessly.

In a makeshift trench dug into the training field, the soldiers were introduced to the brutal realities of trench warfare. With bayonets fixed, they practiced assaulting enemy positions, learning to thrust and parry with deadly precision. The mud and muck of the trench seemed worlds away from their hometowns in Alabama, but this was their new reality.

"Remember, boys, this ain't just about muscle," Sergeant Smith barked during one such practice. "It's about keeping your wits and balance and your comrades alive out there."

For James and Tommy, these training exercises took on a profound meaning. They weren't just preparing for a theoretical war; they were preparing to face the horrors of the front lines in Europe, where gas attacks and close combat would be a constant threat.

As the weeks dragged on, the soldiers of the 167th Alabama Infantry Division were pushed to their limits and beyond. The camaraderie among them grew stronger with each passing day, a bond forged in the rigors of training and shared hardship. They were becoming more than just brothers; they were becoming a cohesive unit, ready to face whatever the European theater would throw at them.

Through gas mask drills, trench warfare practices, and bayonet training, they were honing the skills and discipline necessary to stand their ground against the Germans. They knew that the challenges ahead would test their mettle, but they were determined to prove that they were up to the task. The training at Camp Mills was shaping them into a force to be reckoned with, and they felt like they were ready to face their destiny on the battlefields of Europe.

Amid the regimented routines of Camp Mills, James and Tommy found themselves yearning for something that would set them apart, a symbol of their unity and resilience. It was during a rare moment of respite that inspiration struck like a bolt of lightning.

They were rummaging through a surplus tent that had been designated for discarded uniforms and equipment. The pile of discarded garments held a treasure trove of material, and as they sifted through the items, their eyes fell upon a rainbow of colored fabric.

"Look at this, Tommy," James exclaimed, holding up a stack of cloth in various shades. "This could be it, our symbol."

Tommy squinted at the fabric, his mind racing. "A rainbow patch, to represent the unity of the different divisions?"

James nodded, his excitement growing. "Exactly! In these times, we need something to remind us that we're here with people from National Guard units all around the country getting ready to take on a common enemy."

Their decision made, they set to work, carefully cutting and stitching the colored fabric into a small, rainbow-shaped patch. It was a tangible representation of their friendship and shared commitment to the group that was quickly becoming their own band of brothers. The patch would serve as a reminder of the brighter future they were fighting to protect and the people they had back home for whom they were protecting it.

Their next challenge was finding someone who could sew the

patch onto their uniforms. They asked around the camp, inquiring if anyone had the necessary skills. It was Private Donovan, a soldier from Long Island, who pointed them in the right direction.

"There's a seamstress in town who could do it," Donovan explained. "I've heard she's skilled with a needle and thread."

With newfound determination, James and Tommy set out on a journey to find this seamstress. It was a welcome break from the camp's confines, and the anticipation of seeing their patch proudly displayed on their uniforms added a sense of purpose to their quest.

The town was a quaint Long Island community, a stark contrast to the military camp they had become accustomed to. The seamstress, Mrs. Webb, ran a small shop nestled among the bustling streets. Her sign bore the words "Webb's Tailoring."

Inside the shop, bolts of fabric lined the walls, and the soothing hum of a sewing machine filled the air. Mrs. Webb, a middle-aged woman with a librarian's smile, greeted them as they entered.

"How can I help you gentlemen today?" she inquired.

James and Tommy exchanged a glance before James explained their request. "We've made this patch, and we were wondering if you could sew it onto our uniforms."

Mrs. Webb examined the rainbow patch with a keen eye, her expression thoughtful. "This is a beautiful piece of work. I'd be honored to help you."

As she carefully sewed the patch onto their uniforms, James and Tommy shared stories of their training at Camp Mills, the camaraderie among their fellow soldiers, and their anticipation of the journey to Europe. Mrs. Webb listened with interest, her nimble fingers working the needle and thread with precision.

When she finished, she presented the uniforms, the rainbow patch now a vibrant addition to their attire. James and Tommy admired her handiwork, a sense of pride swelling within them.

"Thank you, Mrs. Webb," James said sincerely. "This means

more to us than you can imagine."

She smiled warmly. "It was my pleasure, boys. Remember, in the darkest of times, a symbol of unity can make all the difference."

As they left the shop, James and Tommy felt a renewed sense of purpose. Their rainbow patch, sewn with care by Mrs. Webb, represented not only their friendship but also the friendship of their unit and the other units that comprise the 42nd division. When they got back to Camp Mills, Sergeant Smith saw them returning and noticed their patches. After giving them a stern look for a few minutes, he commented "Are those patches regulation?" James and Tommy looked at each other with a worried expression on their face that they were about to get in trouble, before Sergeant Smith continued, "Even if they're not, I think it's a great way to show unity amongst the boys. Hopefully, others will follow your lead." As other soldiers in the camp started to notice their patches over the coming days, other soldiers started to copy their example. Eventually, the rainbow became the unofficial patch of the 42nd Division.

Life at Camp Mills was a whirlwind of training, camaraderie, and, occasionally, moments of respite. During the discipline and preparation for the European theater, the soldiers of

James and Tommy's company had found a unique way to unwind – craps.

Craps games had become a common pastime during down times in the camp. The rhythmic rattle of dice on makeshift tables could be heard late into the night, and soldiers gathered around, their faces illuminated by the flickering flames of nearby lanterns.

One evening, as the stars began to twinkle in the dark sky, a heated craps game was in full swing. James and Tommy stood at the fringes of the gathering, watching the game's ebbs and flows. In the center of the action was Corporal Sullivan, the company cook, known for his skill with the dice.

"Roll 'em, Corporal!" someone shouted, and Sullivan obliged. The dice tumbled across the wooden surface, and the cheers and groans of the onlookers signaled the game's fortunes.

But as the night wore on, tension began to simmer beneath the surface. A dispute over a bet escalated into a heated exchange of words, and then, suddenly, fists were flying. It was Sullivan, the cook, and Private Rodriguez, a wiry soldier with a penchant for gambling, locked in a fierce brawl.

James and Tommy rushed forward, attempting to pull the two combatants apart. "Enough, you two! Break it up!" James shouted; his voice strained with urgency.

It took the combined efforts of several soldiers to separate the brawling pair. Sullivan's face was battered, and Rodriguez sported a shiner that would undoubtedly be a badge of honor among the soldiers. The fight had left a palpable tension in the air, and the craps game quickly disbanded.

The following morning, as the sun rose over Camp Mills, word spread like wildfire about the brawl. Sullivan, the company cook, had been injured in the fight and was confined to the infirmary.

James and Tommy couldn't help but feel a sense of irony about the situation. The man responsible for their daily meals had found himself on the receiving end of a punch, and now, he was nursing his wounds under the care of the camp's medical staff.

Curiosity got the better of them, and they decided to pay a visit to the infirmary to check on Sullivan. As they entered the sterile environment, they found him lying on a narrow cot, his face heavily bandaged.

"Corporal Sullivan," Tommy began tentatively, "we just wanted to see how you're holding up."

Sullivan managed a weak smile and thumbs up, though it was clear he was in pain. "Boys, I've been through worse scrapes than this, but I appreciate the visit."

James nodded in understanding. "Seems even the best of us can't resist the allure of a good craps game."

Sullivan chuckled, wincing slightly as he did. "You're not wrong. But let this be a lesson to the lot of us — sometimes, it's best to know when to fold 'em."

As they chatted with the patient, the cook shared stories of his own experiences in the military and offered some culinary advice for their time in Europe. Despite the injuries and the brawl, there was a sense of camaraderie in the infirmary that was hard to ignore.

The incident served as a stark reminder that even during rigorous training and preparations for war, moments of levity and camaraderie were essential for the soldiers' morale.

***

The announcement came as a surprise to James and his fellow soldiers of the 167th Alabama Infantry Division. Their company commander, Captain Mitchell, stood before them, his expression unusually animated.

"Listen up, men," Captain Mitchell began, his voice carrying an air of excitement. "We've been granted a rare opportunity. Tonight, a select few of you will have the chance to visit New York City."

A murmur of excitement and surprise swept through the assembled soldiers. For most of them, this was an unexpected twist in their favor.

Captain Mitchell continued, "We've all been working hard, and we could use a break. The rest of you will remain here and hold down the fort. But for those chosen, get ready for a night out in the Big Apple."

James exchanged a quick glance with Tommy, a mixture of disbelief and anticipation in their eyes. They had heard stories of New York City, a place of towering buildings, bright lights, and a vibrancy unlike anything they had experienced in the South.

The selection process was swift, with Captain Mitchell calling out the names of those chosen for the excursion. James' heart pounded as he heard his own name among the fortunate few. Tommy, however, was not among the chosen, and the friends exchanged an expression of disappointment as they realized that both of them would not be able to go.

As the day dipped below the horizon, the chosen soldiers, including James, assembled near the camp's entrance. They were met by a convoy of trucks, which would transport them into the city.

The drive into New York City was an experience in itself. The soldiers gazed out of the truck, their eyes widening as they passed through the streets of Manhattan. The towering buildings seemed to scrape the heavens, their illuminated facades casting a dazzling glow over the bustling city streets.

Their first stop was Times Square, a place that seemed to pulse with energy. Bright lights illuminated the night, advertisements promoted everything from Broadway shows to the latest wartime propaganda and news. The soldiers marveled at the spectacle, snapping photos and exchanging stories of their hometowns.

Captain Mitchell led them through the vibrant streets, taking in the sights and sounds of the city. They dined at a bustling diner, savoring dishes that were a far cry from the camp's mess hall fare. Laughter filled the air as they shared stories and enjoyed a taste of civilian life.

After dinner, Captain Mitchell led them to one of New York's iconic landmarks—the Woolworth Building. They ascended to the observation deck, where they were treated to a breathtaking view of the city spread out below them. The twinkling lights of New York stretched to the horizon, a testament to the resilience and spirit of the city and the nation.

As they stood atop the Woolworth Building, James couldn't help but feel a profound sense of awe. This was a world far removed from the trenches and training fields of Camp Mills. The city's heartbeat pulsed beneath them, a reminder of the vibrant life that continued despite the war raging overseas.

The soldiers spent the remaining hours of their night out exploring the city, from the tranquil beauty of Central Park to the busy streets of Greenwich Village. They experienced the magic of a city that never slept, where people of all walks of life came together in a shared pursuit.

As the night was drawing to a close, the soldiers returned to Camp Mills, Captain Mitchell addressed them one final time, his voice filled with gratitude.

"Remember this night, men," he said. "It's a reminder of what we're fighting for, the freedom and vibrancy of a city like this. We'll return to our training, but moments like these keep our spirits alive."

***

My Dearest Maggie,

I hope this letter finds you well and full of the same spirit that has always inspired me. I have news that I can't wait to share with you, news that I know will light up your heart.

Imagine a morning like any other at Camp Mills, the sun rising over our tents, and the steady rhythm of drills and duties that have become our daily life. But then, whispers began to drift through the camp like a soft breeze—whispers that made my heart race with anticipation.

Maggie, your idol, the remarkable Helen Keller, was coming to visit our regiment. I can hardly put into words the excitement that rippled through the camp. It was as if a spark of hope had been ignited in all of us, reminding us of the world we're fighting to protect.

The day arrived, and I joined my fellow soldiers in assembling to welcome Miss Keller. She appeared, guided by her loyal companion, Anne Sullivan, and the moment was nothing short of extraordinary. Maggie, her spirit and determination are every bit as awe-inspiring as you've always told me.

Miss Keller communicated through a system of tactile signing, and it was moving to watch as Anne Sullivan translated her words into our ears. The language was one of connection and touch, a powerful reminder of the human capacity for communication and understanding.

I had the honor of shaking Miss Keller's hand and speaking with her briefly. Maggie, she radiated a sense of resilience and hope that I can't adequately describe. In her presence, I felt humbled and inspired, and I knew that her message was one that I had to carry with me.

Miss Keller spoke to us about the importance of resilience, unity, and the belief that every individual has the power to make a difference, no matter what the challenges they face. Her words resonated deeply with all of us, reminding us of the purpose of our mission—to defend the values and freedoms that allow remarkable individuals like her to thrive.

As Miss Keller and Anne Sullivan left, we soldiers erupted in applause and cheers, our hearts filled with admiration and gratitude. Maggie, meeting her was a moment I will cherish forever, and I couldn't help but think of you, knowing how much you've admired her.

I wanted to share this incredible experience with you, Maggie, to remind you of the boundless strength of the human spirit and the difference one person can make in the world. Miss Keller's visit has left an indelible mark on me, and I carry her message of hope and resilience with me as we continue our training and prepare for the challenges that lie ahead.

Please know that I think of you often, and your unwavering support continues to fuel my determination. I look forward to the day when I can return home and share more stories with you.

With all my love and admiration,

James

***

The atmosphere at Camp Mills, New York, was charged with anticipation and excitement as the soldiers of the 167th Alabama Infantry Division received their long-awaited orders. The news had come signaling their imminent departure for the frontlines of the war in France.

For weeks, the soldiers had undergone rigorous training, honing their skills for the challenges that awaited them overseas. Now, the moment they had been preparing for was upon them, and a sense of purpose, unease and determination filled the air.

James, Tommy, and their comrades gathered in the barracks, their faces etched with a mixture of excitement and apprehension. They had formed bonds that went beyond mere friendship; they were a brotherhood, forged in the difficulties of training and shared experiences.

Captain Mitchell stood before them, his voice carrying a gravity that matched the occasion. "Men, the time has come. We have our orders to ship out to France and join the fight. The Rainbow Division is known for its courage and determination, and I have no doubt that each one of you will do our regiment proud."

A round of applause and cheers erupted from the soldiers, a testament to their commitment to their duty and the camaraderie that had developed among them. They knew that they were about to embark on a journey that would test their mettle and resilience like never before.

The preparations for departure were a whirlwind of activity. Uniforms were inspected, weapons cleaned and loaded, and personal belongings carefully packed away. Letters were written to loved ones back home, words of reassurance and love penned in the uncertain hours before departure.

As the day of departure drew near, the soldiers were given briefings on the conditions they would face in France, from the trenches to the gas attacks. It was a sobering reminder of the grim reality of war, but it only served to strengthen their resolve.

Finally, the day arrived. The soldiers of the 167th Alabama Infantry Division, part of the Rainbow Division, gathered at the Camp Mills depot. The air was thick with a mixture of emotions—fear, determination, and a profound sense of duty.

The departure was a somber affair, with soldiers bidding farewell to the familiar surroundings of Camp Mills. They boarded a convoy of trucks that would take them to the nearby railroad station, where a train awaited to transport them to the port of embarkation.

As the train pulled away from Camp Mills, James, Tommy, and the other soldiers gazed out of the train cars, watching as the familiar landscape of New York faded into the distance. They were headed into the unknown, a world of trenches, battlefields, and the weighty responsibility of defending their homeland and the values they held dear.

The journey to the port was a long and reflective one. Soldiers exchanged stories, sang songs, and tried to find solace in the brotherhood that had sustained them throughout their training. They knew that the challenges ahead would test their limits, but they were determined to face them with the courage and unity that had defined them.

191

Chapter 9

The night was dark and cool as James and his fellow soldiers of the 167th rose from their bunks in the early hours of the morning. The camp was shrouded in a deep, velvety darkness. The faint glow of lanterns illuminated the faces of the men as they prepared to embark on the next leg of their journey.

As James donned his uniform and checked his gear, a sense of purpose filled the air. The time for their departure to Europe had come, and the soldiers were ready, their resolve steeled by weeks of training and anticipation.

The camp was a hive of activity as soldiers gathered their belongings and double-checked their equipment. James could hear the soft murmur of conversations and the shuffle of boots on the ground as they readied themselves for the journey ahead.

In the mess hall, they were handed sandwiches—simple fare that would sustain them on the journey to Long Island City, where they would board a train bound for New York City. The sandwiches were a small comfort, a reminder of the meals shared with fellow soldiers in the mess hall.

With their gear in tow and sandwiches tucked away in their packs, the soldiers filed out of the barracks and onto the parade lines that would take them to the train station. The chill of the early morning air cut through their uniforms, but they pressed on, fueled by a sense of duty and anticipation.

The convoy of trucks made its way through the darkened camp, the rumble of boots marching and the jostle of the road a stark contrast to the quietude of the sleeping world around them. The journey to the train station was a short one, but it felt like a symbolic threshold—a point of no return.

As the parade lines marched into the Long Island City train station, the soldiers were met with a sight that filled their hearts with a mixture of surprise and gratitude. The platform was crowded with civilians, gathered in the pre-dawn darkness to bid farewell to the departing soldiers.

The men, women, and children cheered and waved American flags, their faces illuminated by the soft glow of lanterns and torches. It was a display of unwavering support and patriotism that swelled the pride inside of the soldiers.

As James and his friends broke ranks from the parade lines, they were met with smiles and handshakes from the well-wishers. Some of them offered small tokens of appreciation—letters, snacks, and even homemade scarves and mittens. The face of the soldiers betrayed that they were moved by the outpouring of love and support from these strangers who had come to say goodbye.

Captain Mitchell addressed his men; his voice tinged with emotion as he spoke of the significance of the moment. "Men, remember this day," he said. "Remember the faces of these Americans who have come to see us off. They believe in us, and we carry their hopes and dreams for the future with us."

The soldiers boarded the waiting train, their hearts filled with a renewed sense of purpose and determination. As the locomotive pulled away from the platform, the cheers of the adoring crowd faded into the distance, but the memory of that early morning farewell would remain etched in their hearts for eternity.

The journey to Europe had begun.

The units stood in formation on the bustling platform of Long Island City, waiting for the next phase of their journey to begin. The early morning air was crisp, and the soldiers' breaths hung in the chilly darkness. Before them lay the East River, a ribbon of inky blackness that separated them from their final destination: Hoboken, New Jersey.

The ferry that would carry them down the East River and under the iconic Brooklyn Bridge was a massive vessel, its bulk illuminated by the soft glow of lanterns and the occasional flash of a photographer's camera. Soldiers and civilians alike bustled about, the platform a hive of activity as the departure time neared.

James and his brothers-in-arms had grown accustomed to waiting, but the anticipation of this moment was unlike anything they had experienced. They had trained for this day, prepared for the journey across the Atlantic to the battlefields of Europe, and now, it was finally at hand.

Captain Mitchell moved among his men, offering words of encouragement and reassurance. His presence was a source of comfort, a reminder that they were not alone on this journey. He spoke of the challenges they would face and the importance of unity and determination. The men listened, their faces illuminated by the lantern light, their eyes reflecting a mixture of resolve and apprehension.

As the first light of dawn began to break over the East River, the ferry's horn sounded a deep, mournful bellow that echoed through the early morning stillness. It was time to board.

The soldiers filed onto the ferry, their boots clanging on the metal gangplank as they made their way to the deck. The ferry was a massive vessel, its decks crammed with soldiers, equipment, and supplies. The passengers found spots along the railings; their faces turned toward the river as the ferry pulled away from the platform.

The East River stretched out before them, its waters reflecting the first blush of sunrise. To their left, the Brooklyn Bridge loomed, its majestic towers casting long shadows over the water. It was a sight that filled the soldiers with a sense of awe and wonder, a reminder of the grandeur of the city that many of them had never seen before, and some would never see again.

As the ferry glided down the river, the soldiers took in the sights of the city. They passed by the towering buildings of Manhattan, their windows shimmering in the early morning light. The Statue of Liberty stood sentinel in the harbor, her torch raised high in welcome and farewell.

The soldiers on board were a diverse group, representing diverse backgrounds, regions, and walks of life. Some struck up conversations with their fellow soldiers, sharing stories and jokes in an attempt to lighten the mood. Others stood in silent reflection, lost in their own thoughts.

The journey down the East River was a surreal experience, a moment suspended in time between the familiar world they had known and the uncertain future that lay ahead. It was a journey of transition and transformation, a passage from the life they left behind to the life that lay ahead for them.

As the ferry approached Hoboken, the soldiers could see the bustling docks that awaited them with people whose activity would make the busiest ant colony envious. The activity on the docks reminded James of the docks that he worked at in Mobile, which brought back memories of his friends and co-workers there. The skyline of New York City loomed in the distance, a testament to the city's resilient spirit. The ferry docked with a gentle bump, and everyone began to disembark, their boots once again clanging on the metal gangplank.

The journey from Long Island City to Hoboken had been a symbolic one—a bridge between the world they were leaving behind and the world they were entering. The soldiers of the 167th Alabama Infantry Division were ready to face the challenges that lay ahead, united in their commitment to defend freedom and uphold the values they held dear.

As they set foot on the docks of Hoboken, the soldiers knew that their journey was far from over. They were about to board the ships that would carry them across the Atlantic, to the battlefields of Europe, and into the pages of history. But for now, they stood on the threshold of a new adventure, their hearts filled with a mixture of apprehension and determination, ready to face whatever lay ahead as a united and resolute band of brothers.

The men of the 167th Infantry had made their way from Camp Mills to Hoboken and now stood at the docks of New York Harbor, ready to board the Canadian ship Andania. The massive vessel loomed before them, its hull towering above, and its decks brimming with people, equipment, and supplies. This was the moment they had been waiting for, the next step on their journey to the war in Europe.

As they filed up the gangplank and onto the ship, the soldiers were greeted by the ship's crew, who directed them to their respective quarters. James and Tommy found themselves in a dimly lit corridor, their footfalls echoing on the steel deck as they followed the crew's instructions.

The ship was a labyrinth of narrow passages and compartments, and finding their way around was a challenge in itself. They eventually reached their assigned bunkroom, a cramped space filled with rows of stacked metal bunks. The room was already crowded with men stowing their gear and settling in for the voyage.

James and Tommy found their bunks and stowed their bags, their names written on small tags hanging from the bedposts. It was a strange feeling to be in such close quarters with so many men, but they knew that this was the reality of wartime travel.

Mealtime assignments had been posted on a notice board near the mess hall, and the soldiers checked to see when they would be eating. The mess hall was a hub of activity, with people lining up for their rations and finding places at long tables to eat. The food was simple but nourishing, a reminder of the meals they had shared back at camp.

Before departure, the soldiers underwent one last health check by the ship's medical staff. They lined up in a corridor, waiting their turn to have their medical examinations completed. It was a thorough process, with each soldier questioned about his health and screened for signs of illness. It was a precautionary measure, a reminder of the risks they would face during the long voyage and in the trenches of Europe.

Finally, the soldiers were assigned their lifeboat positions. "Reynolds," the crewman shouted. "You're in lifeboat five, starboard side. Remember to get there as quickly as possible, as your boat can't evacuate without you and you don't want your fellow boatmates pissed at you," he continued. "Yessir," James responded. A reminder of the seriousness of the lifesaving safety the smaller boats provided.

As the ship's departure time drew near, the soldiers gathered on the deck to watch as the gangplank was raised, and the ship gently pulled away from the dock. The skyline of New York City receded into the distance, the Statue of Liberty standing tall as a symbol of hope and freedom.

The passengers stood on deck, the sea breeze ruffling their uniform, hair and their faces turned toward the horizon. They were bound for Europe, ready to face the challenges that lay ahead. The voyage across the Atlantic would be long and uncertain, but they were united in their commitment.

As the ship sailed out into the open sea, James and Tommy could not help but feel a mixture of apprehension and determination. They were part of a historic mission, representing Alabama and the United States on the world stage. The journey had begun, and the soldiers of the 167th were ready to face whatever lay ahead with courage and unity, their hearts filled with the spirit of duty and sacrifice.

***

The voyage of the 167th Alabama aboard the Andania was a journey filled with both bonding and challenges. As the ship set sail from New York Harbor, they settled into their new maritime routine, adjusting to life at sea.

The men quickly discovered that shipboard life was a world unto itself. The confines of the vessel were cramped, and the bunks were narrow, making sleep a precious commodity. James and Tommy found themselves in close quarters with their fellow bunkmates, sharing stories and laughter. "One time as we were unloading cotton bales in Mobile, Ronnie, who was hungover, passed out on one of the ships. No one could find him after work that night, and we all thought he just walked off. We saw him the next day getting off a pilot's boat that picked him up after being discovered by the ship's crew and getting roughed up. He swore he would never drink again after that. Yeah, that promise lasted until we all went to the Tavern that night!" James relayed as the men around him started to chuckle.

One evening, as they made their way to the mess hall for dinner, James and Tommy decided to try something new—Australian rabbit, a dish offered as part of the ship's rations. They had heard that it was a delicacy, but their first taste left them less than impressed. "This is disgusting!" Tommy quipped. "Keep your voice down, you don't want the cook to come out here and beat you with his mixing spoon," James retorted. The meat was tough and gamey, and they could not help but long for the simpler meals they had enjoyed back at Camp Mills.

As the days turned into nights, the soldiers grew accustomed to the constant thrum of the ship's engines and the gentle rocking of the vessel. At night, the ship's interior had been dimly lit to avoid attracting the attention of German submarines. It made for an eerie atmosphere, with soldiers navigating narrow passageways with only minimal lighting. "This is creepy," Tommy said as he continually had to make room for passersby on his way to the showers one evening. "Yeah, but it would make for great ghost storytelling." James responded, trying to lighten the mood.

One evening, as James and Tommy were settling in, the ship's alarm started to sound, and they immediately jumped up and started down the corridors of the ship. "Is this a drill?" Tommy nervously asked a passing crewmember. "No, a German sub has been spotted on the aft side." The crewmember responded as he continued in the opposite direction of James and Tommy. The threat of enemy submarines was a constant concern, and the soldiers underwent regular boat drills to prepare for the possibility of an attack. They practiced abandoning ship and making their way to lifeboats quickly and efficiently. It was a sobering reminder of the dangers they faced at sea.

Tragically, the journey was not without its losses. One of James' company mates fell ill with pneumonia during the voyage. Despite the efforts of the ship's medical staff, the soldier's condition deteriorated rapidly, and he passed away. "Man Johnny was a good soul," Sam remarked solemnly as they remembered him later in the mess hall after the news had spread. "Yeah, I'll miss his fishing stories about the times his dad would take him down to the Black Warrior River and they would spend all day down there," James chimed in. "Here's to Johnny!" Tommy exclaimed as they raised their coffee mugs in the air as they toasted his memory. It was a somber moment for the entire company, a reminder of the fragility of life in wartime.

Despite the challenges and the somber moments, there were also moments of camaraderie and solidarity. Soldiers shared letters from home, played cards to pass the time, and even organized impromptu sing-alongs to lift their spirits. Bonds had been forged during those long days at sea, as they looked out for one another in the face of the unknown.

Finally, after two weeks at sea, the shores of England came into view. The soldiers gathered on deck, their faces reflecting a mixture of relief and anticipation. The journey had been arduous, but they had made it safely across the Atlantic.

As the Andania docked in Liverpool, the soldiers disembarked, their boots once again connecting with solid ground. They were in a new land, ready to continue their training and preparations for the battles that lay ahead in Europe. The voyage had tested their mettle and strengthened their resolve, and they were more determined than ever to do their duty.

James and Tommy, along with the rest of the 167th Infantry Division, had crossed an ocean to join the fight in Europe. The challenges of the journey had only steeled them to face whatever lay ahead for James and increased Tommy's level of worry, united in their commitment.

***

Rumors of change ran like wildfire through the ranks of the 42nd Rainbow Division as the news of a change in leadership spread. The division's commander, Major General William A. Mann, was being replaced. The soldiers had grown accustomed to Mann's leadership, and the sudden change left many feeling uncertain about what lay ahead.

It was a tense time in the division's ranks, with men huddled in small groups, speculating about the reasons behind the change and what it might mean for their future. Some feared that the 42nd would be disbanded, its soldiers sent to fill the ranks of other divisions as replacements. The uncertainty hung in the air like a heavy cloud.

One evening, as the soldiers gathered around their makeshift campfires, the topic of conversation inevitably turned to the change in command. James and Tommy sat with their fellow soldiers, their faces reflecting a mixture of curiosity and concern.

"I heard they're bringing in Major General Charles Menoher to take over," one soldier said, his voice hushed as if sharing a secret.

"Is that so?" another replied, raising an eyebrow. "What do you make of it?"

James leaned in closer, trying to catch every word of the conversation. The soldiers around the fire exchanged a series of shrugs and speculative glances.

"I heard a rumor," a third soldier chimed in, "that they might break up the 42nd. Use us as replacements for other divisions that need fresh troops."

The murmurs of agreement rippled through the group. The prospect of being separated from their fellow soldiers they had trained and shared hardships with was unsettling.

Tommy, ever the pessimist, tried to inject a note of hope into the conversation. "Well, we won't know for sure until we hear it from the top brass. Let's not jump to conclusions."

James nodded in agreement. The uncertainty was indeed challenging, but he knew that their duty remained the same: to prepare for the battles that lay ahead, regardless of who was in command or what changes might come.

As the soldiers continued to speculate, they could not help but wonder about the future of the 42nd Rainbow Division. Major General Menoher's arrival would bring new leadership, and with it, new challenges, and opportunities. The only certainty was that their commitment to their country and their friends remained, and they would face whatever came their way with courage.

As the 167th Division had completed their transatlantic journey and arrived on the shores of England in December of 1917, their arrival marked the beginning of a new chapter in their journey, one filled with the challenges of training and acclimating to the unfamiliar English landscape and weather.

The soldiers disembarked in Liverpool, greeted by the characteristic chill of a British winter. The weather was miserable, with cold winds and frequent rain making their arrival less than welcoming. The soldiers wrapped themselves in their coats and scarves, grateful for whatever warmth they could find.

As they disembarked from the ship, the soldiers could not help but feel the difference in the atmosphere. England was quite different from their homes in Alabama, and the unfamiliarity of it all weighed on their minds. The soldiers having been greeted by their British counterparts, their accents and uniforms a stark reminder that they were now on foreign soil.

Food and water were in short supply, a result of the demands of wartime rationing. The soldiers lined up for their rations, receiving a meager portion of bread and whatever canned goods could be spared. "Is this it?" James asked incredulously. "Yep, and if you don't like it you can go without," The British soldier handing out the rations retorted. It was a stark contrast to the hearty meals they had enjoyed back in the United States, and the soldiers had to adjust to the new reality of wartime scarcity.

From Liverpool, the soldiers embarked on a short train ride to Winchester, England, where they would make their camp. The train journey took them through the rolling English countryside, a patchwork of green fields and quaint villages. It was a scenic ride and for a brief moment, the soldiers could forget the challenges that lay ahead.

Upon arriving in Winchester, the soldiers were greeted with a sense of relief. Their new camp offered a sense of stability amid uncertainty. The tents were set up in orderly rows, and the soldiers settled into their new surroundings.

Life in England was quite different from what they had known back home. The soldiers had to adapt to the British way of life, from the tea-drinking customs to the currency and measurements. It was a time of adjustment and learning, as they prepared for the training that would follow.

Despite the challenges of the weather and the scarcity of resources, the men of the 167th Alabama faced their new reality with resilience. They were on foreign soil, far from home, but their commitment to their mission remained unwavering. The journey was far from over, and they were prepared to face whatever lay ahead in the service of their country.

One chilly evening in Winchester, England, James and Tommy decided to take a break from their military routines and enjoy a taste of home. They had heard about a concert in the town square, and the promise of music and an enjoyable time was too enticing to resist.

As they made their way through the cobbled streets of Winchester, the strains of music grew louder, guiding them to the heart of the town. There, in the softly lit square, a stage had been set up, and the 42nd Regimental Military Band, composed of their fellow soldiers, was warming up for their performance.

Soldiers and townspeople alike had gathered, creating a diverse and eager audience. The band members, clad in their military uniforms, took their positions on the stage, their instruments gleaming under the dim lights.

The conductor raised his baton, and the music began to fill the chilly air. The familiar melodies of home resonated through the square, stirring emotions in the hearts of everyone. It was a brief respite from the rigors of training and the uncertainties of wartime.

James and Tommy found a spot among the gathered crowd, their faces illuminated by the warm glow of the stage. As the music played on, they could not help but feel a sense of unity with their fellow soldiers and a connection to their shared American roots.

Between performances, the band members exchanged stories and laughter with the audience, forging connections with the townspeople who had opened their hearts to these American soldiers so far from home.

As the concert ended with the band's performance of Yankee Doodle, James and Tommy applauded enthusiastically, grateful for the opportunity to experience a taste of home in this foreign land. It was a reminder that even during war and uncertainty, moments of coming together and shared culture could provide solace and a sense of belonging.

With the strains of music still echoing in their ears, James and Tommy made their way back to camp, their spirits lifted by the power of music and the knowledge that they were part of a larger community, bound together by their service and their shared love of Alabama.

On a crisp winter day in 1917, the soldiers of the 167th Alabama Infantry Division gathered in anticipation. Their orders to ship out had arrived, and the time had come to embark on the next phase of their journey.

As the soldiers assembled in formation, their officers read aloud the orders that would send them across the English Channel to the battlefields of France. The news came with a mix of emotions—excitement, apprehension, and a deep sense of duty.

The soldiers had spent months training and preparing for this moment, and now it was here. They were going to be a part of history, representing Alabama and the United States on the world stage. Their commitment to their country and to each other remained unwavering, and they were ready to face whatever challenges lay ahead.

The orders specified their departure date: November 25th, 1917. It was a date that would be etched in their memories, marking the beginning of a new chapter in their service. As they left the assembly area and began their preparations, the soldiers knew that their journey was far from over, but they were resolute in their determination to do their duty for their country and their fellow soldiers.

With their gear packed and their hearts filled, the soldiers of the 167th and the 42nd Rainbow Division set their sights on the horizon. France awaited, and they were ready to face whatever challenges and triumphs lay ahead in the service of freedom and justice.

Chapter 10

As the men of the 167th Infantry Division, stood on the shores of England, they were filled with anticipation and anxiety. The day had come for them to cross the English Channel and set foot on the soil of France; a journey that would take them closer to the front lines.

The weather was characteristically English—cold, rainy, and miserable. A fine drizzle seemed to hang in the air, and the soldiers bundled up in their wet gear, bracing themselves for the journey ahead. The gray skies overhead matched the somber mood that settled over the men.

The soldiers were divided among three boats, each one tasked with carrying a portion of the division across the channel. James found himself on one of the three boats that would attempt the crossing. The tension was palpable as they boarded the vessels, their faces illuminated only by the feeble glow of light provided by nature. "This is going to be fun," James said to Sam, trying to lighten the tension before the trip. "Kinda like getting stuck on a dingy in the Gulf during a hurricane," Sam returned as those around them started to chuckle.

As the boats set out, the waters of the English Channel proved as unforgiving as the weather. The vessels rocked and swayed in the rough seas, and the soldiers clung to whatever handholds they could find. The crossing was treacherous, with waves crashing over the sides and drenching the men.

James' boat, battered and tossed by the tempestuous sea, pressed on through the night. The soldiers held onto hope, knowing that their friends were on the other boats, facing the same harsh conditions.

Meanwhile, on Tommy's boat, the situation took a different turn. The weather proved too formidable, and the boat had to turn back to the English coast. The disappointment was palpable among the soldiers as they realized they would not make it to France that night. "Don't worry guys," Tommy said trying to lift their spirits. "It's better to get there late rather than not at all."

For those on James' boat, the ordeal continued through the long, grueling hours of darkness. They clung to the rails; their eyes fixed on the distant horizon. The channel seemed endless, and the cold seeped into their bones.

Finally, as dawn broke on the horizon, James' boat made

landfall on the shores of France. Exhausted and soaked to the bone, the soldiers disembarked, their boots sinking into the wet sand. "If I never have to do that in a thousand years, it will be too soon," James exclaimed as he started gathering his things and trying to dry himself off. They had made it across the channel, but they knew that their journey was far from over.

Back on the English coast, Tommy and the men who had turned back faced a night of disappointment and uncertainty. They knew that their friends had reached France, and they longed to join them. "We will be there soon enough, and we can bet those lucky sons of guns that are already there will be happy to see us," Tommy told his friends as they settled in for a long wait for a second chance to cross the channel.

As the morning rose over the English Channel, the third boat, with Tommy aboard, made its second attempt to cross. The weather had calmed somewhat, and this time, they were successful. "Late to the party as usually 'eh Tommy?" James quipped as he approached his childhood friend. "Yeah, well you know me, I like to make a big entrance." Tommy retorted as they shook hands upon the arrival of the third boat.

The journey across the English Channel had been a grueling experience for the soldiers of the 167th, but now they were on

French soil, ready to face the Germans. Their next leg of the journey involved a lengthy train ride, one that would take them deeper into the heart of France.

The soldiers boarded French trains, their uniforms a stark contrast to the unfamiliar surroundings of the passenger cars. The train cars were unlike what they had seen in the United States, with straight benches and overhead storage racks. "Well, I hope you took your shower this morning, Tommy, I would hate to smell you all the way to Paris!" James teased his friend. "Aww come on James, everyone back home knows you're the smelly one" his friend volleyed back to him. It was a tight fit, and the soldiers settled in as comfortably as they could for the long journey ahead.

As the train rolled through the French countryside, the soldiers gazed out of the windows, taking in the picturesque villages and rolling hills. The landscape was a far cry from the familiar sights of Alabama, and the soldiers couldn't help but be intrigued by the foreign beauty of France. "Peggy would love this place," Tommy mentioned as the scenery passed by. "Maybe you can bring her back here on your honeymoon," James suggested.

Hours passed, and the train continued on its winding path through the French countryside. The soldiers found ways to pass the time, sharing stories, some true, some not so true, to keep their spirits high. The bonds between them grew stronger with each passing mile.

After what felt like an eternity, the train made an unexpected stop at a French Red Cross station. The soldiers disembarked, curious about their surroundings. "I wonder why we are stopping?" Tommy inquired. "I dunno, but I sure am glad we are!" James answered as he looked at the scene outside. French ladies, dressed in the white uniforms of the Red Cross, greeted them with warm smiles.

One of the ladies approached James and Tommy, offering them cups of hot coffee and treats. "Merci" the men said almost in unison. Their faces lit up with gratitude as they sipped the warm brew and enjoyed the simple but comforting snacks. It was a small gesture of kindness in the midst of their long journey, and it left a lasting impression on them.

As the train resumed its journey, the soldiers settled back into their seats, their bodies weary but their spirits lifted by the hospitality of the French Red Cross workers.

The French trains rolled to a slow and creaking stop at the train station in Vaucouleurs, France. The 167th Infantry disembarked, their boots thudding on the wooden platform. They were greeted by the brisk French air, a stark contrast to the confines of the train cars.

James and Tommy gathered their gear and shouldered their packs. The journey from Alabama to this small French town had been a long and arduous one, but they were now ready for the next leg of their mission. "Let's get this show on the road," James said as they started to get into formation.

The train station bustled with activity as soldiers and supplies were unloaded from the train cars. French railway workers, speaking a language unfamiliar to most of the American soldiers, coordinated the effort with hand signals and gestures.

"We're in France, Tommy," James remarked, a mixture of excitement and uncertainty in his voice.

Tommy nodded, his eyes scanning the unfamiliar surroundings. "It's a long way from home, that's for sure."

Their journey was far from over. The men had a six-mile march ahead of them to reach their first destination at Uruffe.

The road stretched before them, winding through the French countryside.

With their packs secured and their rifles slung over their shoulders, the soldiers began their march. The weight of their gear was a constant reminder of the challenges they would face in the days and weeks to come.

As they marched through the French villages, the local residents came out to watch. Children waved, and some of the villagers offered small gifts—a piece of fruit, a loaf of bread—as tokens of welcome and gratitude.

The soldiers walked in disciplined formation, their boots echoing in unison on the cobblestone streets. It was a long and tiring journey, but the brotherhood among the soldiers made it easier to bear. They shared stories and jokes, finding moments of levity amidst the seriousness of their task. "Did you see all those young French women waiting for their American heroes to come rescue them?" James asked Tommy. "I did see them, but were they really waiting on us?" Tommy asked. "Sure, you know that no woman anywhere in the world can't resist the southern charms of us Alabama boys." James quipped with a big grin on his face. "Settle down James," Sam chuckled. "you're going to pass out from lack of oxygen with your head that high in the clouds."

Hours passed, and the landscape gradually changed. Fields of wheat and rolling hills stretched out in all directions as they pressed.

Finally, as the sun dipped below the horizon, they reached Uruffe. The men were weary from the march. They had arrived at their first post in France, ready to face the enemy.

The town of Uruffe was a quaint French village with cobblestone streets and centuries-old buildings. It was a far cry from the small towns, big cities, and rolling fields of Alabama, and the soldiers couldn't help but be intrigued by the Old-World charm that surrounded them.

James and Tommy, having been assigned quarters together, made their way to a modest cattle shed on the outskirts of town. The shed, while not luxurious by any means, would serve as their home during their time here.

Inside the shed, they found a small but functional space. Bunks were lined up along one wall, some equipped with a rough mattress and others with a blanket. Their gear had been haphazardly stacked in a corner, and the dim light filtering through a small window cast long shadows across the wooden floor.

"Well, this is home for now," James remarked, his voice tinged with exhaustion as he dropped his pack onto one of the spaces for a bunk.

Tommy nodded in agreement, his eyes taking in the surroundings. "It's not much, but it's better than sleeping out in the snow."

With a sense of understanding that had grown stronger throughout their journey, the two soldiers set about making their part of the shed as comfortable as possible. They hung their helmets on their propped-up rifles, arranged their gear, and settled in for the night.

Outside, the town of Uruffe went about its business, seemingly untouched by the presence of the Americans. The soldiers knew that their mission was just beginning, and they were eager to contribute to the fight in any way they could.

As the night settled in, James and Tommy exchanged stories

and shared their hopes for the future.

***

Dear Maggie,

I hope this letter finds you well. We've finally arrived in France, and I wanted to share some of the experiences we've had so far. It's quite different from home, but there's something special about this place.

The village kids here are something else, Maggie. They're as excited to see us as we are to be here. When we first arrived, they gathered around, their eyes wide with wonder. They've never seen Americans before, and they seem genuinely happy to have us here.

The other day, a group of these kids challenged us to a snowball fight in the main part of the village. I tell you, Maggie, it was like something out of a storybook. Snowflakes were falling, and we were all laughing and playing like kids again. We may be soldiers, but there's always room for a little fun.

The kids are quick learners, and they gave us quite a run for our money.

Their giggles and cheers echoed through the narrow streets, and for a moment, it felt like we were all just kids enjoying a winter's day.

I couldn't help but think of you, Maggie, and how much you'd love to see the joy on their faces. It's moments like these that remind us why we're here, fighting for a better world.

I'll write to you soon with more updates, but for now, know that we're safe and making the most of our time in this new place. Give my love to everyone back home, especially Ma. I miss you all more than words can say.

Until next time, take care, dear sister.

Yours always,

James

***

The days in Uruffe, settled into a routine for the men of the 167th Infantry. While they trained and prepared for their eventual deployment to the front lines, they also found themselves becoming a part of the daily life in the village.

One crisp morning, as James and his fellow soldiers were busy cleaning up at the village washhouse, several villagers joined them. The washhouse was a bustling hub of activity, with locals and soldiers working side by side to scrub themselves clean and learn about each other.

As James dunked himself into a basin of soapy water, he couldn't help but notice the friendly faces of the villagers around him. They chatted in a mix of broken English and French, trying to bridge the language barrier that separated them.

One elderly woman, her hands worn from years of challenging work, approached James with a warm smile. She pointed to the soap and then to him, repeating the word "savon" with enthusiasm. James nodded, understanding her gesture.

Another villager, a young man with a mop of unruly brown hair, joined in. He pointed to a pile of clothes and said, "Laver," indicating that they needed to be washed. James repeated the word with a grin, trying his best to mimic the pronunciation.

Soon, it became a sort of game. The villagers would teach the soldiers a French word, and in return, they would share an English word. Laughter echoed through the washhouse as they tried to communicate, often resorting to hand gestures and exaggerated expressions to convey their meaning.

"Bon," one of the villagers exclaimed, giving James a thumbs-up when he correctly identified the French word for "water." The camaraderie between the soldiers and the villagers grew stronger with each exchanged word.

After a few hours of washing and laughter, the soldiers were trying to dry themselves in the crisp winter air. James wiped his hands on his towel and looked around at the smiling faces of both soldiers and villagers.

Though they came from different worlds and spoke different languages, they had found a way to connect through simple gestures and shared tasks. It was a reminder that, despite the challenges of war, there was still room for moments of humanity and connection.

As James and his unit headed back to their quarters, they

couldn't help but feel a sense of gratitude for the warm welcome they had received in this small French village. They were not just soldiers passing through; they were becoming a part of the community, forging bonds that would last a lifetime.

The arrival of 30 American officers and two French instructors in Uruffe marked a significant turning point for the men of the 167th. They knew that despite their determination and dedication, they were, in military terms, "green." Many had not seen combat before, and the reality of warfare was a looming certainty.

As the officers and instructors began their training regimen, the soldiers gathered in the designated training area with a sense of weariness and respect. They understood that this additional training was essential to prepare them for the challenges ahead on the battlefields.

The two French instructors, Captain Dupont and Lieutenant Moreau, brought a wealth of experience to the training sessions. Their weathered faces and battle-hardened demeanor spoke volumes about the trials of war. Despite the language barrier, the soldiers found a way to communicate through gestures, broken English, and nods.

Captain Miller, one of the American officers, stepped forward to address the troops. "Men," he began, his voice carrying a sense of authority, "we're here to ensure that you're ready for battle against the Germans. We know many of you haven't faced combat before, but that's why we're here."

He went on to outline the training program, which included marksmanship drills, tactical maneuvers, and simulated combat scenarios. The soldiers listened intently, their eyes fixed on the officers and instructors who would guide them through the process.

The training was rigorous, with early mornings and long days spent in the field. The soldiers learned the importance of teamwork, discipline, and precision. They practiced firing their weapons until it became second nature and honed their ability to navigate challenging terrain.

James and Tommy, in particular, were dedicated students of the training. They knew that their roles as soldiers, as well as their responsibilities to their fellow brothers, required them to excel in every aspect of their training.

As the weeks passed, a sense of fellowship and mutual respect developed between the American soldiers and their French instructors. Captain Dupont and Lieutenant Moreau not only imparted valuable knowledge but also shared stories of their own experiences in the trenches, giving the soldiers a glimpse into the harsh realities of war.

The soldiers were grateful for the additional training, recognizing that it was a privilege to learn from those who had been tested in battle. They knew that the skills and knowledge they were acquiring would not only enhance their chances of survival but also strengthen their unit as a whole.

Through the dedication of the officers, the expertise of the French instructors, and the unwavering commitment of the troops, the 167th Infantry Division in Uruffe transformed from a group of green National Guardsmen into a formidable force ready to face the challenges that awaited them on the Western Front. They may have been inexperienced, but they were determined to prove themselves as capable and resilient soldiers, ready to serve their country with honor and courage.

Chapter 11

The orders came in the early morning hours, a message that roused the soldiers of the 167th from their restless slumber in Uruffe. They had been training diligently, preparing for the inevitable moment when they would be called upon to face the harsh realities of combat. That moment had now arrived.

Captain Miller, one of the American officers who had been instrumental in their training, stood before the assembled men. His voice was steady, a reassuring presence in the pre-dawn darkness.

"Men," he began, "the time has come. We have received orders to march from Uruffe to St. Blin. This is where our journey truly begins."

James and Tommy exchanged glances, their jaw lines revealing their feelings, excitement and determination for James and worry and anxiety for Tommy. They had come a long way since their arrival in France. Now, they were about to embark on a new phase of their journey.

The soldiers listened intently as Captain Miller outlined the details of the march. They were to move quickly but cautiously. The terrain would be challenging, with muddy fields and narrow roads. Every step would bring them closer to the unknown, and they were acutely aware of the dangers that lay ahead.

As the first light of dawn began to break over Uruffe, the men checked their rifles, adjusted their packs, and tightened their bootlaces. The air was filled with a sense of anticipation, mixed with a touch of apprehension.

James looked at Tommy, his lifelong friend and now fellow unit mate. Their journey had brought them to this moment, and they knew they would rely on each other for strength and support in the days and weeks to come. "I got your back, James," Tommy said as they tied their boots up. "I know, Tommy, and you know I have always had yours," James replied.

The men formed up in formation, their faces set in wrinkled brows and clinched jaws. The village of Uruffe, which had become a temporary home, faded into the distance as they began their march towards St. Blin. The path ahead was uncertain, but they were ready to face whatever challenges the journey would bring.

With their boots hitting the muddy ground in unison, they took their first steps on the road that would lead them closer to the front lines. The march had begun, and the soldiers of the 167th Infantry stood together in the face of adversity, no matter what lay ahead.

The 167th Division had trained rigorously in Uruffe, but now it was time for them to put their skills to the test as they embarked on the grueling 22-mile march to St. Blin. "The only part of army life I don't like, and I don't think I will ever get used to is all this marching," Sam remarked to James as they moved towards the formation. "Yeah, but it is something we have to do, not only to get from place to place but also to maneuver on the battlefield," James replied. "Silence, men!" Capt. Miller barked at them as he approached their path. "Only necessary communication while we are moving."

As the morning painted the sky with shades of orange and pink, the soldiers lined up in formation, their breath visible in the damp winter air. James and Tommy took their positions near the front. They exchanged a nod, silently acknowledging the responsibility that rested on their shoulders.

Miller called out orders, and the march began. The soldiers

moved in unison, their boots hitting the mud with a rhythmic cadence. Each step brought them closer to St. Blin, but it also reminded them of the distance they had yet to cover.

The first few miles passed smoothly. The soldiers were in good spirits, chatting quietly among themselves to avoid the wrath and scolding of their commander.

As the hours passed, fatigue set in. The weight of their gear seemed to grow heavier with each step, and the muddy terrain made the march even more arduous. However, the soldiers trudged on, not affording to fall behind their goal.

Tommy, marching beside James, could not help but glance at his friend. James' brow was furrowed with concentration, and his jaw was set. They had faced countless trials together, and this was just another hurdle to overcome. Tommy was thankful for his friend's strength and courage because he was going to need to borrow some to get through this ordeal.

As they continued, the soldiers were fueled by a sense of purpose. They knew that their journey reflected their commitment to the war effort and to each other. Their boots crunched on frozen and muddy ground as the countryside rolled by, with small villages and open fields stretching into the distance.

By midday, the soldiers took a brief break to rest and eat. They sat on the side of the road, their rations providing a meager but necessary source of sustenance. The laughter and fellowship from earlier had been replaced by the quiet determination to consume what food they had available to them.

The march resumed, and as the sun began its descent, the soldiers pressed on into the twilight hours. The chill of the evening air served as a reminder that their journey was far from over.

When night fell, they continued with the aid of dimly lit lanterns and the guidance of their officers. The dark countryside held an eerie stillness, broken only by the sound of boots on the road and the occasional whisper of conversation.

Fatigue weighed heavily on the soldiers, but they drew strength from each other. They knew that they were sending not only their bodies but also their minds into the challenges that lay ahead on the Western Front.

As the first light of dawn broke on the horizon, St. Blin came into view. The soldiers had completed their 22-mile march, a testament to their resilience. They were met with a mixture of relief and pride, knowing that they had faced this challenge as a united force.

The march to St. Blin had tested the soldiers physically and mentally, but it had also reinforced their bond as a unit. They were one step closer to the front lines and they would face whatever came their way with the same unwavering determination that had carried them through this demanding journey.

The soldiers of the 167th arrived in St. Blin on December 12th, 1917, weary from their march. The two weeks that followed were a mix of hard work, camaraderie, and preparations for a memorable Christmas celebration.

Setting up camp in St. Blin was the first order of business. The soldiers pitched their tents in neat rows, transforming a patch of French countryside into a temporary home. The village's residents looked on with curiosity and gratitude, knowing that these Americans were there to help protect their homeland. The mayor of St. Blin walked up to Capt. Miller and said,

"Mon Dieu, les hommes, vous êtes nombreux ici. Je ne pense pas que les Allemands aient une chance" Miller put his index finger in the air and shouted, "Jones, get over here and translate!" The mayor repeated himself as Private Jones translated for his commander who responded, "I certainly hope that is the case."

James, now becoming a seasoned soldier, took on a leadership role in organizing the camp. They worked alongside their fellow troops to establish a sense of order and efficiency. Trenches were dug for drainage, latrines were constructed, and patrols were established to ensure the safety of the camp.

As Christmas drew nearer, the soldiers began to feel a sense of anticipation and excitement. The village of St. Blin welcomed them warmly, and there was a shared feeling of goodwill between the Americans and the French villagers. This feeling was further reinforced when the villagers began to offer gifts of cattle, chickens, and lambs from their personal farms.

One day, a group of villagers arrived at the camp with a special delivery – fresh rabbit and cattle from their farms. It was a gesture of appreciation and an invitation to share in the bounty of the land. Miller expressed his gratitude, and that of his men, who were touched by this act of generosity, as a tear formed in his eye and voice began to crack and he knew that they were forging a bond with the people they had come to protect.

The camp cooks, skilled at making the most of their rations, took these gifts and turned them into hearty meals. Rabbit stew and beef roast became the staples of the Christmas Day celebratory feast.

However, the true highlight of the Christmas preparations was the making of fruitcakes soaked in whiskey. The camp cooks worked tirelessly, mixing the ingredients and carefully adding a generous dose of spirits to each cake. The aroma of the fruitcakes baking in the makeshift ovens filled the camp with a sense of warmth and holiday spirit. "Man, that smells just like Ma's fruitcake back home!" James exclaimed. "That is still the best cake I've ever had," Tommy responded with a distant stare remembering the holiday treat his friend's mother would make for everyone.

In the evenings, after a hard day's work, the soldiers would gather around campfires to share stories and songs. "I hate spending Christmas away from Peggy," Tommy mentioned with sorrow etched across his face. "I know man, but let's get this thing done and whip these German turds so we can get you back home to her," James responded as cheers rang up around them.

Christmas Eve arrived, and the soldiers of the division gathered together in a makeshift mess hall adorned with candles and decorations crafted from whatever materials they could find. The fruitcakes, soaked in whiskey, took center stage as the men shared slices and toasted to their newfound friendships and shared experience.

The villagers of St. Blin were invited to join in the celebration, and together with the American soldiers, they sang carols, exchanged small gifts, and shared stories of their respective homelands.

As the clock struck midnight on Christmas Day, there was a sense of unity and hope that transcended the bleak reality of the war that lay just beyond the horizon for all of them. The troops of the 167th felt a deep connection to the people of St. Blin, and they knew that in this small village in France, they had found a second family as the villagers and soldiers exchanged hugs and farewells as the evening came to a close.

Christmas Day in St. Blin dawned with a crisp, wintry air that hinted at the magic of the season. The soldiers of the Division and the villagers of St. Blin had come together to celebrate, and the spirit of unity filled the air.

The makeshift mess hall had been transformed into a festive gathering place for the previous night's celebration. Soldiers and villagers worked side by side, continuing to decorate the space with evergreen branches, candles, and whatever decorations they could fashion from scraps of cloth and twine. The room had a warm, inviting glow, and the aroma of a hearty Christmas feast filled the air.

James sat at a long wooden table, reading a letter that had arrived the previous day from his beloved sister, Maggie. The letter was a cherished connection to home, and James could not help but share its contents with his buddies.

"Listen up, fellas," James called out to his friends, his voice filled with a mix of homesickness and joy. "I've got a letter here from my sister, Maggie. She sends her love and Christmas wishes to all of us."

His comrades gathered around, their faces reflecting a longing for their own loved ones back in Alabama. As James read Maggie's heartfelt words aloud, there was a collective sense of gratitude for the letters that brought a piece of home to the far-off fields of France.

Amid the exchange of stories and the reading of letters, the soldiers and villagers began to exchange small gifts. Cigarettes, chew, and pipe tobacco were popular choices, and laughter filled the room as they shared stories of how they would put their newfound treasures to use.

Tommy, always resourceful, had managed to acquire a few sweet treats from the village children during their snowball fight, and he offered them as Christmas presents to his friends. The simple act of giving and receiving brought smiles to the faces of those gathered, and it reinforced the bond that had formed between them and the people of St. Blin.

As midday approached, the men and villagers gathered for a Christmas church service led by the unit's chaplain. The chapel in the village, even though it had been damaged by the ravages of war, was adorned with candles, and the air was filled with the timeless melodies of Christmas hymns like Silent Night and O Holy Night, sung in both English and French.

The chaplain's sermon focused on the message of hope and peace that Christmas represented. He reminded the congregation that, despite the hardships of war, that currently have felled them, they had found a sense of unity and friendship in St. Blin. It was a message that resonated deeply with all who were present.

After the service, the soldiers and villagers sat down to a Christmas feast that had been prepared by the camp cooks. Roast beef, rabbit stew, and fruitcake soaked in whiskey were served alongside whatever local delicacies the villagers had contributed. The shared meal was a symbol of the enduring bond between these two communities brought together by the trials of war.

As the day turned into evening and the candles cast a warm, flickering light on the faces of those gathered, there was a sense of contentment and peace in St. Blin. Christmas had brought soldiers and villagers together in a way that transcended language and nationality. It was a day when the spirit of goodwill and the joy of togetherness prevailed, reminding them all that even amid war, the light of hope and humanity could shine brightly.

The morning of December 26th dawned with a biting cold that hinted at the harsh journey that lay ahead for the soldiers of the 167th. The Christmas celebrations in St. Blin had forged bonds of camaraderie and warmth, but now it was time to face the reality of war once more.

As the soldiers gathered their gear in preparation to depart, there was an air of solemnity that contrasted with the festive atmosphere of the previous day. Their orders had come down from the high command, and the march to Rolampont was to commence immediately.

Colonel Douglas MacArthur, the chief of staff of the supreme American commander in France, General John Pershing, who had been with the men along the Mexican border, had issued the orders. He was known for his no-nonsense approach and his unwavering commitment to the success of the division. The soldiers respected him, but they knew that his decisions were driven by the urgency of the war.

The weather, which had been relatively mild, took a turn for the worse on the day after Christmas. The skies darkened with heavy clouds, and a frigid wind whipped through the village. Snowflakes started to fall, and the ground quickly became blanketed in white.

The men of the 167th were seasoned by now, but even they could not help but feel a sense of dread as they shouldered their packs. "Could God have painted a more foreboding canvas of what's to come?" James asked his buddies. Murmurs of agreement cascaded through the immediate surroundings as they started to file into formation. The march to Rolampont was a formidable one, covering a significant distance through challenging terrain.

James and Tommy, having faced adversity together since their days in Thomasville, exchanged a glance that conveyed concern. They knew that this march would test their mettle like never before, and they were prepared to face it side by side.

The first steps out of St. Blin were marked by the crunch of fresh snow and the hushed whispers of soldiers offering words of encouragement to one another. The landscape around them was

transformed into a winter wonderland, but there was little time to appreciate its beauty.

The snowfall intensified as the day wore on, and the soldiers trudged through the deepening drifts. The weight of their packs pressed against their shoulders, and the biting cold gnawed at their extremities. Still, they pressed forward.

The journey to Rolampont was arduous and relentless. The soldiers relied on their training and the bonds that had been forged in the crucible of training that led up to the war. They encouraged one another, shared stories to distract from the harsh conditions, and kept their eyes on the horizon.

By nightfall, the soldiers had covered a considerable distance, but Rolampont still seemed like a distant goal. The weather showed no mercy, and fatigue weighed heavily on their bodies. Yet, they pressed on.

As time passed, the snow-covered landscape became a relentless backdrop to their march. Every step was a battle against the elements, but the men of the 167th were determined to overcome. They knew that each mile brought them closer to the front lines and the challenges that awaited.

***

Dearest Maggie,

I hope this letter finds you well and warm back home. I cannot express how much your Christmas letter meant to me. It brought a touch of you to these cold and distant lands.

Christmas in France was unlike any I have experienced before. The spirit of the season filled the air, even amid this war-torn world. We gathered with the villagers, and the makeshift mess hall was transformed into a festive haven. There were evergreen branches and candles, and the aroma of a hearty feast of fruitcake, beef, and rabbit that would have made Ma proud.

Now, here comes the funny part. During our celebration, one of the villagers mistook me for a "Yankee." Can you imagine that? Me, a Yankee! I must have looked puzzled because they quickly explained that all Americans were Yankees to them. I had to laugh, and I told them that being called a Yankee in France was a badge of honor. It is funny how far from home one can be and still find humor in the unimportant things.

Speaking of news from afar, I have enclosed a newspaper clipping from the London Globe about our arrival in France. Can you believe it? We are in the papers! They even call us "famous." I must admit, it is a bit bewildering to think of ourselves that way, but it is a reminder of the importance of our mission.

I wish you could see the snow here, Maggie. It blankets the landscape like a pristine canvas, and I find a strange sort of beauty in it. But it also makes every step a challenge, especially as we march on. The weather has turned quite harsh, and it is a testament to the strength of our unit that we press on undaunted.

I miss you and Thomasville every day, Maggie, but your letters keep my spirits high. Please give my love to Ma and Pa and tell them that I am thinking of them often. Stay warm and safe and know that I carry you all in my heart.

With love,

James

Chapter 12

The march from St. Blin to Leffonds had been a grueling ordeal for the 167th Division. They had weathered freezing temperatures, biting winds, and treacherous terrain, earning the nickname the "Valley Forge March" among the soldiers. But as they finally arrived, the weary men were met with a sight that rekindled their spirits.

The village, nestled in the Faverolles region of France, welcomed the American soldiers with open arms. The villagers, bundled in thick coats and scarves against the cold, lined the streets to greet the tired troops. Children waved small American flags, their faces beaming with excitement.

James and Tommy, their breath visible in the frigid air, exchanged grateful glances. The warmth of the villagers' reception thawed the chill that had settled in their bones during the long march. They felt a renewed sense of purpose and unity.

The soldiers marched in formation through the village, their boots crunching on the snow-covered cobblestone streets. The rhythmic sound was like a heartbeat, a reminder that life went on even amid war. Villagers offered hearty smiles and gestures of goodwill along with small pieces of candy and wildflowers, and some even passed out hot cups of tea to the soldiers.

As the soldiers settled into their quarters, they could not help but notice the stark contrast between the rugged countryside they had traversed and the quaint charm of the village. The stone houses with their sloping roofs and narrow streets exuded a timeless beauty.

That evening, the villagers and the soldiers gathered in the village square for a simple yet heartwarming celebration. A bonfire crackled in the center, casting dancing shadows on the snow. A local band played cheerful tunes, and the men and villagers alike joined in the festivities.

James and Tommy found themselves sitting around the bonfire, sharing stories and laughter with the villagers. They were offered warm bowls of rabbit soup and chunks of crusty bread, a meal that felt like a feast after the long march. The camaraderie between the troops and the villagers transcended language barriers, and they communicated through gestures and shared smiles.

As the night wore on, they sang songs together, their voices rising into the frosty air. It was a moment of unity, that even amid a world torn by conflict, the bonds of humanity could still prevail.

James looked around at the faces illuminated by the bonfire's glow, both American and French, young and old. In that moment, he felt a profound sense of gratitude for the kindness and resilience of the people of Leffonds. "I think French hospitality can rival that of the Southern hospitality of Thomasville any day of the week," James remarked to Tommy. "Yeah, they are friendly here, I wonder if they are always like this or just see us as their saviors?" a skeptical Tommy inquired. They had welcomed the unit into their village, offering warmth and friendship in a time of uncertainty.

As the night grew late, the soldiers retired to their quarters, their hearts filled with a newfound sense of hope. The "Valley Forge March" had been a test of endurance, but it had brought them to a place where they were not only soldiers on foreign soil but also guests in a village that had shown them the true meaning of hospitality.

The call to action resonated throughout the ranks of the 167th Infantry Unit and the 42nd Rainbow Division. American commanders, well aware of the urgency of the situation on the front lines, pushed the soldiers to prepare for combat with unprecedented speed and intensity. The men knew that they were being readied to reinforce the French troops and bolster the Allied effort in the ongoing conflict.

As the soldiers of the 167th settled into their temporary base in Leffonds, the relentless training began. Days blurred into nights as they honed their combat skills. The biting cold of the French winter was unforgiving, but it only added to the sense of urgency.

Colonel Douglas MacArthur, whose reputation for unwavering discipline was widely known, oversaw the rigorous training regimen. Having shown up on the second day of training, Col. McArthur inspired the men to try harder and push themselves further than they had ever done before. "We can't let McArthur down, he would be badly disappointed," was the common refrain from the soldiers. He pushed the soldiers to their limits, demanding excellence in marksmanship, tactical maneuvers, and physical endurance. Each day, they drilled relentlessly, their boots sinking into the snow-covered ground.

The soldiers were no strangers to hardship. They had weathered the harsh conditions of the "Valley Forge March" and faced the challenges of training camps in the United States,

Great Britain and France. But this was different. The knowledge that they would soon be on the front lines added an extra layer of urgency to their efforts.

Instructors, many of them veterans of the European theater, shared their combat experience with the soldiers. They taught them about the intricacies of trench warfare, the use of gas masks, and the importance of swift and decisive action. The men absorbed these lessons with a sense of gravity, knowing that their lives and the lives of their friends depended on their ability to apply this knowledge.

The sense of brotherhood among the troops deepened as they trained together. They knew that the bonds forged in the crucible of training were unbreakable. Stories were shared around campfires, and laughter rang out even in the harshest of conditions.

As the days went along, the soldiers could feel themselves growing stronger and more capable. They knew that they were being prepared not just for combat but for a pivotal role in it. Their American commanders were relentless in their push for readiness, and the soldiers responded with a fierce response. "Man, this training is rough," Tommy admitted one evening around the campfire when it was just him and James.

News from the front lines served as a constant reminder of the stakes. Reports of battles and the sacrifices made by others who were already there in distant trenches reinforced the soldiers' commitment to their training. "We have to get better at fighting so that we don't end up in here as a statistic!" James exclaimed, throwing the newspaper in his hand down on the mess hall table in disgust.

All of the soldiers knew that their time on the front lines was fast approaching. They could feel the weight of history on their shoulders, but they felt like they were ready. Their training had forged them into a formidable force, and they were prepared to stand shoulder-to-shoulder with their French allies and do their part in the fight for victory.

On a bitter January day in 1918, the 167th Infantry received news that would forever change their role. General John J. Pershing, the commander of the American Expeditionary Forces, had issued orders to create the First U.S. Army Corps, and the 167th would play a pivotal role in this new development.

The soldiers, now seasoned by months of rigorous training and weathering the elements in the French countryside, gathered for a briefing from their commanding officers. The mood was a mix of anticipation and apprehension. They understood that their training had been preparing them for this moment, but the reality of the front lines was a formidable challenge.

The creation of the First U.S. Army Corps signified a momentous step for the American forces. It was a testament to their growing strength and capability. Pershing, a resolute and strategic leader, saw the need for a cohesive command structure to coordinate the efforts of American troops on the Western Front.

Under this new corps, the soldiers of the 167th would be integrated into the larger framework of the American forces in Europe. They would be part of a coordinated offensive effort alongside their French and British allies. This marked a shift from their previous role, which had focused primarily on training and preparation.

As the men processed this news, they understood the weight of their responsibility. They were no longer just training for combat; they were now preparing to face the realities of trench warfare, gas attacks, and the unrelenting challenges of the Western Front.

Their commanding officers emphasized the importance of discipline, cooperation, and steadfastness in the face of adversity. The soldiers had become a tight-knit unit during their training, and this sense of camaraderie would serve them well in the battles to come.

In the weeks that followed, preparations for deployment intensified. Gear was inspected, supplies were distributed, and the soldiers underwent final training drills. The transition from trainees to combat-ready troops was swift and thorough.

The troops knew that they were part of something bigger. They were among the first American forces to be integrated into the larger Allied effort in Europe, and they carried with them the hopes and expectations of their nation.

On January 15th, as they received their official orders to join the First U.S. Army Corps, there was a tangible sense of resolve among the soldiers. Most of them were ready to face the challenges of the front lines, knowing that their training and their unity prepared them for this moment.

The news of Capt. Mitchell's promotion to battalion

commander brought mixed emotions within the ranks. Mitchell had been a respected and beloved company commander, known for his leadership and bond with his men. As the soldiers gathered to bid him farewell, their faces displayed a mixture of pride and sadness.

James had served as Capt. Mitchell's go-to person and his fellow soldiers knew he was more than capable of stepping into the role of company commander. Mitchell had recognized James' leadership qualities and recommended him for the position. It was a testament to James' competence.

The day of the captain's departure was bittersweet. Men gathered in a makeshift assembly area; their breath visible in the frigid winter air. Mitchell addressed the company one final time, "Men, it has been my honor of a lifetime to command this unit. No unit in this whole army has worked harder and trained better than Company B. I will always cherish my time with you, and I want you to remember that every one of you deserves to be here and will make excellent soldiers on the battlefield." He continued, "We have come a long way since our time at Camp Mills and I have no doubt that the 167th and Company B will be instrumental in our future victories against the Germans."

"I'll miss every one of you," Mitchell said, his voice tinged with emotion. "But I know you're in good hands. Lieutenant Reynolds here has proven himself time and again. He's a leader, and he'll guide you well."

There was a round of applause for Mitchell, and a few shook his hand or patted him on the back. Then, as he departed, James stepped forward to take command.

The transition was seamless. James had already earned the respect of his fellow soldiers through his actions on the training field and in their previous assignments. As he addressed the company, he spoke with a firm but reassuring tone.

"I know we've been through a lot together," James began. "And I want you to know that I'm here to lead, but I'm also here to listen. We're a team, and together, we'll face whatever comes our way."

His words were met with nods of approval and a round of applause. The men knew that James was a leader who led by example. He was approachable and had a knack for understanding the concerns of his men.

Under James' command, the company continued their training for deployment. They knew that the war awaited them, and they were going to face whatever lay ahead.

As the time passed, James' leadership style became evident. He was decisive in his decision-making, but he also encouraged open communication within the company. Soldiers felt comfortable approaching him with their ideas and concerns, knowing that their voices were heard.

James' promotion to company commander marked a significant moment in his military career. He carried the weight of responsibility with grace, honoring the legacy of those who had led before him. His men trusted in his leadership, ready to follow him into the Western Front, knowing that they had a capable and compassionate leader at their helm.

James knew that to excel as a company commander, he needed more than just combat experience. He needed the knowledge and skills that would make him an effective leader on the battlefield. So, when the opportunity arose for him to attend a specialty school in France, he seized it.

The school was located in a small town not far from the front lines. As he arrived, he was greeted by the sight of other American soldiers, all eager to enhance their leadership abilities. The instructors, a mix of experienced officers and seasoned veterans, welcomed the new arrivals.

The curriculum was intensive and multifaceted. It covered a wide range of topics, from tactical maneuvering on the battlefield to administrative tasks crucial for effective command. James was determined to absorb as much as he could.

In the classroom, he studied maps and strategies, learning how to read the terrain and anticipate enemy movements. He delved into the intricacies of trench warfare, understanding the importance of fortifications and the use of artillery.

But the training went beyond theory. Out in the field, James and his fellow students practiced leading troops in simulated battles. They honed their communication skills, ensuring that orders were clear and concise even in the chaos of combat.

One of the most valuable aspects of the school was the opportunity to gain knowledge from experienced officers who had already seen action on the front lines. They shared their firsthand experiences, recounting the challenges and victories they had encountered.

As James immersed himself in his studies, he could not help but reflect on his journey from a young boy leaving Thomasville to this moment in France.

The fellowship among the students was evident. They trained together, ate together, and shared stories of their homes and families. Bonds formed as they were all united by a common purpose — to become the best leaders they could be.

One of James's closest friends at the school was another aspiring company commander named Robert Palmer. They often spent evenings discussing tactics, sharing their dreams for when they got home, and finding solace in each other's company amidst the training.

As school concluded, James completed his training with flying colors. He returned to his unit with newfound confidence and expertise, ready to take on the challenges of leading his company on the front lines.

The war continued to rage, and the men knew that they would soon face the stresses of combat. But with James' training and leadership, they believed they had a fighting chance to overcome whatever obstacles lay ahead.

As the days till the men would see the front lines grew shorter and the chill of the air settled over the training grounds in France, the men of the Alabama 167th continued to hone their skills. The war had evolved, and so did their training.

One of the most crucial aspects of their preparation was the construction of training trenches. These were not the elaborate networks of trenches seen on the Western Front, but they provided valuable firsthand experience. Under gray skies, the soldiers dug and reinforced trenches, gaining an understanding of the labor and precision required to create defensive positions.

James oversaw these efforts. He led by example, often joining his men in the muddy trenches, demonstrating that he was not a leader who stayed in the rear but was willing to get his hands dirty. His presence inspired his soldiers, and they respected him not only for his leadership but for his willingness to share their burdens.

Gas attacks had become a horrifying reality of modern warfare, and the men underwent rigorous training with both French and English-made gas masks. They learned how to don the masks swiftly and efficiently, understanding that a matter of seconds could be the difference between life and death in a gas attack.

Amid this intense training, James took the opportunity to refine his command skills. He conducted mock battles and tactical exercises, putting his company through their paces. His clear and decisive orders resonated with his men, and they executed their maneuvers with discipline and precision.

The bonds that developed among the troops remained strong. Even as they faced the grim realities of war, they found moments of levity. They shared stories around campfires, traded jokes, and clung to the bonds they had formed.

One chilly evening, as they huddled around a crackling fire, James shared a story from his childhood in Thomasville. "Tommy and I went down to ol'man Turner's pond one afternoon after school to do some Brim fishing, and Tommy started running down the hill and he tripped over a tree root. He stumbled so fast that he could not stop tumbling down the hill. He didn't stop until he was in the pond!" James relayed as Tommy's cheeks reddened with embarrassment and the others chuckled heartily. His anecdotes about the small Alabama town and the adventures he had with his sister Maggie and Tommy brought smiles to the faces of his men.

"Remember," he said, his voice carrying over the flames, "we're not just soldiers; we're Alabamians. We carry the spirit of our home with us, no matter where we go."

The men nodded; their spirits buoyed by James' words. They knew that their commander understood the importance of their roots and the unbreakable ties that bound them together.

As the training continued, the soldiers felt themselves growing stronger, more prepared for the challenges that lay ahead. They were a unit forged in the trials of training, led by a commander who had proven himself effective.

With their skills honed and their resolve unwavering, the Alabama 167th stood ready for the next chapter of their journey on the Western Front, where they would face the true test of their training and courage in the tests of battle.

***

My Dearest Maggie,

I hope this letter finds you well and in good spirits. It seems like ages since I left our small town and so much has changed since then. I wanted to share some news that I think you will be proud of.

I have been promoted, Maggie! I am now a company commander, responsible for leading a fine group of men in our unit. It is a great honor, but it also comes with immense responsibility. I think about what you always told me about being a leader, that it is not just about giving orders, but about caring for the well-being of those under your command. I will carry those words with me as I take on this new role.

With this promotion has come new orders. We are shipping out soon, Maggie, heading to the front lines to face the Germans. The situation over here is intense, and we are all aware of the challenges that lie ahead. But you know me, I have never been one to shy away from a challenge. I am committed to doing my best to lead my men with honor and courage.

The training we have undergone has prepared us as best as it could. We dug trenches, practiced with gas masks, and drilled tirelessly. I have learned so much, not just about strategy and tactics, but about leadership and the importance of looking out for my men.

I want you to know that, even though I will be far away, you will always be in my thoughts. I carry the memory of our home, the laughter with you and the adventures with Tommy, close to my heart. You are my anchor, Maggie, and the thought of your unwavering support gives me strength.

Please keep me in your prayers, Maggie, as I will keep you in mine. I know this journey will not be easy, but I am determined to come back to you, safe and sound. Until then, know that I love you dearly and that you are always with me, no matter how far away I may be. Give my love to Ma and Pa and give Ma a big hug and a kiss from me.

With all my love,

James

Chapter 13

As the day of departure drew near, the atmosphere in the camp became charged with solemnity. James, now a lieutenant, had been tirelessly preparing his men for the journey to the front lines in the Baccarat sector.

The orders had come in with the precision of a military operation. James and his fellow officers had briefed their men about the specifics of their mission. They were heading to the Baccarat, a region that had seen its share of battles and skirmishes. The seriousness of their destination hung in the air like a heavy fog.

One evening, as the sun cast long shadows over the camp, James gathered his company for a final briefing. The faces of his men bore expressions that ranged from resolve to trepidation. James saw the worry etched all over the brow of his friend and said, "What's wrong Tommy? We have been training for this for a long time and we are ready for this." He knew that this was a crucial moment, and he needed to inspire confidence in his troops.

"Men," he began, his voice steady and commanding, "we're

about to embark on a mission that demands our best. The Baccarat is no place for the faint of heart, but I have every confidence in every one of you. We've trained for this, and we're ready."

His words were met with nods and a few murmurs of "Hooah!" James continued, "Remember your training, trust your instincts, and most importantly, trust your fellow brothers in the trenches. We're a team, and together, there's nothing we can't overcome."

As the time passed, the preparations intensified. Gear was checked and rechecked, weapons cleaned and oiled, and personal letters penned in case the worst should happen. There were moments of levity amidst the tension, with soldiers exchanging stories and sharing mementos from home. It was as if they were trying to capture a piece of normalcy before the impending storm.

The night before departure, the camp was alive with activity. Soldiers gathered around campfires, sharing stories and laughter, attempting to push aside the looming uncertainty of what lay ahead. James, however, found solace in solitude, writing a final letter to Maggie, pouring his thoughts and emotions onto the paper, a last connection to home.

In the pre-dawn darkness, the division assembled, ready to embark on their journey to the front lines. Their faces were set with determination, and the weight of their mission hung heavily in the air. The order to move out was given, and James led his company forward, knowing that the trials of the Baccarat sector awaited them.

The path to the front lines was fraught with challenges, both physical and emotional. But James and his men pressed forward.

As they approached the Baccarat, the distant sound of artillery fire, automatic gunfire, and shouts and hollering served as a stark reminder of the battles that lay ahead. James knew the true test of their training and courage was about to begin, and he steeled himself for the challenges that awaited him in the vice grips of war.

The orders James and his company received were to have them leave the relative comfort of their camp and embark on a train journey that would take them to Baccarat. The soldiers, now seasoned and ready, prepared for this next leg of their journey with a mix of anticipation and resolve.

The morning hung low in the sky as James and his men shouldered their packs and marched to the nearby train station. It was a somber procession, each step taking them further from the familiar and deeper into the unknown.

At the station, a line of 40 and 8 boxcars awaited them. The name, "40 and 8," originally designed to carry forty men or eight horses. They were far from luxurious, with wooden benches and cramped quarters, but the soldiers were grateful for any means of transportation that would bring them closer to their destination.

The loading process was a chaotic affair. Soldiers squeezed into the boxcars, their gear, and rifles piled around them. The atmosphere inside was stifling, the air thick with the combined scents of sweat, leather, and anticipation. James tried to maintain an air of authority as he ensured his men were settled and as comfortable as could be expected.

The train's whistle pierced the air, signaling their departure. With a jolt, the boxcars lurched forward, setting the men inside swaying. The rhythmic clattering of the wheels against the tracks provided a steady backdrop to their thoughts.

Inside the boxcars, conversation was subdued. Some soldiers

spoke in hushed tones, sharing stories and jokes to keep their spirits up. Others stared out of small, grated windows, watching the journey with a mixture of curiosity and apprehension.

As the time passed, and the train rolled on, the landscape gradually changed from the serene fields of France to something altogether different. The signs of war became more evident—the occasional craters left by artillery shells, the barbed wire fences, and the distinct sound of distant artillery fire.

As they neared Baccarat, the tension inside the boxcars grew tense. James could see it in the faces of his men—each of them bracing for the unknown that awaited them. They were no longer just soldiers on a train; they were warriors on a journey to the front lines.

The train's brakes screeched, and the boxcars came to a grinding halt. James stood up, his heart pounding in his chest. He knew that the true test of their mettle was about to begin. They were no longer passengers on a train; they were soldiers at the doorstep of war.

The arrival of the 167th Infantry in Baccarat brought with it a tangible sense of anticipation. The soldiers disembarked from the boxcars, their arrival marked by the clatter of gear and the thud of boots on the platform. Their large equipment, including field artillery and supplies, was unloaded with precision and efficiency.

As the soldiers set up their camp on the outskirts of Baccarat, the local civilian population watched with a mix of curiosity and relief. The town had seen its share of hardships, and the arrival of American troops signaled a turning point. The French villagers watched as the soldiers went about their duties setting up tents, unpacking gear, and getting the other necessities of camp life set up, impressed by their discipline and resolve.

James could sense the change in the atmosphere. The people of Baccarat greeted them with warm smiles and words of gratitude. The soldiers, in turn, tried their best to interact with the locals, bridging the gap between cultures and languages. It was not always easy, but small acts of kindness—a shared meal, a helping hand—forged connections between the men and the villagers.

One evening, James was engaged in a conversation with the town's mayor, a man with weathered hands and a keen sense of duty to his community. Through a combination of broken

French and gestures, they exchanged stories of their respective homelands. "We were founded before America was even a country," the mayor said in broken English. "That's interesting, my area of the world was actually started by your country," James responded, trying to build a connection with the mayor.

The mayor spoke of the hardships his town had endured during the war, the constant fear of German incursions, and the resilience of the people of Baccarat. James listened intently, recognizing the shared sense of sacrifice and that transcended language barriers.

In return, James shared tales of Alabama, of his family, and the small town of Thomasville. He spoke of his sister Maggie, the letters she wrote, and the hopes he held for a better future. The mayor nodded, his eyes reflecting a deep understanding of the universal desire for peace and security.

Over time, the soldiers and the villagers formed bonds that transcended the limitations of language. Children played games with the Americans, and the soldiers shared their rations with grateful families. The once war-torn town of Baccarat began to bloom with a new sense of optimism, fueled by the presence of these young American warriors.

As the men of the 167th settled into their new surroundings, they carried with them not only their weapons but also a commitment to protect and serve. The arrival of the division had brought a glimmer of hope to Baccarat, a town that had weathered the storm of war, and as they looked to the future, they did so with a newfound optimism.

The march from Baccarat to Glonville was a solemn journey through a landscape scarred by the ravages of war. As the 167th Infantry began their trek, they left behind the newfound hope they had brought to Baccarat, venturing into the heart of a region that bore the heavy weight of conflict.

The soldiers trudged through the remnants of once-thriving towns, now reduced to rubble and ash. Buildings lay in ruins, their skeletal structures serving as haunting reminders of the destructive power of warfare. Burned-out shells of homes and shops lined the streets, their shattered windows gaping like empty eyes.

Amidst this desolation, the soldiers passed makeshift graves, marked by simple wooden crosses bearing the names of fallen French soldiers. These graves were scattered haphazardly along the route, a poignant testament to the sacrifices made in the name of freedom. James could not help but bow his head in respect as he passed each one, his thoughts turning to the brave souls who had given their lives in this unforgiving terrain.

The landscape stretched out before them, a monochromatic canvas of gray, dreary, and frozen beauty. Leafless trees clawed at the leaden sky; their twisted branches silhouetted against the backdrop of an endless winter. A bitter chill hung in the air, and the ground crunched beneath their boots as they marched, a stark reminder of the unforgiving cold.

Transporting artillery became a Herculean task as the men approached a frozen river. The horses strained against the weight of the heavy cannons, their hooves clattering over the ice-covered surface. The men worked in unison, their breath forming frosty plumes in the frigid air as they guided the artillery across the frozen expanse.

The journey to Glonville was a stark contrast to the optimism they had brought to Baccarat. Here, in this frozen and desolate landscape, the realities of war weighed heavily on their shoulders. But they marched on, driven by a shared sense of duty and a commitment to each other and the people they had come to protect. Ahead lay Glonville, a place shrouded in uncertainty.

***

Four days after being ordered to depart Glonville, the 167th Infantry Division reached the town of Brouville. The journey, like so many before this one, had been long and arduous, with each step bringing them closer to the ever-present specter of war. As they entered the town, the troops could see that it bore the scars of recent conflict, much like the other towns they had passed through. "Tommy, these towns get sadder and sadder the closer to the front we get," James remarked. "Yeah, it's going to take a lot after the war to return these places to their former glory," his friend returned.

The remnants of shattered buildings lined the streets, a stark testament to the violence that had swept through the region. The civilians who remained offered weary smiles and appreciation as the American soldiers passed by, their faces etched with a mixture of relief and trepidation.

As the division settled into their new surroundings, the soldiers could not help but feel a sense of foreboding. War was no longer an abstract concept discussed in training; it was a tangible presence that hung heavy in the air.

One crisp afternoon, as James and his men prepared for deployment to the front lines of the war, a sudden roar from above shattered the relative calm. They looked up to see a skirmish in the skies. Allied and German warplanes engaged in aerial combat, the machines dancing through the heavens like dueling birds of prey.

The men watched in awe and trepidation as the dogfight unfolded above them. "Look! Have you ever seen anything like that?" Tommy asked excitedly. No," James responded. "But let's not stay out in the open too long and be careful in case they start dropping ordinance on us." The thunderous rumbles of the engines echoed through the streets of Brouville, and the distant chatter of machine guns filled the air. Puffs of smoke and flashes of fire marked the deadly exchange between the aircraft.

It was a stark reminder that the war had evolved beyond the trenches and battlefields. The skies themselves had become a battleground, where young men piloted their machines with bravery and skill, locked in mortal combat high above the earth.

As the aerial skirmish continued, James and his command could not help but feel a sense of admiration for the courage of those who soared above them. They knew that they, too, would soon face their own trials and challenges in the crux of war. For now, they watched the spectacle unfold with a mixture of awe and apprehension, aware that the world around them had irrevocably changed.

In the bleak and wintry February of 1918, the 167th arrived at the trenches east of Baccarat. Their journey through the scarred French terrain had led them to this pivotal moment. As they settled into their new positions, they could feel the weight of history pressing down upon them.

The American soldiers found themselves initially under the command of battle-hardened French divisions that had been holding the line in these trenches for months. These French brethren, with their stoic resolve, welcomed the Americans with a mixture of weariness and hope. "We know they have trained you relentlessly for this moment but remember even the best plans go out the window after the first shots are fired," the French commander relayed to James as they were in the midst of the command transfer discussions. "These German bastards will launch gas canisters and hand grenades at you at the most inconvenient times. They don't ask you if their schedule works for you." They shared other stories of the unrelenting nature of trench warfare, where every inch of ground was paid for in blood and sweat.

Facing them across the desolate expanse of No Man's Land were the formidable 96th German Infantry Division and the relentless 6th German Cavalry Division. The soldiers knew that they were up against a formidable adversary, one that had been entrenched in this unforgiving terrain for a long time.

The trenches themselves were a stark reminder of the unyielding nature of the Western Front. Deep, winding ditches etched into the earth, they were lined with sandbags and wooden supports, offering meager protection from the constant threat of enemy fire. The mud was a constant companion, seeping into every crevice of clothing and equipment.

As the soldiers settled into their positions, they could not help but feel a sense of trepidation. This was the moment they had trained for, the culmination of months of preparation. The legacy of the French divisions who had held these trenches was a heavy burden to bear, but it also served as a source of inspiration.

James felt the weight of leadership on his shoulders. He looked out across the scarred landscape, knowing that his decisions would have a profound impact on the lives of the men under his command. They had come to France as green soldiers, but they were determined to prove themselves.

Chapter 14

As the cold winds of February swept through the trenches, the soldiers steeled themselves for the challenges that lay ahead. The battle-hardened French divisions stood beside them, and together, they were prepared to face the formidable German foe that lurked just beyond the horizon.

Life in the trenches of France was a daily struggle for the soldiers of the 167th. Each day brought its own set of challenges, and they were reminded constantly of the unforgiving nature of war.

Meals were a moment of respite amid the chaos. They arrived in the trenches via mule-drawn carts, the clatter of hooves heralding the arrival of sustenance. The soldiers gathered around, their mess tins in hand, as they received their rations. "Man, I'm starving," Tommy quipped. "I almost charged the enemy so I could eat his rations," Sam continued. "Settle down boys, they know none of us Alabama boys have ever missed a meal, and the trouble we would cause if they tried to deny us," James admonished his men. The food was a simple affair - hardtack biscuits, tinned meat, and whatever could be scrounged up from the limited supplies. The food was a far cry from the hearty meals of home, but it was enough to keep them going.

The rain was a constant companion in the trenches, much like back in Thomasville. It fell in a relentless onslaught, turning the ground into a quagmire of mud and misery. The soldiers' boots squelched with each step, and their uniforms clung to their bodies, heavy and waterlogged. "John, your feet!" James ordered one of his men while holding out his hand to help him up. "I can't boss, they hurt so bad," his soldier replied. "Tommy, help him get to the aid station," James said to his friend as they helped him to his feet. "And remember everyone, keep your feet dry and change your socks daily!" Trench foot, a painful condition caused by prolonged exposure to wet and freezing conditions, was a constant threat.

Despite the discomfort and the ever-present danger, the soldiers found ways to cope. They huddled together in their cramped surroundings, sharing stories and jokes to lighten the mood. Cigarettes were passed around, their smoke mingling with the damp air. Letters from loved ones back home were read and reread, the words providing a brief escape from the harsh reality of the front lines.

At night, the trenches came alive with the eerie glow of flares and the distant rumble of artillery. The soldiers took turns on watch, scanning the darkness for any sign of movement. Sleep was fitful and often interrupted by the deafening cacophony of gunfire and explosions.

Yet, despite the hardships and the constant threat of danger, there was a sense of camaraderie among the men. They relied on each other for support.

As the rain continued to fall and the mud clung to their boots, the soldiers of the 167th Infantry found solace in the company of their fellow warriors. They had to hold the line, to face the challenges of the trenches no matter what the cost. Amid the muck and the misery, they held on to the hope that one day, they would return to the warmth of home and the embrace of loved ones.

The rhythm of life in the trenches was unrelenting, a cycle of eight days that repeated itself endlessly. Each segment of this cycle brought with it a unique set of challenges and a unique perspective on the war.

The first eight days were perhaps the most grueling. The soldiers would take their positions in the trenches, ready to face the enemy. These days were marked by ceaseless vigilance, as the soldiers peered out into No Man's Land, scanning for any sign of movement from the enemy. The trenches were a world unto themselves, with narrow, winding passages that offered meager protection from the constant threat of enemy fire.

The meals were delivered with precision by mule-drawn carts, the clattering hooves were a welcome sound amid the chaos. The soldiers would huddle together to eat their rations, finding solace in the familiar taste of the canned meat and hardtack biscuits. The rain and mud made life miserable.

After their stint in the front, the soldiers would rotate to a different role: eight days in support. During this time, they would help those in the trenches, supplying them with much-needed reinforcements, ammunition, and supplies. It was a crucial role, ensuring that those on the front lines could continue the fight.

Support life was still dangerous, as the enemy's artillery could strike at any moment. Yet, it offered a brief respite from the constant threat of sniper fire and the claustrophobic confines of the trenches. "While this isn't home, it's much better than being up there," James said as he pointed to the front-line trenches. Soldiers would catch up on much-needed rest and sleep during these days, even if it meant resting in cramped dugouts.

The final segment of the cycle was eight days in reserve. This was a time when the men could step back from the front lines and regain their strength. They would rotate out of the trenches entirely, retreating to positions farther from the front. Here, they could clean their uniforms, tend to their equipment, and even enjoy slightly better living conditions.

During their time in reserve, the troops would receive new supplies and equipment, replacing what had been worn or damaged during their time in the trenches. It was a time for reflection, as they prepared mentally and physically for their next rotation back to the front.

This cycle repeated itself relentlessly. It was a brutal rhythm, one that demanded unwavering resilience. The soldiers of the 167th Infantry Division knew that this was the harsh reality of the Western Front.

The stay of the 167th in the trenches east of Baccarat was marked by a grim welcome from the enemy. Within the first 24 hours, German warplanes swooped down twice, dropping bombs with deadly precision.

The initial shockwave of the explosions sent tremors through the earth, rattling their nerves. The first attack occurred during daylight hours, catching the men off guard as they settled into their positions. The deafening roar of the engines was a harbinger of destruction, and the bombs struck with merciless accuracy, causing chaos and devastation.

"Take cover!" James shouted to his men as one of the planes swooped down low over their trenches and dropped ordinance on them. "And will somebody please get some artillery on these bastards!" he continued. As the last of the German planes started to leave the area, James and his men rushed to provide first aid to those wounded in the attack as James ordered them to be evacuated to the rear for treatment.

The second attack, under the cover of darkness, added an eerie sense of foreboding to the already tense atmosphere. Flares illuminated the night sky as the enemy planes once again unleashed their deadly cargo.

These harrowing experiences served as a stark reminder that the trenches were far from safe. The warplanes had left a trail of destruction, and the soldiers knew that they had entered a world where danger lurked above as well as on the muddy ground below. The men of the 167th, including James and Tommy, had learned a bitter lesson: the war would test their mettle from every direction, and survival required courage in the face of relentless adversity.

The Baccarat sector of the Lorraine trench lines was a place where an unusual understanding had developed between the French and German troops. Amid the relentless grind of war, an unspoken truce had emerged during certain routine tasks, a fragile agreement that allowed for a brief respite from the constant threat of violence.

French and German soldiers, despite their enmity, had reached a mutual understanding that when it came to mundane tasks like cigarette breaks and laundry, there would be a temporary ceasefire. During these moments, soldiers on both sides could take a breath, if only for a few minutes, without the fear of sniper fire or artillery shelling.

However, this unwritten accord was not known to the Alabamians of the 167th, including Tommy. When the 167th arrived in the sector, they brought with them a unique perspective on the war. To them, every moment on the front lines was a potential opportunity to engage the enemy.

It was much like any other day when Tommy's impatience and resolve got the best of him. As he and his friends watched a group of German soldiers washing their clothes in a waterhole in No Man's Land, he raised his rifle, aimed carefully, and fired a single shot. The German soldiers caught off guard, scrambled back to the safety of their trench lines.

The story of Tommy's bold action quickly made its way back to James' command post. The commander of the French forces stationed in the trenches with the Alabamians, his eyebrows arched, and teeth clenched, immediately started dressing Tommy down. "Putain, your actions were extremely dangerous and put our men in grave danger. Because you broke this fragile truce among gentlemen, they can now fire at us whenever they want. Private, you better pray to God that I can put this genie back in the bottle." Tommy indignantly responded, "I did not come here to watch the Germans wash their knickers; I came here to shoot 'em." "Get back to your station private, I will clear things up from here," James told Tommy with a wink and pat on the shoulder.

His words reflected the fierce determination of the 167th Infantry Division, a unit that was not content with a temporary truce during moments of respite. They had come to the front lines with a clear purpose: to engage the enemy at every opportunity and to carry the fight to the Germans, no matter the circumstance.

This incident served as a stark reminder that the Alabamians were cut from a different cloth, and their presence in the Baccarat sector would bring a new and unyielding intensity to the war along the Western Front.

One evening in the desolate trenches, boredom gripped James and his fellow soldiers in a way that only those who had endured the relentless monotony of war could understand. The ceaseless rain had turned the trenches into a muddy quagmire, and the distant sounds of gunfire served as a constant reminder of the peril that surrounded them. On this particularly dreary night, James and Tommy hatched a plan to break the monotony and inject a bit of levity into their grim existence.

With a mischievous glint in their eyes, they gathered two other soldiers, fellow brethren who were equally eager for a change of pace. In hushed tones, they discussed their audacious plan. It was an idea born out of restlessness and a desire to thumb their noses at the ever-watchful eyes of the Germans.

Under the cover of darkness, they ventured into No Man's Land, a perilous expanse of barbed wire, shell craters, and uncertainty. Each step was fraught with danger, as the slightest noise could draw the attention of lurking snipers or trigger-happy sentries. They moved silently, their hearts pounding with a mix of excitement and apprehension.

As they approached the German wire obstructions, James and Tommy took the lead. With practiced hands, they unfurled a makeshift sign, cobbled together from bits of cloth and whatever materials they could scavenge. In bold, defiant letters, the sign proclaimed, "Give your world to God because your ass belongs to Alabam."

The act was equal parts audacious and reckless, a fleeting moment of rebellion against the harsh realities of war. With the sign in place, they stole one last glance at their handiwork before retreating into the relative safety of their trenches, hearts pounding with adrenaline.

The sign remained, a silent testament to the daring spirit of the Alabamians in the face of adversity. It was a small act of defiance, a reminder that even in the darkest of times, humor and mischievousness could pierce through the gloom. For a brief moment, the soldiers of the 167th had found a way to push back against the weight of war and assert their indomitable spirit.

On March 4th, men from Company B, led by Lt. Reynolds, embarked on a fateful patrol, venturing into the treacherous land that separated the Allied and German trenches. This was to be their first taste of direct engagement with the enemy, a moment that would test their mettle and bond them even tighter as brothers-in-arms.

The night was draped in darkness, and the biting cold gnawed at their bones as they silently made their way through the labyrinthine trenches. Clad in heavy, rain-soaked uniforms and clutching their rifles with white-knuckled determination, the five-man patrol moved like ghosts, guided only by the faint glow of distant flares.

The tension in the air was thick, each man acutely aware that at any moment, they might come face to face with the enemy. James led the way, his eyes scanning the desolate landscape for any sign of movement. He was flanked by four other Alabamians, their breaths visible in the chilly night air.

As they cautiously advanced, they suddenly stumbled upon an unexpected sight—an unguarded section of the German trench. The element of surprise was theirs, and they seized it without hesitation. Shots rang out, echoing through the night as the Alabamians opened fire. In the chaos that followed, three German soldiers were caught in the deadly crossfire.

Two of them lay wounded, their moans of pain a haunting lament in the darkness. The third, unfortunately, met his fate in the crosshairs of James' rifle. A flicker of remorse passed through his eyes, but he knew it was a matter of survival in the brutal theatre of war.

Amidst the chaotic exchange of gunfire, one German soldier was captured during a desperate hand-to-hand struggle. The sounds of combat soon gave way to a tense silence as the Alabamians regained control of the situation. "Take this man back to our lines and get as much information from him as possible, James ordered one of his men. "We will follow close behind you after we tend to the wounded here."

Their daring patrol had not only left a significant mark on the enemy but also earned them unexpected recognition. For their valor and audacity, the French 4th Army Corps bestowed upon them the Croix de Guerre, a symbol of honor and courage. The American Army, equally impressed, awarded them the Distinguished Service Cross, recognizing their extraordinary bravery in the face of danger.

March 6th marked the arrival of an esteemed visitor to their beleaguered ranks. General John Pershing, the towering figure at the helm of the American Forces in Europe, had come to observe the troops, their morale, and their readiness for the grueling battles ahead.

The field camp hummed with anticipation as the news of General Pershing's imminent arrival spread like wildfire. Soldiers scurried to straighten their uniforms and polish their boots, even though the mud of the trenches seemed eternally determined to defy their efforts. James, who had earned recognition for his role in the daring patrol just days earlier, was no exception. With a sense of pride and responsibility, he made sure every detail was in place as best he could.

As the sun broke through the clouded sky, casting a feeble glow over the desolate landscape, the division assembled in formation. James stood alongside his soldiers, their faces bearing the unmistakable weariness of men who had endured the relentless hardships of war.

Just then, a convoy of vehicles, led by General Pershing's car, rumbled into the camp. The atmosphere tensed as the soldiers stood at attention, their eyes fixed on the distinguished visitor who had traveled there to witness their efforts.

General Pershing, his iconic campaign hat casting a shadow over his stern visage, stepped out of his car. His mere presence commanded respect and admiration from all who beheld him.

He approached the formation, his eyes scanning the ranks, and it was not long before they fell upon James and his troops.

With measured steps, Pershing walked toward James, his boots squelching in the muck. The young Alabamian saluted crisply, his heart pounding with both pride and nervousness. The General returned the salute and extended his gloved hand, a warm smile breaking through his forbidding countenance.

"Lieutenant Reynolds," he said, his voice carrying the weight of authority and experience, "I've heard about you and your patrol. Remarkable work, son. Your bravery and that of your men embody the spirit of the American soldier."

James could hardly believe his ears. Here he was, a down-home country boy, meeting Europe's highest-ranking American military officer. It was a moment of recognition and validation, not just for him but for his entire division.

As General Pershing continued to make his way through the ranks, stopping to chat with other soldiers and commanders, James watched with a renewed sense of purpose.

When Pershing departed, leaving behind a division reinvigorated and inspired, James could not help but feel a surge of pride in his heart. Meeting the legendary military leader had reaffirmed his dedication to the cause, and he knew that, together with his fellow soldiers, he would continue to forge their path through the gauntlet of war

Chapter 15

June 18, 1918, dawned with a mixture of relief and apprehension for the 167th Infantry. After months of grueling trench work on the French-German border, they had received a new and urgent mission: to defend the beloved city of Paris, the heart of France.

The orders had come in swiftly, and the soldiers of the Rainbow Division knew that this shift in location meant they were about to face an entirely separate set of challenges. The trenches and the familiar terrain of the Lorraine theater were left behind as they embarked on a journey toward the City of Light.

As James and his command boarded trains bound for Paris, the atmosphere was a mix of anticipation and anxiety. The move to defend such a renowned and culturally significant city added weight to their shoulders, unlike anything they had experienced before.

The journey itself was a testament to the logistical complexity of moving a large military division. Troop trains rumbled along the French countryside, passing through quaint villages and rolling fields. They carried not only soldiers but also their equipment, supplies, and the mental burden of responsibility.

The journey back to Paris was a stark contrast to their earlier arrival. This time, they traveled by rail, leaving behind the muddy trenches and the chilly borderlands. The train cars clacked and rattled as they sped toward the capital city, and the soldiers watched the landscape shift from rural to urban.

As they approached Paris, the skyline came into view, a testament to the resilience of a city that had faced the ravages of war. The Eiffel Tower stood proudly, a symbol of French determination. But beneath the surface of this iconic city, the war's scars were visible in the form of damaged buildings and lingering memories.

Upon their arrival in Paris, the Rainbow Division was greeted with a sense of urgency. The city's defenses had to be bolstered quickly, for the threat of a German advance loomed large. The soldiers were tasked with setting up defensive positions on the outskirts of the city, preparing for the possibility of an enemy invasion.

The change in scenery was striking. The urban environment of Paris contrasted sharply with the trenches and the rural landscape they had become accustomed to. The soldiers found themselves patrolling the city's outskirts, guarding key points, and maintaining a vigilant watch.

As the soldiers of the 167th arrived in Paris, they disembarked from the trains and found themselves in the heart of Paris, a place of rich history and vibrant culture.

But amidst the challenges, there was also a sense of unease. The citizens of Paris, who had endured so much during the war, welcomed them with gratitude and a shared commitment to safeguard their city.

In the evenings, as James and his fellow soldiers looked out over the Paris skyline, they could not help but feel a profound sense of responsibility. They were now the guardians of this iconic city, standing resolutely against the specter of war that threatened to encroach upon its streets. "This is such a beautiful place, I hope the Germans don't ruin it with their bombs," James remarked to Sam one evening while on guard duty.

Their departure from the rugged trenches and the familiar landscapes of the Lorraine came as a mix of relief and apprehension.

Their presence was met with appreciation and gratitude from the people of Paris. The civilians, who had endured the hardships of war, greeted them with cheers and warm welcomes. "Everybody here in France has been so nice. This is the best welcome we have gotten so far," Tommy remarked while on patrol one day. "You would be grateful too, if our homes and town had been ravaged by war too," James responded.

As they settled into their new positions on the outskirts of Paris, the soldiers knew that their mission had taken on even greater significance. They were not only defending a city; they were also defending the indomitable spirit of the French people.

The days in Paris were a mix of hard work and vigilance. As they patrolled the city's boundaries, maintained defensive positions, the people prepared for any eventuality.

Nights in Paris had a different feel compared to the trenches. The city's lights illuminated the sky, and the soldiers could catch glimpses of life returning to normalcy amid war. It was a reminder of what this place once was and what it could be again.

As James and his comrades looked out over the Parisian skyline, they could not help but feel a sense of awe. They were part of an extensive line of defenders, joining the ranks of those who had stood firm in the face of adversity throughout history.

Paris had a way of inspiring courage and imagination. It was a reminder that even in the darkest of times, the human spirit could prevail. And as they stood guard over the City of Light, James and his fellow soldiers were determined to do just that.

In the bustling heart of Paris, the 167th underwent a transformation. They had been called upon to defend the city, and with this new mission came the need for reinforcements and supplies. The arrival of fresh troops and much-needed provisions breathed new life into the division.

Reinforcements streamed into Paris from various parts of the United States. Young men, eager to do their part and get back home after being drafted, joined the ranks. They came from diverse backgrounds, representing the melting pot of America. Still, they all shared a common purpose—to stand against the enemy and protect a city that symbolized freedom.

As these new soldiers integrated into the division, they were greeted with a mixture of fellowship and guidance from the veterans who had weathered the trenches. "Everybody, welcome Dave to the unit," James announced one day as they got their start. "He is from Ohio, but we won't hold that against him as long as he doesn't hold us back," he continued playfully with a sly grin on his face. Bonds were formed quickly, as the shared experiences of military life forged connections that transcended differences.

The arrival of fresh troops brought a renewed sense of strength.

With the reinforcements came a steady stream of supplies. Trucks laden with ammunition, rations, and equipment rumbled through the city streets. The logistical machinery of war was in full swing, ensuring that the 167th would be well-prepared for the challenges that they may face.

The resupply efforts extended beyond the basics of warfare. The soldiers received letters from home, a lifeline to loved ones across the ocean. Care packages, filled with familiar treats and comforts, brought smiles to their faces and a taste of home to foreign shores. "Look what Peggy sent me!" Tommy exclaimed, showing the box he had just received. "Her famous homemade fudge!" James said excitedly as he reached in the box, Tommy swatting his hand away before he could get a piece. "You know the rule, you will get some, but I always get the first piece!" he admonished, breaking off his own piece before handing the box over to his friend.

Medical supplies were replenished, and field hospitals were established to care for the wounded. The division's medics and corpsmen worked tirelessly, knowing that their skills would be needed in the days to come.

As Parisians went about their daily lives, they looked upon the American soldiers with gratitude. The presence of these young men from across the Atlantic served as a symbol of solidarity and hope. The city's cafes and shops welcomed the soldiers, offering a taste of French culture and cuisine. The children would regularly walk up to them and hand them small trinkets like flowers and stones.

Nights in Paris were marked by a blend of anticipation and vigilance. The soldiers knew that the enemy was not far away, and they remained vigilant in their defensive positions. But they also found moments of respite and camaraderie, sharing stories and laughter amidst the backdrop of a city that had seen it all.

The unit had become an integral part of the Parisian landscape. Their resolve was unwavering, and their commitment to their mission burned brighter than ever. They were prepared to defend this city and to stand shoulder to shoulder with the French people.

In the heart of Paris, amid the echoes of history and the promise of a better future, the 167th awaited the next chapter in their journey—a chapter that would test their mettle and cement their place in the annals of wartime valor.

Amidst the bustling streets of Paris, where the city's heartbeat with an undying vitality, Lt. James Reynolds found himself captivated by the spirit of a city that had endured much but never lost its allure. It was here, in the City of Light, that he had a chance encounter that would stir his heart.

One sunny afternoon, as James strolled along the Seine, the river's shimmering waters seemed to reflect the city's vibrant energy. Parisians and soldiers alike reveled in the beauty of their surroundings. The Eiffel Tower loomed majestically against the cloudless sky, its iron lattice an iconic symbol of the city.

As he meandered along the quays, taking in the view, he

noticed a group of young Parisians enjoying a picnic by the riverbank. Among them was a striking young woman of about eighteen, with golden blonde hair cascading down her back like a waterfall of silk. Her laughter rang out like a melodic chime, drawing James' attention like a magnet.

He could not help but be captivated by her radiant smile and the sparkle in her eyes. It was as if the sun itself had decided to shine from within her. She was dressed in a simple, yet elegant, sundress that billowed gently in the breeze. Her friends adored her, and her presence seemed to infuse the gathering with infectious joy.

Caught in the currents of fate, James felt a magnetic pull towards this enchanting Parisian maiden. His steps, which had been purposeful, slowed to a halt, and he found himself discreetly observing her from a distance.

As the day turned into evening, the group's picnic evolved into an impromptu dance by the river. This is when James decided to boldly make his move, taking a leap of faith and introduce himself to the young woman and her friends, asking her to dance. A local musician with an accordion serenaded the gathering, and with that, James and the young woman, with an effortless grace that seemed innate to Parisians, glided across the cobblestones. Her laughter was like the tinkling of crystal, and her dance was a mesmerizing blend of tradition and modernity.

James watched in awe, feeling a stirring within him that he had not experienced in a long time. The war, the trenches, and the ceaseless duty had forged him into a warrior, but here, in the heart of Paris, he felt a boyish connection to life that transcended conflict.

As the night descended, the young woman and her friends bid adieu to the riverside revelry, leaving James with an indelible memory and a burning desire to know more about the captivating Parisian he had seen. It was a fleeting encounter, yet it left an imprint on his heart—a testament to the enduring allure of Paris and the promise of life beyond the battlefield.

In the days that followed, James could not help but find himself returning to that riverside spot, hoping for another glimpse of the girl who had unknowingly ignited a spark within him. Paris had become not just a battleground but a place where dreams and desires flickered like stars in the night sky, and he was determined to seize whatever chance fate might offer.

As the day dipped below the horizon, casting the city of Paris into a tapestry of twilight hues, Lt. Reynolds strolled along the Seine's edge with Ellie Marie, the captivating Parisian girl he had met just the day before Their day had been one of serendipity and laughter, and their connection had grown stronger with every shared moment.

The gentle breeze carried the laughter of Ellie Marie's friends as they picnicked on the riverbank earlier that day, a vibrant reminder of the joyous hours they had spent together. "I think I am falling in love," he blurted out in a moment of quiet togetherness. "Aww, you Alabama boys are such romantics," she quipped in her heavily accented English with a coy smile on her face. "Naw, it's just me," he returned with a hint of laughter in his voice as he tried to keep the mood playful. James could not help but feel a profound sense of contentment as he walked beside her.

The city's landmarks, which had once seemed distant and foreign, now felt like old friends. The Eiffel Tower, aglow with thousands of shimmering lights, served as a radiant backdrop to their evening. It was a picture-perfect Parisian scene, a memory etched into James' heart.

As they walked, their conversation flowed effortlessly, crossing the boundaries of language and culture. James' Alabama drawl and Ellie Marie's melodic French accent seemed to harmonize in the enchanting evening air.

But fate, ever the capricious force, had other plans for the pair. As they approached a lamppost, its soft glow casting an amber halo around them, a man suddenly emerged from the shadows. Tall and imposing, he wore a uniform that was unmistakable to James—a fellow soldier.

The man, with a stern expression and an air of authority, looked directly at James and asked, "Which unit are you from?"

James, caught off guard by the abrupt interruption, momentarily forgot himself. His response, tinged with a touch of defiance and a hint of his Southern drawl, escaped his lips before he could temper it. "The Ala-goddamn-Bama," he replied, his voice infused with the indomitable spirit of his homeland.

Ellie Marie, standing beside him, watched the exchange with a mixture of curiosity and concern. She knew that the world beyond Paris was a place of turmoil and conflict, and this encounter reminded her of the very real war that loomed on the horizon.

The soldier's gaze lingered on James for a moment, as if assessing his response. Then, without another word, he turned and disappeared into the night, leaving James and Ellie Marie in the quiet embrace of the Parisian streets. "I'm sorry, my sweet dear, I didn't intend to be so vulgar," James said as he turned towards Elle, "but he startled me, and it just came out before I could stop myself." Her expression softened as she responded, "it's okay, he frightened me too."

For a brief moment, the spell of their idyllic evening was broken. The weight of the war, the uncertainty of the future, and the stark reality of his role as a soldier in a distant land hung heavily in the air. But as they continued their walk, hand in hand, there was a shared understanding that, for now, they would savor every precious moment of peace and connection that Paris had to offer—a city that had become the backdrop for their own fleeting love story.

***

Amid the grandeur of the city's boulevards and the whispers of its storied history, James Reynolds faced a new challenge as the leader of his company. The Rainbow Division had received reinforcements, fresh-faced young men from all corners of

America, eager but untested in the crucible of war. James knew it was his duty to integrate them seamlessly into the fold.

His meeting with these new arrivals took place in an aging yet dignified building commandeered by the division as a temporary barracks. The room was dimly lit, and the air was thick with anticipation. These young men had left their homes and families to venture into the unknown, guided by a sense of duty that mirrored James' journey.

As James stood before them, he could see the mix of emotions in their eyes—uncertainty, apprehension, but also a fierce determination to prove themselves. He started with a warm smile, welcoming them to the Rainbow Division and emphasizing the importance of their role in the upcoming battles.

"Now, I know some of you are fresh off the boat, so to speak," James said, his Southern drawl resonating through the room. "But we're all brothers here. We watch each other's backs, we fight for each other, and we'll make it through this together."

He introduced them to the veterans of the company, men who had weathered the storms of battle and now wore their experiences on their worn and hardened faces. There was a sense of brotherhood among the soldiers, a recognition of the shared hardships, and the unbreakable bond forged in the trials of war.

In the coming days, James and his seasoned non-commissioned officers worked tirelessly to train the newcomers. They drilled on the basics—weapon handling, trench warfare, and the importance of vigilance on the frontlines. The Parisian streets became their training grounds, and the city itself seemed to bear witness to their preparations for the battles ahead.

But it was not just about military training; James wanted these young men to feel like part of a family. He organized gatherings where stories were shared, laughter echoed, and the burdens of war were momentarily set aside. One evening after training was done for the day, Lt. Reynolds took his entire company for a night of fun and drinks at the nearby pub. "First round is on me," James announced as a roar of applause and cheers erupted from the group. They explored the city together, taking in its beauty and history, an experience that helped these soldiers feel connected not only to their comrades but also to the world they were fighting to protect.

James made it a point to learn each man's name, to understand their fears and aspirations. He encouraged them to lean on each other for support and emphasized the importance of trust and unity within the company.

As days turned into weeks, James witnessed a transformation in these young soldiers. They grew more confident, their hesitations replaced with a sense of purpose. They became an integral part of the company, each one contributing to the collective strength that would soon be tested on the frontlines.

And so, in the heart of Paris, amid the echoes of its history and the promise of its future, James Reynolds, the Alabama son who had ventured far from home, continued to lead his company with unwavering resolve. They were a band of brothers, ready to face whatever challenges lay ahead, bound together by the bonds of camaraderie.

On a warm July morning, the 167th Infantry Division prepared to leave the comforts and joys of the French capital behind. Their destination was Château-Thierry, a name that would soon become synonymous with courage and sacrifice on the battlefield.

Amidst the bustling platform of the train station, James stood tall in his uniform, his face reflecting a mixture of emotions— duty, anticipation, and the weight of leaving behind a city that had become a sanctuary of respite and love amidst the chaos of war.

The soldiers had spent weeks in Paris, receiving reinforcements and refocusing their spirits. The city welcomed them with open arms, offering respite from the trenches, reminding them that life continued beyond the horrors of war. For James, Paris held a special place, not just for its beauty but for the romance forged with Ellie Marie.

As he scanned the platform, he saw her, her blonde hair shimmering in the morning sunlight. Ellie Marie was there to bid him farewell, just as she had been there during their precious moments together in the city. Her light blue dress flowed like a summer breeze, a stark contrast to the soldier's olive drab.

"James," she said softly, her eyes brimming with both sadness and pride. "You take care of yourself out there. Promise me you'll come back."

James could not help but smile, even as he fought to hold back his own emotions. He stepped closer to her, and in that bustling train station, amidst the cacophony of departure, they shared a quiet moment. He took her hand, its warmth and tenderness searing into his memory.

"I promise," he replied, his voice filled with conviction. "I'll come back, Ellie Marie. I'll come back to you."

With their promise lingering in the air, she leaned in, and their lips met in a gentle, heartfelt kiss—a kiss that carried with it the hopes and dreams of two souls brought together by the tumultuous currents of war. It was a moment that would stay etched in James' memory, a beacon of light in the dark days to come.

As James boarded the train and settled into his seat, he could not help but steal one last glance at Ellie Marie on the platform. Her eyes followed the departing train, and her hand waved goodbye, a small yet unwavering figure amidst the bustling crowd.

The train pulled away from the platform, and Paris, the city of love and dreams, slowly faded into the distance. His buddies, including Tommy, mercilessly teased and ribbed him about Ellie Marie, as young men do. They were bound for Château-Thierry, where they would face the uncertainty of battle once more. But he carried with him not only the weight of his duty but also the memory of a promise, a kiss, and a love that would endure the trials of time and war.

Chapter 16

The journey from Paris to the Champagne region of France had been arduous, and the once cheerful atmosphere among the troops had grown somber. The soldiers of the 167th, including their leader, knew that they were heading into the heart of the battle. They had left behind the comforts of the big city, along with James' fond memories of Ellie, and now they stood on the precipice of a new and dangerous mission.

Their orders were clear: attack the German front lines at Crioux Rouge Farm, a name that carried with it tales of previous battles and fierce resistance. As the men settled into their new camp, they underwent rigorous preparations, knowing that the days ahead would test their mettle and courage like never before.

James, as company commander, bore the weight of leadership on his shoulders. He spent long nights poring over maps and battle plans, trying to devise a strategy that would minimize casualties for his men. But deep down, he knew that the horrors of war often defied the best-laid plans.

One evening, as the sun dipped below the horizon, James

gathered his company for a briefing. The faces of his men were a mix of resolve and apprehension, their eyes reflecting the shared understanding of the perilous task ahead.

"Men," James began, his voice steady and commanding, "we have received orders to advance on Crioux Rouge Farm. We have trained for this, and we are ready. But I will not lie to you; it is going to be tough. The Germans will hold that ground with determination, and they won't give it up easily."

A murmur of agreement rippled through the ranks. The soldiers knew that they faced a formidable adversary, but they also knew the importance of their mission.

"Our objective is clear," James continued. "We take Crioux Rouge Farm. And we do it together, as a team, watching each other's backs every step of the way. We've trained for this, and we have the courage."

As the time drew closer for the attack, preparations intensified. The soldiers cleaned their weapons, checked their gear, and rehearsed their movements. The tension in the air was palpable, but so was the camaraderie. In the darkest hours, James found solace in the brotherhood that had formed among his men.

Finally, the day of the attack arrived. The soldiers donned their helmets, shouldered their rifles, and lined up in formation. James looked at their faces, each one a portrait of strength and determination. He could not help but feel a sense of pride in the courage and resilience of his company.

With a nod, he signaled the advance. The 167th Infantry marched toward Crioux Rouge Farm. They were ready to face the crux of battle once more, united in their purpose, and led by a commander who would never ask his men to do something he would not do himself.

As they marched, the distant rumble of artillery and the echoes of war grew louder, but so did the resolve of the Alabama soldiers. They were the 167th, and they were ready to face whatever lay ahead on what would become the blood-soaked fields of Crioux Rouge Farm.

The artillery shells came down like a thunderclap. As James was preparing to give the orders to advance of the enemy positions, he looked over at the moment that Tommy fell over. "Tommy!" James yelled as he ran towards his friend. Once James reached his friend, Sam and another soldier had already gotten to him first and were tending to him. "He's unconscious," Sam told his commander as he arrived. At that moment, the medic arrived and started to evaluate Tommy when he started to come to. The medic reached into his bag, pulled out some smelling salts, and put it under Tommy's nose, which prompted him to react. "Just looks like he was knocked off his feet, he might have a concussion," the medic told James. "Get him to the aid station," James ordered the medic. "And take good care of him."

The 167th were prepared to go over the top of the trench walls immediately for the German lines near Croix Rouge Farm. James knew that this would be one of the most critical battles they would face. The farm had become a symbol of stubborn German resistance, and it was perched atop a ridge that provided a strategic advantage.

The soldiers had scrambled to ready themselves for the assault that was now here. They loaded wagons and carts with ammunition, rations, and medical supplies. The air buzzed with a mixture of anticipation and anxiety. James, with his map spread out before him, carefully explained the battle plan to his men.

"Listen up, everyone," he began, his voice firm and commanding. "Our objective is Croix Rouge Farm. The Germans have held it for too long, and it is our job to dislodge them. We've trained for this, and I have confidence in every one of you."

His men nodded in agreement; their faces etched with determination. They had been through battles before, but this felt different—more significant, more momentous.

The preparations had continued into the night. Rifles were checked, grenades were distributed, and the soldiers engaged in last-minute individual rituals. James made the rounds, offering words of encouragement to his men. Some sought solace in prayer, while others wrote letters home, not knowing if the men would ever see their loved ones again.

As the following morning had arrived, the men of the 167th assembled on the outskirts of the camp. The air was crisp, and a sense of solemnity hung heavy in the ranks. While James looked at his men, he could not help but feel a deep sense of responsibility for their lives.

General Douglas MacArthur, now commanding the Rainbow Division, stepped forward to address the troops. His voice boomed across the field, rallying the soldiers with words of courage and purpose. James listened intently, his jaw set, and his gaze unwavering. "Today we take the fight to the enemy,"

MacArthur started. "They have been entrenched in this position for too long, and it's time we sent them scurrying back towards their own country. Right here in this place at this time marks the beginning of the end of their reign of terror over this land, and we begin the process of liberating these people and giving them back their homes."

Then, the order to advance came. The soldiers moved out in formation, their boots crunching on the gravel road. The weight of their gear pressed against their shoulders, a reminder of the gravity of their mission. James led his company with purpose, his eyes scanning the horizon for any sign of the enemy.

As they neared Croix Rouge Farm, the tension mounted. Artillery shells exploded in the distance, and the sound of distant gunfire echoed through the air. The soldiers tightened their grip on their rifles, each step bringing them closer to the unknown.

The battle for Croix Rouge Farm would be fierce and unrelenting. The Germans were well-entrenched, and they defended their positions with unwavering determination. But the men of the 167th and the Rainbow Division were just as stubborn to prevail.

Amidst the chaos of battle, James drew on every ounce of leadership he had developed over the months. He led his company through the mud and the smoke, barking orders and rallying his men when the situation seemed dire. "Advance men!" He encouraged them when their progress would stall, and it seemed like the enemy was gaining the upper hand.

As the hours drug on, the battle raged on. The farm's buildings, once standing proudly, were reduced to rubble. The ground was churned into a muddy wasteland. But still, the Alabama soldiers pressed forward, inch by inch, refusing to yield.

***

The Battle of Croix Rouge Farm had begun with a deafening roar of artillery and a furious exchange of gunfire. The 167th Division had been tasked with capturing the heavily fortified German position atop the ridge. The farm had become a symbol of the enemy's resilience, and it was clear that taking it would not be easy.

The American soldiers advanced across the torn landscape,

their boots sinking into the mud with every step. James led the charge. "When we take this farm, there is a beer with everyone's name on it!" James exclaimed, encouraging his men to keep up the attack. The distant rumble of artillery shells and the crackle of rifle fire provided a constant soundtrack of battle.

The Germans were well-prepared, their trenches and bunkers offering formidable defenses. Machine gun nests spat a deadly stream of bullets, and artillery shells exploded with shattering force. The Alabama soldiers pressed on; their courage unwavering despite the fierce resistance.

As they advanced, the casualties began to mount. Men fell to enemy fire, their comrades pulling them to safety if possible. The wounded cried out in pain, their pleas mixing with the chaos of battle. As they were pressing forward, James heard Sam cry out, "God dammit!" James turned to see Sam fall to the mud yelling, "Medic! Corpman!" as he ran towards his friend. Medics worked tirelessly, doing their best to tend to the injured amidst the relentless onslaught.

James watched as some of his closest friends were cut down by enemy fire. It was a painful reminder of the brutal reality of war. The farm, which had seemed so distant when they received their orders, was now a place of death and destruction.

But the troops did not falter. They knew that they had a duty to fulfill, and they were going to see it through. James continued to rally his men, leading by example as he charged forward through the mud and smoke.

The battle raged on, with neither side willing to yield. The Alabama soldiers fought with reckless abandon, their bodies and spirits tested to the limits. The farm's buildings, once symbols of a peaceful existence, became smoldering piles of monuments to the destructive power of war.

Despite the heavy losses, the 167th pressed forward. They launched coordinated attacks, attempting to breach the German lines. Each advance was met with fierce resistance, and the casualty count continued to rise.

The battle became a brutal, grueling contest of attrition. The men dug in, determined to hold their ground. They endured relentless shelling and the constant threat of enemy counterattacks.

Through it all, James remained a steadfast leader. His voice carried above the chaos, offering words of encouragement and reassurance to his men. He knew that their sacrifices were not in vain and that they were part of something much larger—a battle that could tip the scales of the war.

Amidst the relentless turmoil of the battle, James huddled in a makeshift command post alongside Captain Bunn, the leader of Company D. The battle had taken a heavy toll on both their companies and the need for a new strategy was evident.

The constant roar of artillery shells and the staccato bursts of machine gun fire provided the backdrop for their discussion. The farm, which had been the epicenter of brutal combat lay ahead, still heavily fortified with German troops. It was a formidable adversary, and the casualties on both sides were mounting.

James wiped sweat and dirt from his brow, his face etched with determination. He turned to Captain Bunn; his voice steady despite the chaos around them. "Captain, we can't keep pushing straight ahead like this. We're losing too many men."

Bunn nodded grimly, his eyes reflecting the same resolve. "You're right, Lieutenant. We need a new approach, something that'll catch the Germans off guard."

They studied the tactical map spread out before them, tracing their previous advances and the positions of the entrenched German forces. It was a complex puzzle, and they needed a solution that would break the stalemate.

"I've been thinking," James began, "what if Company D approaches from the east, using the cover of those woods? We could create a diversion, draw their fire away from you."

Captain Bunn considered the idea for a moment, then nodded in agreement. "That could work. While they are focused on you, my men could advance from the woods, moving through that trench system. It might catch the Germans off guard."

Their plan began to take shape, the two officers working out the details of their coordinated attack. It was a risky strategy, but they knew they had to try something different. The lives of their men depended on it.

As they finalized their plan, the rumble of approaching artillery shells served as a stark reminder of the urgency of their situation. The battle was far from over, and the farm still lay ahead, its defenses steadfast.

With their new strategy in place, James and Captain Bunn left the makeshift command post and returned to their respective companies. "Listen up guys!" James announced as he returned to his men. "We are going to create a distraction over here for the Germans," he continued pointing to a spot on a map. "Company D is going to swing around here to these woods and catch them off guard from the other direction," James finished up pointing to another spot on the map. "It's not going to be easy, and we are probably going to lose a lot of men, but we are going to lose a lot continuing this way and we feel like this is the best way to break their defenses" They had a challenging task ahead, but they were determined to see it through. The soldiers under his command looked to him for leadership and honesty, and he would not let them down.

The Battle of Croix Rouge Farm had already tested their mettle in ways they could never have imagined, but James and Captain Bunn knew that the fight was far from over. The men would continue to adapt, to innovate, and to lead their men with unwavering resolve as they pressed forward into the crucible of war.

***

As the evening came upon them, casting long shadows over the blood-soaked fields of Croix Rouge Farm, the men of the 167th set to work. The decision had been made, and the orders had come down from division headquarters: the depleted companies were to be consolidated into two, each under the command of a capable leader. Lieutenant James Reynolds of Company B and Captain Ronald Bunn of Company D, each respected for their unwavering resolve and tactical acumen, were chosen to lead this final assault on Croix Rouge.

The men, wearied by days of relentless combat and the heavy toll it had exacted, rallied around their chosen leaders. The moon rose in the night sky, casting an eerie glow over the makeshift assembly area where the soldiers gathered. It was a somber scene.

Lt. Reynolds addressed his men, his voice steady and resolute. "We've been through hell and back on this farm, and we've lost brothers along the way. But now, we have a chance to make a difference, to take that damned farm."

Captain Bunn echoed the sentiment with a nod. "We're consolidating our forces, making our units stronger. It will not be easy, but we have faced worse odds. We're going to hit them hard and fast."

The consolidation process was swift and efficient. The soldiers from the depleted companies were divided among the two new companies, their ranks now bolstered by fresh reinforcements that had arrived in the nick of time. Weapons were cleaned, ammunition checked, and spirits lifted as the men prepared for the final assault.

In the pale light of dawn, the two companies moved out, leaving their assembly area behind and advancing toward Croix Rouge. The farm had been a symbol of relentless struggle, a place where courage and sacrifice had become the norm. But now, with the two companies united under the leadership of James and Captain Bunn, there was a renewed sense of purpose.

As they approached the formidable German defenses, the soldiers felt a surge of adrenaline. The farm's fields, once a battleground of despair, now lay before them as a challenge waiting to be conquered.

The assault on the farm was fierce and unrelenting, but the combined strength of the two companies, led by James and Captain Bunn, proved to be a formidable force. The Germans fought tenaciously, but the Alabama soldiers pushed forward.

Amidst the chaos of battle, the two leaders coordinated their efforts, ensuring that their men moved in unison. It was a testament to the trust and camaraderie that had developed among the soldiers, a bond forged in the fire of war.

The battle raged on, but the determination of the 167th remained. The farm, which had been a symbol of relentless struggle, was now within their grasp. With one final push, the Alabama soldiers overwhelmed the German defenders, and Croix Rouge Farm was secured.

The victory came at a heavy cost, with many brave men paying the ultimate price for their valor. But the farm, which had been a symbol of German resistance, was now a symbol of their triumph. The soldiers of the 167th had achieved what had seemed impossible, and they had done it as a united force under the leadership of these two men.

While they looked out over the fields, they had fought so hard to claim, the soldiers knew that the battle was far from over. But they had proven that, even in the darkest of times, their courage could overcome any obstacle. The consolidation of their forces had made them stronger, and they were ready to face whatever challenges lay ahead on the path to victory.

Chapter 17

The battlefield at Croix Rouge Farm had become a nightmarish landscape, scarred by trenches, craters, and the detritments of war. For days, the men had fought with unwavering resolve, inching ever closer to their objective: Cross Street. It was a pivotal point in the battle, a stronghold the Germans were determined to defend at all costs. But James, now leading a combined force of the leftover numbers of several companies, was equally determined to break through.

As the sunlight began its descent on that fateful day, James gathered his men, his voice a beacon of unwavering resolve amidst the cacophony of battle. "We've come too far to turn back now," he declared, his gaze steely and unwavering. "Cross Street is within our reach, and we're going to take it."

His words were met with a resounding cheer from the men, their faces smeared with mud and sweat, but their spirits high. The consolidation of their forces had made them as whole a unit as possible, and they were ready to take on the Germans who had been equally decimated.

The initial approach to their objective was treacherous. German machine gun fire raked the ground, forcing the Alabama soldiers to advance with caution. James led from the front, his helmet pulled low, and his rifle at the ready. The enemy's defensive line was fierce, but the Alabamians were relentless.

As they closed in on their objective, the battle reached a fever pitch. Artillery shells burst overhead, and the air was thick with the stench of gunpowder and smoke. But James and his men pressed forward, undeterred by the chaos around them.

Amidst the hail of bullets, grenades, and the deafening roar of battle, James spotted a moment of opportunity. With a signal, he led a charge that caught the Germans off guard. The Alabama soldiers surged forward, their bayonets fixed, and their cries of "Roll Tide" echoed across the battlefield.

In a furious and bloody melee, hand-to-hand combat ensued. The Alabamians fought with a ferocity born of desperation. James clashed with a German officer; their bayonets locked in a deadly dance. With a final thrust, he dispatched his adversary, and his men followed suit.

As the day came to a close, Cross Street was finally secured.

The Germans had been driven back; their defenses shattered by the unyielding assault of the 167th. It was a hard-fought victory, one that had come at a tremendous cost, but it was a testament to the valor and unity of James and his men.

With the objective secured, the Alabama soldiers could see the path to further victories unfolding before them. The consolidation of their forces and their unwavering leader had carried them through one of the most challenging battles of their lives. The road ahead would still be perilous, but they had proven that they could overcome any obstacle in their path.

The battlefield around them lay littered with the fallen from both sides. The eerie stillness that followed the intense battle was broken only by the indistinct groans of the wounded and the distant rumble of artillery. The moon cast a pallid glow over the torn earth, revealing the grim aftermath of combat.

James knew that they could not leave their fallen brethren to rot on the field. It was a solemn duty to ensure that each man received a proper farewell, and their personal effects returned to their grieving families. He gathered a group of non-combatant soldiers, including medics and clerks, and outlined the grim task ahead.

"We owe it to these men to honor their sacrifice," James declared, his voice heavy with the weight of responsibility. "We'll form search parties to comb through the battlefield, identify our own, and collect any personal effects. Each man deserves to be remembered."

The search parties set out under the cover of darkness, their lanterns casting flickering shadows on the red tinged torn ground. The medics attended to the wounded, while the clerks carefully cataloged the belongings of the fallen. It was a somber and painstaking process, as they worked methodically.

James joined one of the search parties, his heart heavy as he knelt beside fallen comrades, some of whom he had known for years. Their faces, once full of life and mischief, were now etched with the pain and finality of death emphasized by the blank gaze in their eyes and the slack in their jaws. Each man was gently turned over, and their personal effects were collected.

Dog tags, letters from home, photographs of loved ones — these were the tokens of humanity that connected these soldiers to the lives they had left behind. James could not help but wonder about the families awaiting news, the mothers and fathers, wives and children, who would never see their loved ones again.

As the night wore on, the search parties worked diligently, their lanterns casting a soft glow over the field of the fallen. The wounded were evacuated, and the fallen were gathered together in a makeshift burial site. It was a solemn and respectful ceremony, a final farewell to those who had given everything.

When the task was completed, and the personal effects cataloged, James planned for the items' return to the soldiers' families. Each item held a story, a connection to a life that had been cut short by the brutal realities of war. It was a small comfort to know that these mementos would find their way home, providing solace to those left behind.

With heavy hearts, the search parties returned to camp, their duty fulfilled. James knew that the memory of this night would linger, a reminder of the cost of war and the bonds of brotherhood that bound them together. It was a reminder that amid battle, even amidst the chaos and destruction, humanity and honor could prevail.

In the wake of the hard-fought victory at Croix Rouge Farm and Cross Street, James and the commander of Company D found themselves summoned to division headquarters, a place that had seen more than its share of grim decisions and war-worn officers. Colonel Screws, the steadfast leader of the Division, awaited them there.

The two company commanders entered the room, their faces etched with the weariness of battle but also the satisfaction of knowing their efforts had not been in vain. Colonel Screws, a grizzled veteran with years of military experience, regarded them with a mixture of sternness and respect.

"Gentlemen," Colonel Screws began, his voice carrying the weight of command, "what you accomplished at Croix Rouge Farm was nothing short of extraordinary. Your leadership, courage, and the sacrifices of your men have not gone unnoticed."

James and Capt.   Bunn exchanged glances, acknowledging the truth in the colonel's words. It had been a brutal battle, one that had tested their resolve and tenacity.

"As a result of your actions, it's clear that we need to reorganize and consolidate our forces," Colonel Screws continued. "The 167th has suffered heavy losses, but we cannot let that deter us. We must adapt and press forward."

James and the other commander nodded, understanding the necessity of such a decision. War demanded flexibility and innovation, and their depleted ranks required an innovative approach.

Colonel Screws leaned forward, his eyes locking onto theirs. "Both of you have proven yourselves capable leaders in the heat of battle. As a result, I am entrusting you with a significant responsibility. You will lead consolidated companies formed from the remnants of all the companies remaining from the 167th."

The weight of this news settled on James' shoulders, and he could see the same realization dawning on the face of Captain Bunn. Leading such a unit would be challenging, but it was a testament to their leadership and the faith that Colonel Screws had in them.

"We're reorganizing, but we're not retreating," Colonel Screws declared. "This war is far from over, and we'll continue to fight with the same determination that brought us to this point. Your consolidated companies will play a vital role in the battles to come."

With those words, the meeting concluded, and James and the other commander left division headquarters with a renewed sense of purpose. They would face the challenges ahead with the same resilience and camaraderie that had carried them through Croix Rouge Farm. Together, they would lead their consolidated companies into the uncertain future of war, driven by a shared commitment to their comrades and their duty.

James led his consolidated company, a unit born from the ashes of multiple companies, on a march northward along a winding road that seemed to stretch endlessly through the French countryside. The weariness of battle had been replaced by a sense of purpose and determination, for they were not retreating but advancing into fresh territory.

The road was flanked by tall trees, their leaves rustling in the breeze like a soft, melancholic song. The fields beyond were dotted with wildflowers, their colors a stark contrast to the drabness of war. James could not help but steal a glance at the men under his command. They marched with the weary but resolute gait of soldiers who had seen too much and yet were prepared to see it through to the end.

As they continued their journey, the road gave way to a meandering path through woods, the dense canopy providing some respite from the relentless sun. The dappled sunlight played on the faces of the troops, creating a shifting mosaic of light and shadow. Conversations among the men were hushed, for they understood the importance of stealth in these unfamiliar woods.

The march stretched on for miles, the monotony of the landscape broken only by the occasional rustling of wildlife and the distant sound of artillery, a constant reminder of the war that raged nearby. James kept a watchful eye on his men, ensuring they stayed on course and maintained their formation. His responsibility weighed heavily on him, but he drew strength from their shared experience.

Finally, they emerged from the woods into a vast open field, the Ourcq River shimmering in the distance like a ribbon of hope. James knew that their destination lay ahead. The men quickened their pace as they approached the river, anticipation mingling with exhaustion.

After a mile's march along the riverbank, they found a suitable spot to make camp on the west side of the Ourcq. It was a place where the terrain offered some natural defenses, and the river provided a source of water. The soldiers set to work with practiced efficiency, pitching tents and preparing for the challenges that lay ahead.

As the sky turned to shades of orange and purple, James stood on the riverbank, gazing across the water. The reflection of his men, weary but unyielding, mirrored in the calm surface of the Ourcq, filled him with a sense of pride and camaraderie. They were soldiers of the 167th, forged in the furnace of war, and they would face whatever the future held together.

With their camp established along the west bank of the Ourcq, James and his company settled into their makeshift positions. It was a relief to finally have a moment's respite from the relentless march and the recent battle. Yet, there was no escaping the ever-present reminders of the war that raged around them.

As the evening ascended, the men gathered around meager fires, their faces illuminated by the flickering flames. They shared what remained of their rations, a simple meal of hardtack and canned meat. The conversation was hushed, a mixture of weary humor and whispered tales of home. For a brief moment, they could almost forget the horrors they had witnessed.

The sound of distant artillery echoed through the night, a haunting reminder that even in these fleeting moments of rest, the war never truly ceased. German artillery shells sporadically found their mark, their explosions lighting up the night sky with fiery bursts. The earth trembled beneath the soldiers' feet, a testament to the sheer power of the munitions.

James moved among his men, offering words of encouragement and ensuring that each man had what they needed. "Do not despair men, we will be back home in Alabama before you know it." He repeated as he made his way through the ranks. There was an unspoken understanding among them, a bond forged in the tests of combat. They were brothers, bound together by a shared purpose and the determination to see this war through to its end.

As the night wore on, the sporadic artillery fire gave way to the harsh staccato of German machine guns. Tracers streaked through the darkness, illuminating the battlefield like malevolent fireflies. The soldiers sought cover in hastily dug trenches and foxholes, their fatigue battling with the instinct for self-preservation.

Sleep was elusive that night. Instead, they lay in their muddy, rain-soaked positions, their bodies tense, and their senses heightened. The sound of German voices carried across the river, a reminder that the enemy was never far away. In these long hours of darkness, their thoughts turned to the loved ones left behind, to the uncertainty of the future, and to the unspoken fear that each night could be their last.

Through it all, James remained a steady presence, his leadership unwavering in the face of danger. He knew that rest was a luxury and that they must remain vigilant. As the night slowly gave way to dawn, the men of the 167th Infantry Division clung to the hope that a new day would bring them one step closer to the end of this brutal conflict.

The morning cast a pale light on the Ourcq River as James and his men prepared to cross it. The night had been long and restless, the constant artillery fire and sporadic machine gun chatter had kept them on edge. But now, as the dawn broke, a new day brought renewed hope.

"Alright, boys, it's time to move out," James called to his men, his voice carrying a note of both command and camaraderie. They had become a tight-knit group, bound by shared experiences and trust.

Tommy, who had rejoined the unit a few days before, wearily rose to his feet. He glanced at James, a faint smile playing on his lips. "You know, James, this river ain't much to speak of. Back home in Alabama, we'd call this a creek."

James chuckled, the tension of the night slowly dissipating. "You're right, Tommy. This Ourcq might look imposing, but it's nothing compared to the rivers back in the South."

As they approached the riverbank, the soldiers carried their rifles nestled in their shoulders, their uniforms weighed down by mud and rain. The Ourcq, which had appeared as a formidable obstacle, indeed seemed more like a creek compared to the mighty rivers of Alabama. The water barely reached their knees, and the current was manageable.

One by one, they waded through the shallow waters. The crossing was surprisingly uneventful, and within minutes, they were on the opposite bank, water dripping from their uniforms as they continued their march.

The landscape stretched out before them, a patchwork of fields and small villages. Their destination lay beyond the horizon, and their resolve was unwavering. They had faced the worst that war could offer, and yet they pressed forward, determined to see it through to the end.

***

The battle raged on around Mercury Farm as James and his men fought to secure it for the Rainbow Division. The once tranquil fields and rolling hills were now a chaotic battleground, strewn with the remnants of war—craters, barbed wire, and the echoes of gunfire.

James had taken point, leading his men through the perilous landscape. Bullets whizzed past, and the sharp crack of rifle fire filled the air. They moved cautiously, each step forward a testament to their resolve.

As they approached the farmhouse, they encountered pockets of resistance. German soldiers, entrenched behind hastily constructed barriers, put up fierce resistance. The fight was brutal, and James knew that every inch of ground gained came at a heavy cost.

Amidst the chaos, James could not help but reflect on the irony of their situation. "I wonder what the Kaiser thinks of Alabama now?" he muttered, a touch of defiance in his voice.

Tommy, who was fighting alongside him, overheard and let out a brief chuckle. "I reckon he's got more than he bargained for, James."

They pressed on with every step, they inched closer to their objective. The battle raged on, Alabama had come to France, and they were making sure their presence was felt.

As the time passed, the fighting gradually subsided as the Germans retreated. The fields of Mercury Farm were littered with the fallen, a somber testament to the price of war.

As the dust settled, James stood amidst the battered landscape, his uniform caked in mud and sweat. Victory had been achieved, but it was a victory that came with a heavy toll. However, they had secured their objective.

The night was silent, save for the distant sounds of artillery in the distance. James and his men took a moment to catch their breath, knowing that their journey was far from done. They had faced the enemy head-on, and they had shown that Alabama was more than a distant name on a map—it was a force to be reckoned with on the front lines.

The initial triumph of securing Mercury Farm was short-lived.

As the sun dipped below the horizon, casting long shadows over the battlefield, James and his men settled into their hard-won positions, exhausted but relieved. They had fought valiantly, paying a heavy toll to secure this patch of French soil.

The farm itself bore the scars of battle—buildings reduced to rubble, fields churned into mud, and the stench of gunpowder and death hanging in the air. In those brief moments of respite, James could not help but think of Alabama, of home, and the faces of his family. He knew he had to push such thoughts aside. There was a war to win, and the battle was not over.

As James and his men caught their breath, they began fortifying their positions. They knew that the Germans would not easily relinquish what they had just taken. They reinforced the hastily dug trenches, positioned machine guns, and set up a rudimentary communication network with runners darting back and forth.

But the night held an ominous stillness, broken only by the distant rumble of artillery. Then, out of the darkness, came a sound that sent shivers down their spines—the low, guttural roar of German voices drawing closer.

"They're coming back," one of James' men whispered, peering

into the blackness.

James nodded grimly, his fingers tightening around his rifle. "Hold your positions. We will give 'em hell when they come."

And come they did. In the darkest hours of the night, the Germans launched a furious counterattack. Flares lit up the sky, revealing the advancing enemy forces. The battlefield that had been silent only moments ago erupted into chaos once more.

The men fought valiantly, trading shots in the inky darkness. It was a brutal, close-quarters battle, illuminated only by the sporadic bursts of gunfire and the eerie glow of flares. James barked orders, his voice carrying over the din of combat as he directed his men to hold the line.

For three grueling hours, they fought tooth and nail, pushing back wave after wave of German attackers. But the relentless assault took its toll. Ammunition ran low, and the men were exhausted, their faces etched with blank stares and lost expressions of weariness.

Finally, as the first light of dawn broke on the horizon, James made a difficult decision. "Fall back, boys! We cannot hold 'em any longer!"

Reluctantly, they withdrew from Mercury Farm, retreating through the fields they had fought so hard to claim. The Germans pursued, but the Americans managed to establish a new defensive line, digging in once more to halt the enemy's advance.

Mercury Farm, for which they had paid such a high price, was lost. But the battle-hardened men knew that the war wasn't over. They had proven their mettle, and as they regrouped, they steeled themselves for the challenges yet to come.

The weeks of unrelenting combat had left the men physically and emotionally drained. As dawn broke over the battlefield, they had retreated, dug in on new defensive lines, and prepared to hold the position once more.

Suddenly, a brief respite came. Orders were issued for a temporary withdrawal from the front lines to a support position. It was a small reprieve, a mere respite from the continuous onslaught they had endured. But it was a chance to catch their breath, to eat a hot meal, and to close their eyes for a few precious moments. "Move out men," James ordered as he folded up the new orders. "We're heading back to camp for some rest!"

James and his men collapsed in the makeshift camp; exhaustion etched into their faces. Fatigue had worn them down, and their nerves were frayed from the relentless combat. They huddled around fires, trying to ward off the chill that had settled in their bones.

As they ate, conversation was scarce, and what little talk there was consisted of grumbling about the situation. The men were cranky, irritable, and rightfully so. They had faced an unending barrage of artillery, machine gun fire, and close-quarters combat. Sleep had been a luxury they had not known for days.

James sat with Tommy; their shoulders slumped in weariness. "I don't know how much more of this I can take," he muttered, his voice hoarse from shouting commands and battle cries.

Tommy nodded; his eyes heavy-lidded. "I reckon none of us are built for this kind of relentless fighting."

Around them, other soldiers echoed similar sentiments. They longed for the tranquility of home, for the simple pleasures of a warm meal, a soft bed, and the reassuring presence of loved ones. But the war showed no mercy, and duty called them back to the front.

Their respite was fleeting, and soon the orders came. The 167th had to return to the front lines, to the grim reality of the battlefield. They rose, their bodies aching, and shouldered their rifles once more. The exhaustion weighed heavily on them, but they knew there was no choice but to press on.

As they trudged back towards the front, their faces etched with exhaustion, the men steeled themselves for what lay ahead. They were weary, but their spirit remained intact, for they were bound by duty and the unshakable brotherhood forged in the trials of war.

The Battle of Ourcq had raged on for days, and the men led by James' company, had been at the forefront of the brutal fight. They had pushed the Germans back, hill by hill, yard by yard, as the sun set on another day, the artillery shells continued to explode around them.

The final charge up the hills along the bank of the Ourcq River was a desperate push. James had led his men with unwavering resolve, his voice rising above the chaos as he shouted orders and encouragement. The Germans had fought fiercely, and the Alabama troops had met their determination with their own.

As the American flag waved atop one of the captured hills, James and his men could not help but feel a sense of triumph and let out a rebel yell. They had achieved their objective, albeit at a heavy cost. The hillside was littered with the fallen.

Tommy, who had fought alongside James throughout the ordeal, caught his breath and wiped the sweat and grime from his face. "We did it, James," he said, his voice a mixture of exhaustion and elation.

James nodded, his gaze sweeping across the landscape. "We did, Tommy. But there is no time to rest. We need to consolidate our position and prepare for what comes next."

As night fell, they dug trenches and set up defensive positions on the hard-won hill. The battlefield was eerily quiet, except for the occasional distant rumble of artillery. The men knew that the Germans would not give up easily, and the battle was far from over.

Hours passed, and the weariness settled in once more. The men huddled together for warmth, sharing stories and cigarettes in the darkness. They had fought with unwavering courage, but the toll of battle was etched on their faces.

Just as they were settling in, an officer arrived with new orders. They were to withdraw from their hard-won position and move to a reserve position at the Forêt de Fère. It was a bitter pill to swallow, leaving behind the ground they had fought so hard to claim. But they were soldiers, and they knew that their duty was to follow orders without question.

James gathered his men, their faces etched with disappointment. "We've done our part here," he said, his voice steady. "Now, we march to the rear. We'll rest there, regroup, and be ready for whatever comes next."

The men nodded. They had faced the crucible of battle together, and they would face whatever lay ahead with the same unwavering determination. With one last look at the hill, they had fought so hard to take, they began their march to the Forêt de Fère, the darkness of night shrouding their weary figures as they moved forward, ready for the next chapter of their harrowing journey.

349

Chapter 18

My Dearest Maggie,

I hope this letter finds you well and in good spirits. It's been some time since I last wrote, and for that, I must apologize. The front lines have been relentless, and there's been little time to sit down and pen a letter. However, I wanted to share with you an extraordinary experience I had recently.

We were granted a brief respite from the unrelenting horrors of the battlefield, and I found myself in a quaint little village not far from our current position. The villagers, brave souls who've endured the trials of this war alongside us, had organized a special event to lift the spirits of the weary soldiers.

The highlight of the evening was a performance by none other than Elsie Janis! I had heard of her talent before but witnessing it in person was a unique experience. Maggie, her voice was like a soothing balm for our battle-worn souls. She sang songs that spoke to our hearts, evoking emotions I hadn't felt since strolling the streets of Paris with Elle. Her melodies carried us away from the grim reality of war, if only for a short while.

And her dancing! Oh, Maggie, you would have been enchanted by her graceful movements. With each step, she seemed to defy the weight of the world, reminding us that beauty and art still exist amidst the chaos of this conflict. The entire audience was captivated by her performance, and for a few precious hours, we forgot the horrors of the trenches.

After the show, I had the opportunity to meet Miss Janis briefly. She's a kind and gracious woman who took the time to speak with each soldier who approached her. I thanked her for bringing a glimmer of light into our lives during these dark times, and she seemed genuinely touched by our gratitude.

As I sit here in my makeshift tent, writing by the dim glow of a lantern, I can't help but feel a renewed sense of hope. Elsie Janis reminded me that even amid war, there are moments of beauty and humanity worth cherishing. Her performance was a gift, and I wanted to share it with you, even if only through words.

Please know that I think of you constantly, and I pray for the day when this war is but a distant memory, and we can be reunited. Until then, hold onto hope, as I do, and let the memory of Elsie Janis's performance bring a smile to your face, just as it did for me.

With all my love,

James

***

The predawn hours were shrouded in thick, eerie darkness as James and the men of the 167th Infantry Division rose from their makeshift bivouac on the outskirts of a village in northeastern France. The damp chill of early morning permeated the air, and the soft murmur of whispered conversations and the clinking of equipment filled the stillness.

James gathered his gear, checking the straps on his helmet and rifle. As he looked around at his men, he could see the weariness etched into the furrowed brows and distant stares of their faces. These were men who had seen the horrors of war up close, who had weathered the storms of battle and emerged stronger, if only by sheer force of will.

Their orders were clear: they were to march to Château-Thierry, a pivotal town that had witnessed the ebb and flow of this brutal conflict. The distance was considerable, and they were to complete the journey in two grueling days.

The march began, and the rhythmic trudge of boots on the dirt road echoed through the pre-dawn darkness. The weight of their rifles and packs dug into their shoulders, a constant reminder of the burden they carried – not just in terms of equipment, but the weight of their fellow soldiers and the mission ahead.

As they walked, the sound of distant artillery fire served as a haunting backdrop, a grim reminder of the violence that awaited them. Occasionally, they passed other troops heading in the opposite direction. Fresh-faced soldiers, newly arrived from the States, their eyes filled with a mixture of excitement and trepidation.

"God help them," James muttered to Tommy. "They're in for a wake-up call."

Tommy agreed, his eyes reflecting the wisdom of experience. "They'll learn soon enough what this war is really like."

Along the way, they encountered supply columns – trucks loaded with crates of ammunition, food, and medical supplies. The sight of these precious resources was a reassuring one. It meant that reinforcements were coming, that the war machine continued to churn, and that they were not alone in this fight.

The hours stretched on, and fatigue set in. The men grew silent, their thoughts turning inward as they pushed their bodies to the limit. Each step brought them closer to Château-Thierry, closer to their goal, and closer to the end.

By the time the dusk started to set in, casting a golden hue across the landscape, the division had covered a significant distance. Their determination was fueled by a shared sense of duty and camaraderie. They were not just soldiers; they were a brotherhood.

As the first day of the march neared its end, James stole a moment to look up at the sky. The heavens seemed vast and unending, a stark contrast to the confines of the trenches. He prayed for strength, guidance, and the safe passage of his men.

Château-Thierry awaited; its destiny entwined with theirs. The 167th Infantry marched forward, ready to face whatever challenges lay ahead and to fight with all their might for a cause they held dear — the cause of freedom and justice in a world torn by war.

As James, his men, and the other units approached Château-Thierry, they encountered a sight that struck them deeply amid the turmoil of war. There, in the fields that stretched out beyond the town's outskirts, French farmers and villagers toiled diligently, harvesting the golden grain that rippled in the summer breeze.

The contrast between the soldiers, bearing the weight of rifles and the scars of battle, and the civilians bent over their work was stark. James couldn't help but feel a sense of admiration for these tenacious people who continued their daily lives despite the ever-present threat of war. "Man, I think I'd rather be doing that," James mentioned as they passed the fields of workers. "Even in this hellhole."

He halted his men for a moment, allowing them to observe this scene. "Look at them," he remarked to Tommy, his voice tinged with a mixture of respect and wonder. "Even amid all this chaos, they carry on with their work. It's as if life goes on, no matter what."

Tommy nodded in agreement; his gaze fixed on the diligent farmers. "They've seen hardships we can't even imagine. But they don't let it break them."

The soldiers watched in silence as the farmers moved methodically through the fields, their scythes slicing through the tall stalks of wheat. It was a reminder that amidst the horrors of war, life still flourished, and the resilience of the human spirit endured.

When James and the rest of the unit arrived in Montreuil-aux-Lions, they were met with a sight that both lifted their spirits and brought new challenges. The sleepy French town had become a hub for the arrival of much-needed reinforcements and supplies from the United States. Among the bustling activity at the makeshift camp, the men of the 167th could see fresh faces – the draftees from back in the States who would join their ranks.

James understood the importance of integrating these new soldiers into their unit. As Company B of the 167th, they had seen their fair share of combat and had forged a strong bond through shared hardship. James knew that it was his responsibility to ensure that the newcomers felt welcome and prepared for the challenges that lay ahead.

He gathered his men and addressed them. "Boys, we've got some new faces among us," he said, his voice carrying a note of authority and warmth. "These are our reinforcements, and we must make them part of this family."

The men listened attentively, some nodding. They knew that the success of their unit depended on the cohesion of its members, old and new. Still, the lines between those who had already tasted combat and the fresh draftees were delineated.

As the days passed, James observed the dynamics within the unit. The veterans shared stories of their experiences, both harrowing and humorous, with the newcomers. They offered advice, teaching them the finer points of survival on the front lines – from digging a foxhole to recognizing the distant whine of incoming artillery.

But despite the camaraderie and James' efforts, there was an unspoken division. The combat-hardened soldiers possessed a level of trust that could only be earned through shared danger. The newcomers, although eager and willing, had yet to prove themselves in the crucible of battle.

James recognized this gap and knew that time would be the ultimate equalizer. As the unit continued its training, the distinctions between old and new began to blur. Shared challenges, sleepless nights, and the looming prospect of returning to the front forged bonds that transcended experience.

In the crucible of war, the 167th would become a cohesive force. James understood that the strength of their unit lay not only in their skills but in their ability to function as a seamless whole, where every soldier, regardless of their background or experience, played a vital role in the greater mission.

It was an ordinary evening in Montreuil-aux-Lions as James gathered with his company for roll call. The sun was beginning its descent, casting a warm hue across the makeshift camp. The soldiers stood in rows, fatigue etched into their faces from a day of drills and training.

James was about to begin the roll call when he noticed something unusual about one of the fresh faces in the formation. A young soldier, fresh from the United States, had a picture clutched tightly in his hand. The soldier's eyes were filled with a mix of excitement and nervousness as he waited to be recognized.

James, ever vigilant and attentive to the well-being of his troops, stepped forward. "Name and hometown," he barked in his customary manner, but his eyes lingered on the photograph.

The young soldier cleared his throat, trying to stifle his nerves. "Private Daniel Cowan, sir. I'm from Thomasville, Alabama."

Recognition dawned on James, and he couldn't help but feel a surge of curiosity and pride. "Thomasville, you say?" he inquired, now fully focused on the young man before him.

"Yes, sir," Daniel replied, standing tall despite his evident unease.

James extended his hand, a rare and warm smile gracing his face. "Well, Private Cowan, it's good to have you here. You see that flag in the window of the house in the picture?"

Daniel nodded, a hint of a smile forming on his lips. "Yes, sir. Your parents asked me to bring this picture with me, as a reminder of home."

James was deeply moved by this gesture. He shook Daniel's hand firmly, the bond between them forged in that simple exchange. "Thank you, Private. It means a lot."

Daniel quickly became an integral part of the company. The soldiers, both new and old, welcomed him with open arms, and his connection with James' family served as a unique bridge between the officer and his men. James often found himself seeking Daniel's perspective on various matters, valuing his input as a representative of their shared hometown.

Life in the reserve position offered a temporary respite for James and his unit. Nestled along the banks of the tranquil river, their current station was a world apart from the relentless horrors of the front lines. As they settled into this newfound stability, the men relished simple pleasures, like taking a bath and swimming in the river, washing away the grime and exhaustion that clung to them like a shadow.

One warm afternoon, James was down by the riverbank, the soothing sound of flowing water providing a momentary escape from the harsh realities of war. Nearby, some of his men frolicked in the river, their laughter echoing through the air. It was a welcome change from the constant tension and danger they had faced for so long.

James waded into the river, the cool water soothing his aching muscles and washing away the accumulated dust and sweat. He couldn't help but smile as he watched his men, now shirtless and carefree, splashing and playing like boys let out of school.

As the day dipped lower on the horizon, some of the soldiers took to boiling their clothes by the river's edge, attempting to rid themselves of the persistent lice and other critters that had taken up residence in their uniforms. Laughter mixed with grumbles as they scrubbed at fabric and chatted about their hopes for their return home.

One soldier, a young private, glanced over at James and approached, a hint of bashfulness in his expression. "Sir, this river, it's like a piece of heaven," he said, his Alabama drawl evident.

James nodded in agreement. "It certainly feels like it, soldier. It's moments like these that remind me of home."

The private smiled, taking a deep breath of the clean, fresh air. "I can't wait to get back there, but I reckon I'm supposed to be here, making a difference."

As they watched the sun sink lower, painting the sky with hues of orange and pink, James couldn't help but share in the private's sentiment. Despite the hardships, despite the ever-present threat of battle, there was a sense of camaraderie among these men that transcended the horrors of war. The river, with its cool embrace and cleansing waters, offered them a brief respite, a brief hope that would return to a peaceful home, free from the ravages of war.

A solemn dusk settled over the camp, the last remnants of daylight slowly giving way to the soft glow of lanterns that illuminated the makeshift medical tent. James stood at the entrance, the flap held open with one hand, while the other clutched a clipboard holding a list of names.

He glanced around, the flickering lanterns casting eerie shadows on the faces of the men lined up before him. They were a mix of expressions: some stoic, some nervous, and others resigned. James understood their discomfort, but he also understood the gravity of the situation.

"Alright, fellas," he began, his voice firm but kind. "We've been ordered to conduct a 'short arm' inspection today. You all know why. The Colonel wants to make sure we're keeping this camp clean and disease-free."

A low murmur rippled through the men, a few awkward chuckles breaking the tension. James continued, "I know it's not a pleasant task, but it's necessary for our health and the health of those around us."

He motioned to the medical personnel, who had gloves and equipment at the ready. "Sergeant Sellers and his team here are going to take a quick look. It won't take long, and it'll be as discreet as possible."

During inspections James maintained a serious demeanor, trying to set an example for his men. He knew that this was not just about following orders; it was about responsibility and discipline.

One of the soldiers, Private Anderson, cleared his throat nervously. "Lieutenant, ain't this a bit personal?"

James met Anderson's gaze. "Yes, Private, it is. But we have got regulations in place for a reason. We cannot afford to have our men falling ill during a crucial time like this. Besides, you all know the rules – no frequenting bordellos or brothels. We need to maintain discipline."

Anderson nodded, a hint of embarrassment in his eyes. "I understand, sir."

As the inspections continued, James could not help but think about how far they had come. From the trenches to this moment of scrutiny, every step had been a challenge. He knew that by enforcing these rules they were safeguarding the mission ahead.

After what felt like an eternity, the inspections were completed. James gathered his men, his voice filled with reassurance. "Thank you for your cooperation, gentlemen. I know it is not easy, but it's necessary. We're all in this together, and we need to look out for one another."

There was a collective nod as the soldiers dispersed, heading back to their quarters. James watched them go; his mind already focused on the next steps of their journey. Amid war, even the most uncomfortable tasks had to be faced with resolve and unity.

***

My Dearest Ellie Marie,

I hope this letter finds you in the best of spirits, my love. Each moment away from you feels like an eternity, and with each passing day, my heart longs for your presence more and more. There is so much I wish to say, to share with you, and to dream about for our future together.

First and foremost, I want you to know the depth of my love for you. It is a love that grows stronger with every sunrise and sunset I witness in this far-off land. Your memory is a constant source of warmth and comfort amidst the harsh realities of war. You are my guiding star in these dark times.

I yearn for the day when I can hold you in my arms again when I can see your smile and hear your laughter. I dream of us walking together, hand in hand, under the Alabama sun, exploring the beautiful countryside of which I have often spoken. I long to introduce you to my family and friends, and to proudly call you mine.

Ellie, my darling, I want nothing more than for you to come live with me in Alabama once this wretched war is over. You, with your grace, your spirit, and your unwavering support, are the missing piece of my life's puzzle. We will build a home filled with love, laughter, and the warmth that only two hearts deeply in love can provide.

I must admit, my love, that not all is well on my side. My men, as much as I care for them, continue to visit bordellos and brothels against regulations. It pains me to see them succumb to such temptations, especially when we have rules in place to protect their health and discipline. I find myself endlessly frustrated by their actions, as I fear for their well-being and the consequences that might follow.

But please, let us not dwell on such matters. Instead, let us focus on the dreams we share, on the love that binds us across the miles. Together, we will overcome all obstacles, my love, and write a beautiful chapter in the book of our lives.

Until the day we are reunited, I will carry your love in my heart, Ellie Marie. Be safe, be strong, and know that you are cherished beyond measure.

Forever Yours,

James

**"

The 167th Infantry found themselves in a peculiar situation. The green recruits and draftees, fresh from America, were thrust into the harsh realities of war. It was a far cry from the training grounds back home, and they needed to be acclimated quickly to become useful in combat.

James, now a seasoned company commander, took it upon himself to ensure that these new soldiers were integrated into the unit effectively. He understood that the strength of their division relied on the cohesiveness of the men.

"Alright, listen up, everyone!" James called the troops together. The faces before him were a mix of anxiety and determination. "I know you're new here, and this isn't what you expected. But remember, you are not alone in this. We are a team, and we look out for each other. You've got brothers here who'll watch your back, just as you'll watch theirs."

The veterans in the unit agreed, offering reassuring smiles to the newcomers. James continued, "You've had your training, but nothing can prepare you for the real thing. We learn on the battlefield. We adapt, we improvise, and most importantly, we stick together."

With that, he set about pairing experienced soldiers with new enlistees, creating mentorship bonds to fast-track their understanding of combat tactics and survival skills. The seasoned soldiers shared stories, tricks of the trade, and practical advice, all the while reassuring the fresh faces that they'd make it through.

Days turned into nights as the men practiced drills and maneuvers. They learned to dig trenches, to navigate the treacherous landscapes, and to communicate effectively under fire. James, with the support of his fellow officers, emphasized the importance of discipline and camaraderie.

In the evenings, as they gathered around campfires, the soldiers swapped stories and sang songs from home. The newcomers began to understand that they weren't just part of a division; they were part of a brotherhood.

James often found himself offering words of encouragement, reminding them of their purpose. "We're here to defend our values and everything we hold dear. We'll do it together, as a unit. When we march into battle, remember the men by your side. We've got your back, just as you have ours."

Over time, the green recruits transformed into seasoned soldiers, forged in the irons of experience. They learned to trust their fellow soldiers, to rely on their training, and to face the unknown with courage.

Through the dedication and leadership of officers like James, the unit became a formidable force, ready to face the challenges that lay ahead on the battlefields of Europe. Their unity and strength would be tested, but they were prepared to stand together, as brothers in arms.

The respite in Montreuil-aux-Lions had been a brief interlude of relative peace, but war, like an unrelenting storm, was never far away. The 167th Division had used this time wisely, integrating recruits and draftees, acclimating them to the rigors of military life, and training them for the harsh realities of the front lines. Now, their orders had come—once more, they were destined for the front lines, this time at Saint Mihiel.

The soldiers had become a tight-knit unit, a brotherhood bound by hardship and the shared burden of battle. They had weathered the storm together, and there was a sense of determination that ran deep within their ranks. James Reynolds felt a profound sense of responsibility for the men under his command.

"Gather 'round, everyone," James called his men together, his voice carrying the weight of his authority and experience. "We've received our orders, and it's time to move out. Saint Mihiel awaits, and we've got a job to do."

The faces before him were a mix of resolve and concern. They had been through this before, but the uncertainty of the battlefield always hung heavy in the air. James continued, "I won't lie to you; this won't be an easy fight. But we've trained for this. We're a cohesive unit, and we've got each other's backs. That's what sets us apart."

The soldiers agreed, their trust in their commander unwavering. They knew that James would lead them through the crucible of war as he had done before. He had become more than just a commander; he was a symbol of strength and leadership.

As the 167th prepared to move out, there was a solemn air to the camp. Gear was checked and double-checked, rifles cleaned and loaded, and goodbyes exchanged with the soldiers from other units who had shared this temporary respite. Amid this somber atmosphere, there was an unspoken understanding—a shared determination to face whatever awaited them in the trenches.

The journey to Saint Mihiel was a mix of anticipation and apprehension. The soldiers passed through towns and villages, some still bearing the scars of previous battles. The locals watched them pass, their eyes reflecting a mixture of gratitude and sorrow. They understood the sacrifices these men were making, for they, too, had borne the weight of war.

Along the way, the 167th crossed paths with fresh troops heading in the opposite direction—fresh faces, eager yet unsure, about to embark on their journey to the front lines. James couldn't help but think back to his arrival in France, and the naivety and uncertainty he had felt. He hoped that these new arrivals would find the same strength and camaraderie that had carried his unit through the darkest hours of battle.

The closer they came to Saint Mihiel, the more the landscape bore the scars of war. Cratered fields, shattered buildings, and the ever-present rumble of distant artillery fire served as a grim reminder of what lay ahead.

As the 167th approached their destination, James couldn't help but steal a glance at the soldiers under his command. They were a band of brothers, forged in the fires of war, ready to face the challenges that lay ahead. They had been through so much together, and their bonds were unbreakable.

With a firm resolve, James spoke to his men one last time before they entered the fray. "Saint Mihiel is our next battleground, and we'll meet it head-on. Remember your training, trust in each other, and fight with all you've got. We've faced worse odds, and we've come out stronger. Now, let's show them what the 167th is made of!"

Chapter 19

The command meeting convened under the canvas of the makeshift headquarters in the heart of the camp. James stood among the other officers, the weight of responsibility pressing upon him as Lieutenant Colonel Screws addressed the assembly. His voice was grave, a reflection of the gravity of their upcoming mission.

"Men, we've just received our orders," Lieutenant Colonel Screws began, his gaze sweeping over the assembled officers. "The 42nd Division will be manning the center of the American line for the assault on Saint Mihiel, and the 167th will be right there with them."

A hushed silence settled over the officers, the reality of the impending battle sinking in. James exchanged glances with his fellow officers; they knew this was their moment, a chance to prove their mettle in a battle of immense significance.

Lt Colonel Screws continued, "Lt. Reynolds, your company has been selected to lead the first assault. You'll be at the forefront, setting the pace for the entire division. It's a heavy burden but I trust you and your men to execute it flawlessly."

James nodded, his heart pounding with a mixture of apprehension and trepidation. Leading the first assault meant that they would be the ones to breach the enemy's defenses, to face the initial onslaught. It was a perilous task, but it was their duty.

"As for the rest of you," Colonel Screws addressed the officers, "we need to coordinate our efforts closely with the rest of the division. This will be a joint operation, and teamwork will be crucial. We've trained for this, and we're as prepared as we can be."

James exchanged nods with the other company commanders, a silent acknowledgment of their shared commitment to the mission. They had trained for this moment, and now, they were ready to put their skills to the test.

Lt Colonel Screws concluded, "Gentlemen, we've faced adversity together before, and we've emerged stronger each time. Saint Mihiel won't be an easy fight, but with our unity and resolve, we will prevail. May we meet on the other side of this battle with our heads held high and victory in our grasp."

As the officers dispersed to relay the news to their respective companies, James couldn't help but feel the weight of the impending assault. His men, his brothers, were counting on him to lead them through the battle ahead once more. With a resolute spirit and a firm sense of duty, he steeled himself for the challenges that lay ahead, knowing that they would face them head-on, just as they always had.

James gathered his company under a makeshift canopy, the weathered faces of his men glistening with a mixture of anticipation and apprehension. It was a pivotal moment, and he wanted to share the news with them.

"Men," he began, his voice firm, "I have important news to share. We've been selected to lead the first charge at the upcoming attack. This is an honor, a testament to your training, your discipline, and your accomplishments."

A murmur of acknowledgment rippled through the assembled soldiers, their expressions a blend of pride and determination. Leading the charge was a perilous task, but they understood the significance of their role.

Tommy, ever the one to interject with a dose of humor, couldn't resist a quip. "James, for this attack to succeed, we need submarines for tanks, ducks for carrier pigeons, and alligators for soldiers!" he exclaimed, eliciting a round of laughter from the men.

James chuckled, appreciating Tommy's ability to inject levity even in the gravest of moments. "Tommy's right," he said with a grin. "The conditions out there are challenging. It's muddy, it's rainy, but we're Alabamians, and we don't shy away from a little mud, and hell, we're used to the rain in southern Alabama, this rain won't even wet our beaks."

He continued, his tone growing more serious. "This mission won't be easy. We'll face heavy resistance, but we're prepared. We've trained for this. Our comrades in the 42nd are counting on us, and we won't let them down."

The men nodded; their determination mirrored in James's eyes. They were a band of brothers, and their camaraderie was their greatest strength.

James concluded, "Remember why we're here, why we wear this uniform. It's for our families back home and for each other. Let's make Alabama proud, and let's bring victory home. We're leading the charge, and we'll lead it with honor."

With those words, James instilled in his men a sense of purpose and unity. They might have been facing challenging conditions, but their resolve was unshakable. As they dispersed to prepare for the impending battle, they did so knowing that they would have to face whatever lay ahead.

The start of the assault on Saint Mihiel had arrived, and James, along with Colonel Screws and the other company commanders, gathered at the base of a muddy hill. It was an overcast morning, and the air was thick with anticipation and a tangible tension.

Lt Colonel Screws, his uniform caked with mud from the ascent, addressed the group. "Gentlemen, today's the day we've trained for, the day we take part in a battle that could change the course of this war. But before we move out, we need to understand what we're up against."

The commanders nodded. The hill they were about to climb would provide a vantage point to observe the German positions. However, it was no easy feat, given the recent rains that had turned the terrain into a quagmire.

With determination etched on their faces, they began their ascent, slipping and sliding in the mud. The hill seemed to stretch endlessly upward, the incline growing steeper with every step. It was a testament to their resolve that they persevered, inching closer to the summit.

Finally, they reached the top, breathless and covered in mud. Below them, the front lines stretched out, a vast expanse of trenches, barbed wire, and fortified positions. German artillery could be seen in the distance, and the constant rumble of distant gunfire served as a haunting reminder of the battle to come.

James couldn't help but think of the men under his command, their faces etched in his mind. He knew their lives rested in his hands, along with those of his fellow commanders. It was a heavy burden that James carried with him every day as a company commander.

Colonel Screws, his gaze fixed on the enemy positions, spoke solemnly. "Gentlemen, take a good look. These are the obstacles we'll face today. Our objective is to break through, to advance, and to seize victory. Our comrades in the 42nd are counting on us."

The commanders observed in silence, taking mental notes of the German positions and fortifications. It was a sobering sight, a stark reminder of the challenges that lay ahead.

As they descended the muddy hill to rejoin their respective units, James couldn't shake the feeling that they were on the cusp of something. The battle for Saint Mihiel would be fierce, but the Alabama 167th was prepared to face it head-on, their determination unwavering in the face of adversity.

As they prepared for the assault, James gathered his men in a small clearing within the woods near the front lines. The tension in the air was thick, and the soldiers listened attentively to their company commander's instructions.

"Alright, boys," James began, his voice firm but filled with authority. "Today's the day we break through those German lines and pave the way for the 42nd. But to do that, we need to be swift and nimble. Leave your packs here in the woods; we're traveling light."

His words were met with understanding, and the men quickly removed their heavy packs, placing them in a neat pile amidst the trees. They knew that in the chaos of battle, every extra pound could slow them down.

"Now," James continued, "all you should carry is your rifle, ammunition, and a ration of hardtack and corned beef. Make sure your basic aid kits and canteens are securely fastened. We don't know how long we'll be out there, so conserve your supplies."

As the soldiers complied, adjusting their gear and ensuring their weapons were in working order, James couldn't help feeling a sense of responsibility for these men. Many were fresh reinforcements, untested in battle, and it was his duty to lead them through the crucible of combat.

Tommy gave James a reassuring pat on the shoulder. "We'll get through this, Jim. Just like we always have." Tommy only called James, that when he knew something was bothering him.

James nodded; his gaze filled with concern. "You're damn right, Tommy. We've faced tough odds before, and we've always come out stronger. Today will be no different."

With their packs left behind in the woods, the men of Company B stood ready, their faces grim. They were about to step onto the battlefield, to face the unknown, but they did so as a brotherhood, bound by duty, honor, and the unbreakable spirit of the Alabama 167th.

As night descended upon the rain-soaked landscape near Saint Mihiel, the 42nd Division prepared to slip away from the US 89th Division's position along the front-line trenches. The cover of darkness, coupled with the relentless rain and biting cold, created the perfect conditions for their movements to go undetected by the enemy.

Lieutenant Col William Screws had meticulously planned this operation, and James, along with the rest of the company commanders, had been briefed on every detail. The men knew the importance of their mission – to advance swiftly and seize key objectives, thereby opening the way for the rest of the division.

James gathered his company in a small stand of trees, their faces smeared with dark, wet mud to help blend in with the night. He whispered instructions to his men, their breaths visible in the frigid air.

"We've got to move silently and quickly," James emphasized. "Stay low and stay together. The less we can be spotted the safer it will be for us."

The soldiers nodded; their faces set with the grim realities of war. They knew that the element of surprise was their greatest ally. The rain continued to pour, drenching them to the bone, but they pressed on.

As they made their way through the mud-soaked trenches, the absence of enemy contact only heightened their tension. The Germans, it seemed, were hunkered down in their own trenches, unaware of the impending assault.

Tommy, walking beside James, leaned in close to speak over the rain's persistent patter. "Feels like we're ghosts, Jim. The Boche won't even know what hit 'em."

James gave a tight smile. "Let's keep it that way, Tommy. Onward, boys."

In the dark, with mud squelching beneath their boots, the 42nd Division moved quietly and invisibly. They were warriors in the night, a silent force with a mission to change the course of the battle.

As the clock struck 1:00 a.m. on September 11th, the stillness of the night was shattered by the thunderous roar of American artillery barrages. The earth trembled beneath the relentless pounding as shells screamed through the night sky, heading toward the German lines.

James and his men lay in the muddy trenches, clutching their rifles and awaiting the impending assault. The trench walls quivered with each explosion, showering them with dirt and debris. Flares from the German positions burst forth, casting an eerie, ghostly glow over the battlefield. It was a chaotic symphony of destruction, the prelude to a deadly dance that would follow.

The German artillery responded with equal ferocity, sending their shells screaming back towards the American lines. The night sky erupted into a terrifying display of light and fire, as if the heavens themselves were engaged in a battle.

James, with his eyes fixed on the distant enemy trenches, felt a mix of anxiety and trepidation. He knew that this artillery barrage was a crucial part of their strategy. It was meant to weaken the German defenses, disrupt their communication lines, and sow confusion among the enemy ranks.

Tommy, huddled next to James, shouted above the cacophony of explosions, "This is it, Jim! The big show!"

James nodded grimly. The deafening noise and the sheer power of the bombardment were unlike anything he had ever experienced. He couldn't help but think of the men on the other side, enduring the same relentless storm of steel.

The night wore on, with the artillery duel showing no signs of abating. The ground shook, the trenches trembled, and the soldiers clung to their positions, their hearts pounding in their chests.

Hours passed, but to James and his comrades, it felt like an eternity. Each minute brought them closer to the moment when they would rise from the trenches and advance into the maelstrom of battle. They knew that the success of the assault depended on this relentless barrage softening the enemy's defenses.

Amidst the chaos and destruction, James whispered a silent prayer for strength and courage. The long night was a stark reminder of the harrowing task that lay ahead – to break through and secure victory for their side.

At 5:00 a.m. on that fateful September morning, as the last echoes of the artillery barrage faded into the horizon, James and his company received the order they had been waiting for. It was time to go over the top.

With their bayonets fixed, rifles at the ready, and hearts steeled for what lay ahead, James led his company out of the trenches. The heavy thud of their boots against the mud and the sound of their ragged breaths were the only noises that broke the eerie silence of the dawn.

As they ventured into no man's land, the sky overhead was still obscured by the lingering darkness, but the sporadic flashes of artillery fire and the relentless chatter of machine guns lit up the horizon with fiery bursts. The world around them was a nightmarish landscape of craters, tangled barbed wire, and the remnants of battles past.

James' company moved with purpose; their eyes locked on the enemy trenches looming in the distance. The sound of German artillery shells whistling through the air and the sharp crack of rifle fire filled their ears. The atmosphere was thick with tension, but James couldn't allow fear to grip his men.

"Steady, boys! Keep moving!" he shouted above the chaos, his voice unwavering. "We've got a job to do."

As they approached the first line of German trenches, they encountered a sight that left them momentarily stunned. Hundreds of German soldiers, hands raised in surrender, emerged from the trenches. They were tired, disheveled, and undoubtedly overwhelmed by the ferocity of the American assault.

James' instincts kicked in, and he quickly assessed the situation. He ordered his men to secure the prisoners while maintaining a vigilant watch on the remaining enemy soldiers in the trenches. It was a surreal moment amid the chaos of battle, as the two sides faced each other with a mixture of relief and trepidation.

Some of the captured Germans attempted to communicate in broken English, their voices trembling with fear. James, always the diplomat, called for interpreters among his men to assist in the communication. He wanted to ensure the safe and orderly surrender of the enemy.

"Tell them to drop their weapons," he instructed one of the interpreters, his gaze unwavering. "We'll treat them fairly, but we can't take any chances."

As the German soldiers reluctantly relinquished their rifles, James couldn't help feeling a strange mix of emotions. Here, amid battle, he was tasked with ensuring the humane treatment of prisoners. It was a testament to the complexities of war, where duty and compassion often intermingled.

With the German prisoners under guard, James' company continued their advance, pushing through the captured trenches and moving deeper into enemy territory. The battle was far from over, and more challenges were awaiting them. But for that moment, they had achieved a remarkable feat — hundreds of German soldiers had surrendered, and James had led his company through it with courage and resolve.

***

As James led his men over the top of the first German trench line, the air was thick with tension and the deafening roar of artillery. The heavy thud of boots against the mud was now accompanied by the ominous shriek of incoming shells. The world had descended into chaos.

"Push forward, men! Keep moving!" James shouted; his voice determined despite the chaos surrounding him. His company pressed on, their hearts pounding with adrenaline as they advanced toward the second line of German trenches.

But amid this hellish storm, tragedy struck. A deafening explosion rocked the ground, sending a shockwave of dirt, debris, and sheer terror through the ranks. A barrage of heavy German artillery and gas shells had found their mark, unleashing their devastating payload upon the advancing Americans.

James, who had been at the forefront of the charge, was caught in the deadly maelstrom. Shrapnel from the exploding shells tore through the air, and a gas cloud billowed around him. He fell to the ground, wounded and gasping for breath.

His men, disoriented and reeling from the sudden onslaught, rushed to his side. Through the acrid haze of gas, they could see their beloved commander, bloodied and struggling to breathe. Panic and anguish swept through the ranks as they desperately tried to render aid.

"Medic! We need a medic here!" one of the soldiers cried out, his voice strained with emotion.

Amid the chaos, medics quickly arrived on the scene, their faces obscured by gas masks as they worked tirelessly to save James' life. The gas had left him choking and gasping for air, and his wounds were severe. It was a race against time to stabilize him and get him to safety.

As they struggled to treat his injuries, James remained conscious, his eyes reflecting a mixture of pain, determination, and concern for his men. He attempted to speak, but his words were drowned out by the persistent coughing brought on by the gas.

The situation was dire, and the battlefield around them continued to erupt with violence. The fight for the second line of German trenches raged on, but James' focus was solely on the brave soldiers who had become his family.

"Get... them... home," he managed to wheeze out between coughs, his voice barely a whisper. His last thoughts were of his men, his duty, and the immense responsibility he had carried on his shoulders.

The medics continued their efforts, but it was clear that the wounds were too severe, and the effects of the gas had taken a toll too great to bear. James Reynolds, the courageous leader of Company B, the man who had inspired his men with his unwavering dedication, had given his all on that battlefield.

It was at this time, when his men started to gather around, and the medics were attempting their last bit of life-saving heroics, It would all be in vain, for the sound of an incoming artillery shell could be heard. Before anybody could get out of the way, the shell exploded in a direct hit over the scene.

Chapter 20

Maggie sat on the front porch swing of their home in Thomasville bathed in the warm glow of the late afternoon sun. She held a letter in her trembling hands, its envelope bearing the return address of Paris, France. Her heart raced as she didn't recognize the handwriting on the envelope, the elegant script that could belong to anyone, but this Ellie Marie was unfamiliar to Maggie.

With a mixture of curiosity and trepidation, Maggie carefully opened the letter. The familiar scent of James' favorite cologne, something James had told Ellie to do if she ever wrote Maggie, so that Maggie wouldn't think that she was a scammer, wafted from the pages, instantly transporting her back to those stolen moments when they had held each other close before he left for war.

The words on the page blurred momentarily as Maggie's eyes filled with tears. Ellie Marie's letter was written with such warmth and sincerity that it was impossible not to be touched by her words. In a neat, precise French script, Ellie Marie had poured out her thoughts and feelings.

"Chère Maggie," the letter began, addressing her as 'Dear Maggie' in French. Switching to English, Ellie wrote, "I hope this letter finds you in good health and high spirits. I wanted to write to you because James often spoke of you with such love and admiration. Amid war, your name was a beacon of hope and love for him, and I felt compelled to reach out."

Maggie's heart swelled with a mixture of emotions – gratitude, curiosity, and a tinge of anxiety. She continued reading Ellie Marie's words, painting a vivid picture of the time James had spent in Paris.

"He spoke of your home in Thomasville, your warm and welcoming family, and the swing on your front porch where you both dreamed of a future," Ellie Marie wrote. "In those quiet moments, he found solace and strength in the thought of you. He wanted you to know that you were always in his heart, even across the vast ocean that separated you."

Tears welled in Maggie's eyes as she absorbed Ellie Marie's words. It was both a comfort and a reminder of the deep connection she shared with her brother, a connection that transcended distance and time.

Just as she reached the final paragraphs of the letter, a car pulled up in front of their house. Maggie's heart skipped a beat as she saw a man in an army officer's uniform step out, accompanied by their church's preacher.

With a mixture of surprise and concern, Maggie hurriedly folded Ellie Marie's letter and tucked it into her pocket. She rose from the porch swing, her footsteps echoing the nervous fluttering of her heart as she approached the unexpected visitors.

The officer and the preacher greeted her with somber expressions. The preacher, a kind and familiar face from their church, spoke gently. "Maggie, we've received some news about James," he said, his voice heavy with solemnity.

Maggie's heart pounded in her chest as she braced herself for the news. She knew that war carried with it the weight of uncertainty, and every message from the front lines held the potential for both joy and sorrow.

As they asked where Maggie's mother was, the world around Maggie seemed to blur, and the echoes of Ellie Marie's letter lingered in her mind. The swing on the front porch, the dreams they had shared, and the love that had sustained them through the trials of separation – all of it seemed to converge in this moment.

The warm breeze gently rustled the clothes hanging on the line as Maggie's mother, Elizabeth, diligently went about her daily chores in the sideyard. The sun hung low in the sky, casting a warm, golden hue over their small homestead. Birds chirped merrily, blissfully unaware of the approaching storm.

Maggie, having just returned from the front porch after reading a letter she had received from France had two other people with her, and watched her mother's silhouette from a distance. Elizabeth was a pillar of strength, a woman who had faced adversity with unwavering resolve, yet today, something was amiss.

As Maggie approached, Elizabeth noticed the grim expressions etched on the faces of the men who accompanied her daughter. The preacher, a figure of faith and fortitude for the community in times of joy and sorrow, wore a solemn visage that she had seldom seen before. Beside him stood an army officer, his uniform adorned with medals that glittered in the sunlight.

A feeling of unease settled in Elizabeth's stomach, and she quickened her pace. "Mama," she called out gently, "there are some gentlemen here to see you."

Elizabeth turned, her hands still clutching a clothespin, and looked towards the approaching trio. Maggie could see the momentary confusion in her mother's eyes before it was replaced by a deep-seated worry. She released the clothespin, allowing a shirt to sway lazily in the breeze as she approached the visitors.

"Good afternoon, gentlemen," She greeted them politely but with a quiver in her voice. "Is there something I can help you with?"

The preacher cleared his throat, struggling to find the right words to convey the heavy message they bore. "Elizabeth, we've come with news about your son, James," he began, his voice gentle but filled with sorrow.

Her hands trembled as she clutched the clothespin tighter. Maggie, standing by her mother's side, felt her heartache mirrored in the lines etched on her mother's face. James had been their source of pride and concern, the son who had gone off into the world to make his way and ended up going to war to protect their country.

The army officer stepped forward, his eyes reflecting a profound sense of respect and empathy. "Ma'am, James' unit was involved in a recent engagement," he continued, his voice steady. "I regret to inform you that your son has been classified as missing in action and presumed dead."

A gasp escaped Maggie's mother's lips as she clung to the clothespin with trembling fingers, her eyes welling up with tears. Maggie's heart ached, and she reached out to support her mother, who seemed on the verge of collapse.

The preacher offered his condolences, speaking of faith, resilience, and the community's unwavering support. Elizabeth nodded, her grief-stricken eyes never leaving her daughter's. Maggie, overwhelmed by the heaviness of the moment, could only offer a reassuring squeeze of her mother's hand.

As the visitors slowly made their way back to the car, Maggie and her mother stood side by side, their bond stronger than ever in the face of the devastating news. The world around them continued to turn, birds still chirped, and the sun dipped below the horizon. Yet, in that fleeting moment, their lives had been forever changed by the weight of a message carried by grim expressions and a mother's unspoken grief.

Elizabeth looked at her daughter, her eyes glistening with tears that were on the verge of spilling over. She slowly extended the telegram to Maggie, her hand trembling like a leaf in the wind. Maggie took it, her heart pounding, and read the message:

Mr. and Mrs. Reynolds,

We regret to inform you that your son, Lt. James Reynolds, is missing in action. And is presumed to have been killed in action. He was a brave and dedicated soldier, and our nation is grateful for his service. Please accept our deepest condolences.

Sincerely,

U.S. Army War Department

Maggie's breath caught in her throat as the words sank in. She glanced at her mother, who had been trying to hold back her emotions, and saw her lips quiver as tears welled up in her eyes.

"Oh, Mama," Maggie whispered, her voice choked with emotion, "I'm so sorry."

With a heart-wrenching sob, Maggie's mother suddenly burst into tears, her shoulders trembling. The telegram slipped from Maggie's grasp as she rushed forward to hold her mother. Reverend Wilson, sensing the depth of their grief, moved closer and gently placed a comforting hand on Elizabeth's back.

Her mother clung to Maggie tightly, her tears soaking her daughter's shoulder. "My boy," she cried, "my sweet James."

Maggie held her mother, offering the only solace she could in this moment of devastating loss. The yard filled with the sounds of a mother's grief, the raw, unfiltered anguish of a mother who had just received the news that her son, her brave soldier, would probably never return home.

Reverend Wilson bowed his head, offering a silent prayer for the family and the soul of James Reynolds. As time passed, Elizabeth's sobs subsided, and Maggie continued to hold her mother, offering the comfort of their shared grief.

At that moment, the weight of the telegram and the reality of their loss hung heavy in the air. The world outside continued its bustling routine, unaware of the deep pain that had settled within the confines of the Reynolds' estate.

As Maggie and her mother sat on the porch steps, their grief-laden hearts aching, Reverend Wilson gently rose from his chair. His kindly eyes held the depth of understanding that only comes from years of guiding souls through the trials of life and death. He moved with a certain grace, his suit pants rustling softly as he approached the heartbroken mother and daughter.

"Mrs. Reynolds, Miss Maggie," he said, his voice a soothing balm in their moment of despair, "perhaps some fresh tea might do you both some good."

Maggie nodded, her eyes still filled with tears, while her mother managed a weak, grateful smile. With the minister's suggestion, they rose from the steps, and he went into their kitchen to pour them three glasses of sweet tea.

The breeze whispered through the leaves of the ancient oak trees that lined their street, carrying the sweet scent of magnolia blossoms. Birds chirped in the distance, their melodies a stark contrast to the heavy sorrow that hung over the porch.

As they settled into the swing, Maggie's father raced down the street toward their home. He had been working at the local sawmill when he received a cryptic message that something was amiss at his house. His furrowed brows and the urgency of his steps revealed the worry that had seized him.

Samuel reached their front yard, his eyes scanning the porch with a mixture of relief and concern when he saw his wife and daughter. His steps quickened, and he approached them, a deep crease forming between his brows.

"Elizabeth, Maggie," he said, his voice quivering with a father's fear, "what's happened? Why did I get word at work that something's wrong?"

Maggie's mother, her eyes red from crying, looked up at her husband and managed to speak through her sorrow. "Honey," she said in a quivering voice, "It's James. He's... he's not coming home."

A stricken silence enveloped them. Samuel's face went pale as he absorbed the weight of his wife's words. Maggie and her mother had already shared their grief, and now they must pass it on to him.

"No," Samuel whispered, his voice barely audible. "No, not my boy."

As the realization sank in, Samuel dropped to his knees beside the porch swing, his shoulders shaking with the weight of his sorrow. Elizabeth reached out to hold him, and Maggie wrapped her arms around her father, tears flowing freely from her own eyes.

Reverend Wilson stood nearby, a pillar of strength in this moment of despair. He knew that sometimes; words were inadequate to offer comfort. In such moments, the presence of loved ones, a gentle touch, and the solace of shared grief were the most profound forms of support.

They remained there on the porch swing, a family bound by love and loss, their hearts intertwined in the deep pain of James' absence. The world around them continued to move, but in their grief, they found a stillness, a sacred space where they could honor their beloved son and brother, and together, bear the weight of their sorrow.

Samuel's trembling hands clutched the telegram, its paper crisp and official, bearing news that every parent dreads to receive. His fingers traced the edges of the envelope as he swallowed hard, trying to muster the strength to read aloud the words that would shatter their world.

As Maggie and Elizabeth sat on the porch swing, their eyes were locked on Samuel, their hearts aching in the dreadful news. The sun hung low in the sky, casting long shadows across their front yard, but it couldn't dispel the darkness that had descended upon their home.

Samuel unfolded the telegram, his hands trembling with each unfolding crease. He took a deep breath, his voice barely more than a whisper as he read, "It is with deepest regret that we inform you of the loss of your son, James Reynolds."

The words hung heavily in the air, a crushing weight that threatened to suffocate them all. Maggie's tears flowed freely, and her mother buried her face in her hands, sobbing uncontrollably. Samuel's gaze remained fixed on the telegram, his eyes brimming with tears that he refused to shed.

"Lieutenant Reynolds," he continued, his voice breaking, "went missing in action during the assault on the German lines near Château-Thierry on September 11th, 1918."

The date seemed to echo in the stillness, marking the moment when their lives had been irreparably changed. It was a date etched into their hearts, a day that would forever be associated with loss and sorrow.

Samuel clenched the telegram in his fist, his knuckles turning white. He couldn't bring himself to read the rest of the official message, the words that offered condolences and gratitude for James' service. None of it could fill the void left by their beloved son and brother's absence.

The porch swing creaked softly as Maggie and Elizabeth wept, their grief mingling with the warm breeze. Samuel, his eyes now filled with tears, folded the telegram back into its envelope, a painful artifact of a moment they would never forget.

Their home, once filled with laughter and love, now felt emptier than ever before. The news of James' sacrifice had shattered their world, leaving behind a void that could never be filled. As they clung to one another on that porch swing, they knew that their lives would never be the same, and they would carry the memory of their brave son and brother with them, always.

ABOUT THE AUTHOR

David Preston is a lifelong avid reader and student of History. He studied Political Science at the University of South Alabama. David is a recovering politician, reporter and current business owner. He was born in Gurden, Arkansas and has lived in Plano, Texas and Hernando, Mississippi. He currently resides in Mobile, Alabama where he has lived for 30 years.